Murder Spins a Tale

A Flock and Fiber Mystery

Veryl Ann Grace

Pele's Hair Publishing

This is a work of fiction. Any names, characters, businesses, organizations, places or events are either the product of the author's imagination or used fictitiously.

Copyright © 2010 Veryl Ann Grace

Cover Art: Charlene Lofgreen
Interior Art: Kary Miksis
Author photo: Glenn Grace
Interior Book Design: Linda M. Au

For more information, contact:
Pele's Hair Publishing
PO Box 1330
Kea`au, Hawai`i 96749

ISBN: 1453751300
EAN: 9781453751305

In Memory of

Martha Ellen Eskridge
who gave me the love of mysteries

and

Sierra's Denali Princes
Lion of Tahoma
Euzkotar Love's Ring of Fire
Euzkotar Taylor Made for Love
&
Euzkotar Marathon Man
who taught me the magnificence of big white dogs

Acknowledgments

A s is often said, no first novel is ever written without the help of many. My list is long. Thank you to Linda Weisser, who trusted me with a ten-week-old ball of fluff that we named Denali. It was the start of a great friendship and a long love affair with big white dogs. Thank you to Michael Floyd, who brought one of his mother's handspun, handknit hats to a GPCA regional and started me on the road to so many fiber arts. A great big hug to Catherine de la Cruz and Sharon Betker, who nurtured my desire to spin Great Pyrenees hair. Thanks to the members of the Great Pyrenees Club of Puget Sound, who brought a novice a long way in the lore of livestock guardian dogs.

Thank you to all of those on the Warpies list, past and present, who read early renditions of this story, with special thanks to Carolyn Agosta, who read and critiqued carefully multiple drafts. Thank you to Linda M. Au, who has walked me through many technicalities over the last few months. You see her work here. A big hug and very big thanks to Yasmine Galenorn, who has encouraged me along the way and who introduced me to Warpies. Our friendship of many years is treasured.

And to those online friends, in no particular order, who kept me going when I would think about stopping on many projects, including this one: Stasia, Alicia, Denise, Nannette, Kary, Helen, Judy, Mike, Pamela, Ann, and Talia.

Big hugs to Judy Gustafson, who supports me in so many ways and who has been my cheerleader on this project from its inception. Bless the big white dogs that connected us in the beginning.

Thanks to Barrie and Dale, who helped with an early version of the story. And thanks to all my family and friends, who kept saying, "When do we get to read the book?" Here it is.

Thanks to Charlene Lofgreen (www.ArtWanted.com/clof green) for the beautiful cover art, and to Kary Miksis (http://sheepatthebeachartstudio.blogspot.com) for the interior art.

Last, but never least, thank you to my husband, Glenn, who has supported me and put up with me for forty-six years. Love ya, mister.

You can connect with me on my blogs at http://flocknfi bermysteries.blogspot.com and http://fiberinparadise.blogspot. com and, by late autumn 2010, at my website, http://www. verylanngrace.com.

You will also find me on Facebook and Twitter. Both accounts are under my name, Veryl Ann Grace. Hope to meet you out there.

Chapter 1

It wasn't as if I were unfamiliar with death coming without warning in a brutal fashion. It had happened before. But one was never ready for it; and it always, as is the nature of such things, came as a terrible surprise. But I'm getting ahead of myself. There was nothing that winter morning to warn me except the call of the great horned owl, who in some Native American cultures is the portent of death.

Enjoying the call of the owl, I snuggled a little deeper into my wool jacket and settled my Pyr hair hat down around my ears. My breath steamed in the still morning air. A layer of frost glistened from the fence posts and the gravel crunched under-foot as I walked to the barn to feed the animals. The stars were still bright; it was not often that February skies were so clear. A cold nose went under my coat and a white shoulder gave me a nudge as Falcor reminded me that there was a job to do that didn't involve star gazing. A large white shadow emerged from the side of the shop and Denali joined us as we moved toward the barn. The Great Pyrenees were my livestock protection dogs and companions. Nothing made a coyote more uncomfortable than a guardian the size of a large gray wolf with equally sharp teeth.

"Maaaa," Koa, the Icelandic sheep, greeted me as I started to pull down the hay. Coco, the angora goat, gave me a gentle nudge. The rest of my eclectic spinning flock began to move in for their share of the food. I caught a glimpse of Sable, the Siamese cat, as she stalked a mouse real or imaginary in the straw of one of the stalls. The warmth of the barn, the gentle sounds of my animals eating and the pungent odors that came from the mixture of hay, straw, grain and one goat, five sheep and two alpacas surrounded me as I opened the large barn doors that gave them access to the outside world. Lost in early morning musings, I was gazing across the pasture when a white streak went past me and Falcor raced across the pasture with Denali in hot pursuit. They were barking alarms as they went. Then I heard the coyote yip and his call echoed by another. Both dogs were at the fence line now and telling the world in no uncertain terms that this pasture and this flock belonged to them. No predators were allowed.

It was time for me to leave the barn and start my day. My flock was safe and the Pyrs would make sure that they stayed that way. As I walked up the back steps to my porch, I turned for one more look at the dawn streaked sky before day claimed it.

My name is Martha Williamson. Nearly five years ago, the Air Force moved my husband John and me from the sun-drenched beaches of Honolulu, Hawai`i, to the mist-shrouded forests of Puget Sound. While John flew C17s, I worked as a personnel trainer with the state of Washington. John was going to retire after this tour; so when we were house hunting, we looked for a place that would be a comfortable, permanent home. We knew we'd found it when we were shown this small 25-acre farm nestled among the trees just outside Black Hills, Washington. At the time, it was a long way out and a major commute for both of us, but we fell in love with the tranquility and peace it provided at the end of a busy day.

However, life has a way of turning the best plans upside down, and it did with ours. John was killed on Halloween four years ago while driving to work on Interstate Five. A trucker fell asleep at the wheel and smashed John and his Toyota into the center barrier. John had flown many hours in combat operations and arrived home safely only to be killed on our highways.

I was in shock, but the small community of Black Hills rallied around and helped me through this most difficult of times. Gradually I began to make the changes necessary under such circumstances. I left my job with the state of Washington and opened The Spider's Web, where I sell supplies and teach classes in spinning, weaving, knitting and crochet. It has become a gathering place for people who enjoy fiber arts and allows me to make a living while combining my passions for fiber and teaching. It's a peaceful life and one I have come to savor and enjoy.

Today I had a breakfast date with my best friend, Ellen. Following John's death, we did this on a weekly basis to help keep me on an even keel. Now we manage it about once a month just for the fun of it. Realizing I would need to hustle a bit if I was going to be on time, I showered quickly, combed my waist-length auburn hair into a single braid and pulled on jeans, a flannel shirt, and handspun, handknit socks. I slipped my feet into Birkenstocks and grabbed my coat as I went out the back door and to the Ford pickup. Bright red and my workhorse vehicle, it had been my first major purchase after John died.

Black Hills Road makes a loop off of State Highway 8 to get to the town. My farm is at the west end of the loop not far off the highway. Black Hills is mainly a wide place in the road that once served timber families as home. With the downturn of the timber industry, it has become a bedroom community for Olympia, the state capital, and a place where tourists can stop for a quick bite to eat, obtain gas or find lodging.

As I started to follow the curve of Black Hills Road, I noticed something odd. The door to the beauty parlor was wide open. Janelle was not an early riser and didn't usually open until ten. The shop was in the corner of a small cluster of stores, none of which opened early. I pulled into the empty parking lot and got out of the truck. Looking around, I saw nothing out of the ordinary except the open door.

"Janelle," I called out as I walked closer to the shop. "Janelle."

Getting no answer and hearing nothing except the sound of my own voice and the hum of traffic on the highway some distance away, I decided to poke my head inside.

"Jan…" My call died on my lips as I saw the disaster in the shop. Furniture was overturned and drawers were open. Someone had gone through here in a very big hurry. I could see the TV, on continuously when Janelle was there, was not in its usual spot.

Pulling my cell phone out of my purse, I pressed 911 while I walked over to my truck.

"Emergency operator. How may I help you?"

"This is Martha Williamson. There appears to have been a burglary at Janelle's Hair Spot on Black Hills Road."

"Are you there now?"

"Yes, I'm standing in the parking lot. I just looked in the door. The shop appears empty but boy, is it a mess," I said.

"I have a car on its way. They should be there momentarily. Please stay on the line until they arrive."

The police station wasn't more than a half mile away and as she finished her sentence, I could see the patrol car coming toward me.

"They're here," I said. "Thank you for your help."

"No problem; that's what we're here for."

The patrol car pulled into the parking lot and I could see that it was Walter Jackson. His Doberman, Blackie, was riding shotgun.

"Hey, Martha," he said as he got out of the car. Blackie followed taking his position at Walter's side. Together, they would impress any bad guy. Walter was over six feet tall and muscular. He was smiling and his eyes, which could go steel hard when necessary, were currently twinkling in his black face. Blackie was also muscular and ready for action, if required. "You found trouble here," Walter continued.

"Yes. The door to Janelle's shop is open and the place is a mess inside. I was driving to town when I noticed the open door. Since Janelle never opens until ten, I decided to check on it."

"And what would you have done if the burglar had chosen that moment to run out the door?" Walter asked.

"I know, Walter. I just didn't think about it until after I had looked inside."

"Well, I have help on the way and I believe you were heading into town for a reason. I'll call you if I need more information from you."

"Uh, I couldn't just hang around a bit?" I asked.

"Nope. Get yourself to the café or wherever you were going. But don't say anything to anyone. I'd like Janelle to hear it from me, not some idiot with a cell phone in the café."

"OK, but you will let me know how things come out?"

"If I don't, that brother of yours probably will," Walter answered. "I'll make sure you have what information can be released to you."

My brother, Sean, worked for the Thurston County Sheriff's Department, and Walter was a good friend of his.

I got back in my pickup and drove to the Black Hills Café. I was late and Ellen was probably wondering if I had stood her up. Although my cell phone hadn't rung so maybe she was late too.

"It's about time you got here," a voice said as I walked in the door to the café. I looked around to see Ellen holding a cup of coffee at a table in the corner.

Ellen is tall, slender and as dark as I am fair. All my Celtic heritage shows in my light skin and freckles but Ellen shows none of her known heritage of Swedish and British ancestors. Her olive coloration, dark hair and single eye fold spoke of some ancestor back there who was Asian, but she had no idea who or when they came into her family. Anyway, it adds up to my best friend being one lovely woman.

I waved and made my way across the small restaurant. Every table and most of the seats at the counter were full. Sally had turned this once dreary, rundown diner into a cheerful, homey place with blue check tablecloths of real cloth and flowers on every table. The best way to find out what's happening in Black Hills is to stop in here in the morning when the regulars are grabbing their coffee before they head out to whatever tasks they have for the day. Along with your serving of gossip, you can get a good cup of coffee—not Starbucks fancy but a good strong cup of coffee—and breakfast for a reasonable price. You can also get malasadas, one of my favorites because it brings back memories of our years in Honolulu. Sally came back from one winter on the Big Island of Hawai`i with a knack for making the square Portuguese donuts that are so popular in the islands. This sweet, light treat had become a real favorite with her customers.

"Sorry," I said as I slid into a chair opposite Ellen. "I got sidetracked along the way and didn't have time to call you."

"That's OK. You couldn't have gotten me anyway. I forgot to charge my cell phone. That's why you didn't get a call from me. But I was about to give up and eat without you."

"What else can I get you?" Sally said as she filled my cup with coffee.

"I'll have two eggs, scrambled, and a malasada," I said.

"Coming up," Sally said. "I've just been holding off on yours until she showed, Ellen, so I'll get them both started."

Her bright smile filled her face as she added some additional coffee to Ellen's cup. Her blonde hair was pulled up into a ponytail and bounced as she moved on to fill other cups on her way back to the counter. As usual, she seemed to be everywhere at once making sure that her customers were well taken care of.

"So what are you having?" I asked Ellen.

"Oatmeal with raisins and dates and a bowl of applesauce."

"Ugh! Sounds like something out of the winters of my childhood."

"It is out of mine. That's why I like it. It comes under the heading of soul food," Ellen answered.

I encircled my coffee cup with my hands and inhaled the nutty fragrance. I hadn't made coffee at home this morning. That first cup was always the day's best cup of coffee. I looked over the edge of the cup at Ellen. "Now what's happening in your life this week?" I asked.

"I have a meeting on the program from hell in Seattle Thursday. Hopefully these people will finally have it hashed out as to what they really want this program to do and I can get it finished. So far I have rewritten pages of code because they can't decide how they want it to interact with their employees. Would you remind me why I decided that this was the work I wanted to do?"

I laughed. Ellen went through this particular stage on almost every program she wrote. We both knew why she was doing this for a living. It afforded her the freedom to live her own schedule and have her little farm, and she was a very good programmer who made a nice living doing it.

"Tomorrow I have my annual physical with Dr. Tom," Ellen continued, "which is of course about three months late. You know how well I keep track of things like that. Angie called last week and reminded me."

Thomas Walker is our wonderful family physician and friend. Angie is his office manager and a much appreciated right hand.

"So, I made an appointment when she called," Ellen continued. "But you haven't said why you were late. Spill."

I was saved from answering by Sally showing up with the coffee pot.

"Thanks, Sally," I said.

"Your food is coming right up," Sally said as she topped our coffee cups.

I took a lingering sip of my coffee while Ellen glared at me because I was obviously ignoring her question. While I was trying to figure out how I was going to answer her, she looked up toward the door. I turned to see Dr. Tom walking in. At six-foot-six, he filled the doorway of the café. His sunlined face and large weathered hands, as well as his blue jeans, soft leather boots, Pendleton shirt and stockman's leather jacket, made him look more like a prosperous rancher than a physician.

"Hey, Doc, where you been the last few weeks? Haven't seen you around," Sally hailed as he walked in.

"Had to take a trip to New Mexico. Black Hills looks mighty green after returning from desert country."

"Not thinking about leaving us and going back there, are you, Doc?"

"Not hardly. Too much water under the bridge there. I was just winding up some business and taking a little vacation." Tom continued across the room toward us at a slow pace because everyone had a greeting for him.

"May I join you two?" He flashed his wonderful smile at us as he pulled up a chair at the end of the table. That smile, which starts in his eyes and moves to a full grin, is the feature you notice most after his size.

Sally followed Tom and filled his coffee cup. "I'll be back for your order in just a sec," she said to Tom. "I need to pick up their food."

"Understand you had a bit of excitement this morning," Tom said just as Sally arrived with our food. He gave her his order and then turned his attention back to me.

"It's on the street now?" I asked.

"Well, I heard it from Bob Mitchell when I bought my gas so I'd say so."

"What's on the street?" Ellen jumped in. "Just what were you doing when you were supposed to be meeting me for breakfast?"

"Sorry, Ellen, I told Walter that I wouldn't talk; but if it's gossip now, I guess I can. I was the first to discover that Janelle's shop had been burglarized."

"What? And I suppose you stuck your head into it without thinking about the fact that you just might get it blown off?"

"I did. I'll probably hear from Sean about that too. But I didn't go in. Went back to the truck and called the police. Walter sent me on my way, so now I know no more than you do."

"That is pretty much all that Bob told me too," Tom said. "If they know more, they've managed to keep it from the grapevine so far. I am glad that you didn't find someone, though. I wouldn't want to be patching you up."

"You guys are letting your breakfast get cold," Sally said as she brought Tom's over.

"You're right," I said as I took a bite. "But it's still good."

We all decided that our breakfast needed some attention and ate in silence for awhile.

"Have you all heard of any burglaries in our end of the county lately?" I broke the silence with my question.

"None," Tom answered, "and I hear quite a bit of gossip in the course of a day."

"I think Sean's working on some in the Yelm area but that's quite a distance from here," I said. "I may have to talk to him about them."

"Probably no connection." Ellen said. "I mean, why would anyone jump Olympia, with all the places there, to come here to our little town?"

"Maybe because we are a little town," I answered. "Maybe they feel that we are less apt to have a competent police force."

"Well, they will have guessed wrong then," Tom said. "Jonathon does his job very well and he has put together a great force."

"I just hope this isn't the first of many," I said. "We don't need that kind of excitement around here."

"Thanks, Sally," Tom said as she refilled all our coffee cups. He then turned toward Ellen. "Changing the subject, how's that new pup of yours? Last I talked to Martha, you were wondering if you had rocks in your head."

Ellen had a new Great Pyrenees puppy, Shasta, who would join her male, Tahoma, to guard her flock of Navajo Churro Sheep.

"I haven't killed her yet but it could happen soon. The little monster dug up my favorite rose bush yesterday. It is an old-fashioned one along the side of the house. How she managed to do it, I'll never know. The thing is large and almost a thicket but somehow, she squirreled under it and decided to dig a sleeping hole right there. Thank goodness I found it quickly and got the hole filled in. It helped that Tahoma turned tattletale on her. However, her days near the house are numbered. She is going to be moving out into a small pasture near the barn with some four-month-old lambs. Time for her to learn her job."

Tom and I laughed.

"Just sounds like a pup to me," I said. "She'll grow up soon."

"I know it," Ellen responded shaking her head. "But what a rascal in the meantime."

Tom's cell phone went off just as she finished her sentence and it was obvious that he was going to need to leave. I glanced at my watch and realized that I too needed to leave if I was going to open my shop on time.

"Sorry, but looks like a patient needs attention now," Tom said as he hung up.

"No problem. I think we both have to get back to work too. Why don't you come by one afternoon for a glass of wine, Tom?" I asked. "I've got some real good Cougar Gold cheese to go with it."

"I'd like that," he answered. "I'll call you. I think my schedule on Thursday may be pretty light."

All three of us walked out of the café together. Tom headed down the street toward his car and I walked Ellen to her truck, which was parked a few spots sooner than mine.

"Call me," I said. "Maybe we can get together this weekend, and don't forget that you are coming over Friday night to take the spinning class."

"I want to take the class, but you better call me Friday and remind me. I'm as apt as not to get busy and forget all about it."

Ellen was well known for not remembering dates, times, etc. Her friends just dealt with it, and somehow, she managed to get the important ones for her work remembered.

"OK, I will."

I walked on to my truck. The sun was out and it looked like it was going to be a glorious day—one of the absolutely beautiful ones that we get once in a while in February. It was crystal clear, and if we were lucky, the temperature would get into the low 50s by afternoon in spite of the chilly start to the day.

Chapter 2

I was greeted with deep Pyr barks as I pulled into my driveway and parked. I climbed up to the back porch, kicked off my shoes and entered the house. Even with the colder northwest weather, I still followed the Hawaiian custom of removing my shoes before I went into the house. It was almost ten. I made a quick change into a calf-length denim skirt with a light handknit sweater. With low-heeled boots, an added scarf for accent and some earrings, I was ready to walk over to the shop. I loved being able to commute to work on foot.

The Spider's Web is located in the property's original barn. It is a beautiful old building and was the obvious choice when I decided that I wanted to open a spinning and weaving shop on the property. I had the new barn built to the back of the house for the critters and remodeled the old one. I kept as many of the old barn's features as I could. I left the stairs up the back inside wall of the building to the old hay loft. The loft provided storage for additional stock, supplies and complete fleeces. On the main floor, some of the stall walls remained to mark off different sections of the shop and to give an area for classes to be held.

One stall was enclosed with a picket fence in front and a doggy door was placed in the barn wall behind so that Falcor and Denali could visit without being a problem to customers in the shop. The picket fence kept them in their area but allowed them to see through it and people to visit with them over it. I kept the old wood stove that was in the barn and had a sitting area arranged around it where people could gather to spin or knit or just visit.

The morning went by quickly with a private knitting lesson and a number of customers coming in. Some wanted supplies, some needed help and one only wanted to chat and have a cup of tea.

Just as my stomach started telling me that it was time for lunch, Denali wandered into the shop. She had obviously been rolling and was covered with grass. "Outside with you, big girl. You are a mess. I'll join you in a minute. Outside!" Heading outside, Denali turned her head and I swear she laughed at me as she disappeared through the dog door.

I grabbed a jacket that I keep in the shop, shut the front door and hung my note telling customers to ring the bell if they needed me. A large Japanese temple bell hung near the door of the shop. I could hear it anywhere on my property, and it allowed me the freedom to do other tasks without missing a customer when things were slow.

Denali barked at me as I walked toward the gate. It was such a beautiful afternoon that I decided to walk across the pasture. Other than a few fluffy white clouds, the sky was a clear, bright blue. With the bright sunshine, it seemed warmer than it probably was.

"Is this what you wanted?" I asked as Denali leaned in to get a good ear scratch. After a minute or so, she shook her head, gave me a look that said "we're wasting time," and preceded me across the field. The grass was a deep green from the winter rains and our rather mild weather this year. Falcor and the alpacas, Juan and Joseph, came up to get their share of petting and then joined us as we strolled toward the back fence where I could see that the witch hazel was in full bloom. I loved having this winter blooming plant to brighten my days. I'd come back later and cut some sprigs to put in the house. I led the animals back to the pasture gate, where I gave each of them a hug and left them inside while I headed to the house for lunch.

Back in the shop, I decided to work on some yarn that I was spinning for a customer. It was dog hair from the customer's beloved fourteen-year-old Samoyed. She had been saving the hair for years. It was beautiful. The skein that I had completed was lovely and soft. It would be perfect for knitting the shawl that she had planned; and finished, it would be incredibly warm and have a beautiful halo. I put some CDs on the player and sat down at my wheel.

Falcor barked and I looked up from my spinning to see my kid brother coming up the path to the shop. The bell on the door jingled as he walked in and the dogs came through the doggy door at the same time. Sean was one of their favorite people.

"Hey, Sis. What's this I hear about your morning adventures?"

Sean is seven years younger than me and I always marvel, when I see him, at how good looking that scrawny kid turned out to be. He's not too much taller than I am at five-foot-ten, dark and gives the impression of being muscular without being heavy. He often stopped by when he was out and about on business at this end of the county.

"I just noticed an open door and had to check it out. But what brings you here today?" I asked. "I thought you had a big job up at the Yelm end of the county."

"We do but Dorothy Swanson called. Something had gotten into her sheep so the captain sent me down to check it out. Looks like dogs but nothing I can do about it as she has no real idea of where they came from and not a smidgen of proof if she did have an idea," Sean said.

"I've told her more than once to get a couple of Pyrs but can't get her to listen. This must be the second attack in the last six months."

I'm a firm believer in livestock guardian dogs for flock protection and it goes without saying that the LGD of choice as far as I'm concerned is a Great Pyrenees. I preach the faith about their usefulness to the farmers around here every chance I get.

"She sure could have used a couple of them last night," Sean said. "Something got one of her ewes and hurt a second one pretty bad. Lucky she didn't lose more. Well, can I grab a quick cup of coffee for the road, Sis? Since the captain was sending me this way anyway, he wants me to pick up some information at the Grays Harbor County Sheriff's Office that may help with the burglary; and I need to check in with Walter about your burglary. Any chance of snagging dinner afterward?"

Sean was still struggling with the after-effects of a divorce and dinner was a lonely time for him. I could well understand that sentiment.

"Sure, guy, see you when you get here. I can rustle up something for us to eat."

He poured himself a cup of coffee and scratched Denali and Falcor behind the ears. Then I walked out onto the porch with him. After sending him off with a hug, I stood there savoring the warm sunshine and light breeze before turning back into the shop.

It was a little before three and I don't close the shop until four so I still had time to get some things done. I had lost my momentum on the spinning with Sean's appearance so looked for another task. I hadn't unpacked the shipment that came in Monday from Ashland Bay nor the one from Brown Sheep. Opening them was always a little bit like Christmas as I loved the look and feel of fiber. I opened the box from Ashland Bay. Out spilled a rainbow of color. The soft as a duck's down merino/tencel blends were in bright jewel tones of teal, fuscia, red, purple, yellow and green. The cashmere just begged to be fondled and the silk glistened. I pulled myself from the joy of just fondling the fiber and got busy cataloging and pricing the beautiful roving.

Soon it was time to close up for the night. The yarn from Brown Sheep would have to wait until tomorrow. Sable rubbed against my legs as I walked toward the house. She knew it was getting close to time for her dinner. But first, I had the farm critters to take care of. The early darkness during the winter made for early barn duty too. I went into the house and changed into my jeans before heading back out to the barn. The sounds of hay being pulled down and grain being taken from the covered bins had the sheep and goat joining me pretty quickly. I whistled and Juan and Joseph joined the rest of the barnyard crew. I made sure they were all closed into their respective areas in the big barn and shut the large doors. After finishing their dinner, Falcor and Denali had made their rounds of the stalls to make sure that all were safe and accounted for and then flopped down on the hay for an early evening snooze. I returned to the house where Sable told me of her displeasure at having to wait. Nothing is so distinctive as the voice of a Siamese who is not happy with you.

"OK, girl, let's see what we have for you tonight."

I filled her bowl, which was inside the laundry room and on a ledge above Pyr nose level. It was not totally foolproof but usually enough to keep them out of it.

Then I went looking to see what Sean and I were going to eat. The refrigerator yielded some leftover chili that would probably be better tonight anyway. We'd have that and some fresh cornbread and a green salad. If Sean wanted dessert, there was always ice cream in the freezer and cookies in the cookie jar. I was not much for fancy desserts so people seldom got them at my house.

I saw lights illuminate the fence and then the porch as Sean pulled into the drive. It would be nice to have company for dinner and I always enjoyed my little brother.

"Come on in," I said. "We're having chili so would you like a glass of beer before or just more coffee?"

"A beer would be nice. Got any dark ale?"

"I think so. Check the fridge and get one for me too, please. Did you get what you needed from Montesano?" I asked.

"Yes and no," Sean answered as he handed me a beer and settled onto one of the bar stools beside the kitchen island. "I was able to get the information that the captain wanted but doubt that it is going to help solve this robbery. But fill me in on this morning."

"Not much to tell," I answered. I ran him through my trip to town.

"I probably don't have to say that putting your head in that door was pretty stupid," he said in his tough cop tone of voice.

"I know it. I just didn't think about it. But then you know me, often heading where angels fear to tread."

While I was talking, I'd put the cornbread in the oven and broken up the washed greens for salad. Wouldn't be long until we ate.

"Want to start a fire for us, Sean? I'll get the table set and then I think we will be ready to dish this up."

I had a large country kitchen and loved the fact that there was a two-sided fireplace that separated the kitchen and dining area from the living room. I could enjoy a cheery fire during the long evenings of a Northwest winter no matter which room I was in. With the fire going and the table set, we settled down for a good dinner and our conversation continued.

"What did you learn from Walter this afternoon?" I asked.

"Something very interesting. Our burglar is getting a bit sloppy and left finger prints at his last hit in Yelm. Well, those prints matched some left in your burglary here so it looks like he may have moved south in the county."

"You haven't been able to get a name for the prints?" I asked.

"They've been submitted but so far we've had no response," Sean answered.

"I wonder why he has moved south." I said. "Most of us function in our own little rabbit runs and don't usually branch out to other parts of the county."

"My guess is it was getting a little hot for the guy in the Yelm area," Sean answered. "We now have four break-ins— three homes and one business. Because all have similarities, we are assuming at this point that they were all the work of one person. We now have people pretty well alerted in that area and they are becoming more security conscious."

"Why should that stop him?"

"Because (and this is not for publication) the burglar has only gone into places that were open. We call him the 'opportunist burglar,'" Sean answered. "Janelle admitted to Walter that she may have forgotten to lock the door last night. She couldn't remember doing it and Walter didn't find evidence of a forced entry. We haven't had a recent break-in up north. All of this adds up to the possibility that the 'opportunist' has moved south."

"So your effort at getting people to lock up and stop the opportunity may be working up north and he may have moved down here," I said. "I don't know whether I should thank you for that one. I usually leave my house and shop both unlocked when I'm here. Guess I may need to rethink that."

"You do have the advantage of Falcor and Denali. No place that was hit had a dog but I think it would be a good idea at least until we catch him. We will do that and my guess is fairly soon. When they start getting sloppy in one thing like the fingerprints, they end up getting sloppy in another area. He'll mess up. I'll stake my badge on it. Any dessert?" Sean continued.

"Ice cream and cookies. Check out the freezer and get what you want. You can bring me a small bowl of the macadamia nut," I answered.

While Sean got the dessert, I put the dinner dishes in the dishwasher.

"Let's take this into the living room. It's cozier," I said as I walked in there and curled up on the couch.

Once settled in, our conversation turned to other things. Sean was thinking about making a trip this year into the canyon lands of Utah, probably in October when it wouldn't be quite so hot. He filled me in on his current plans and the pros and cons of various areas to visit. First thing I knew it was almost nine o'clock.

"Well, Sis," Sean said. "I'd better head out of here. The captain will want me there early tomorrow with his information."

"Would you close the gate to the road when you leave?" I asked. "That way, I can let the dogs into the whole area for the night."

I had an outer gate that closed off the house and shop from the road. During the day, I kept it open so customers and friends could come and go easily and kept the inner fenced area gated to keep the dogs in. But at night, I liked them to have access to all the property and I wanted them to be able to visit with me. They had a dog door into the laundry area that provided them entry into the house.

"OK," Sean said. "I'll take off. Talk to you in the next few days. However if I get real busy with this robbery, it may be longer than that. Thanks for dinner and good company. Much better than I would have gotten at my house. The microwave doesn't cook half as well as you do."

I gave him a hug and walked him to the door. I'd let the dogs out as soon as he had the gate locked. I gave him a wave and turned to put my boots on. It had cooled down again, although not as cold as yesterday evening. The clouds had come in and it looked like we would have rain before morning. I walked to the barn and went in through the small door. The critters were settled down for the night and didn't raise a head except for Falcor and Denali who were standing there, tails moving gently, ready to walk back with me.

"OK, monsters, time for us to get settled in for the night. Let's go."

The dogs made a beeline for the area that they had been kept out of all day. After sniffing and catching up on the comings and goings of the world, both marked to make sure that any interloper would know that this was their territory and off-bounds to outsiders. Then with a couple of large woofs, they followed me into the house. If they followed their normal pattern, they would go out a couple of times during the night, make their rounds of the fence lines, checking on everything, and then come back to sleep on the porch or in the house.

Because my number of animals was small and the area that I had actually fenced for them only about half of my acreage, I could let the Pyrs be house pets as well as guard dogs. If I had a large flock or larger areas for them to roam, the Pyrs would need to stay with their flock all the time. I liked this arrangement as I enjoyed their company.

Back in the house, I curled up on the couch with Sable on my lap and settled in with a cup of tea to enjoy the fire for a while longer. I picked up the mystery I was reading. It was a classic that I had somehow missed up until now, *Daughter of Time* by Josephine Tey, and I was enjoying the references to both Shakespeare and English history.

However, I soon found myself wondering about the robbery. Was it Sean's burglar? If so, were we in for more in the area? I picked up the book again but couldn't get interested. It was time for bed. The dogs raised their heads but didn't follow me into the bedroom. I kept the door slightly open so they could come in if they wanted to check on me during the night. I was tired and would have no problems sleeping tonight.

Chapter 3

A bark from Denali alerted me just before I heard the classic sounds of a large, commercial truck backing up. I put down the last skein of yarn I was putting in the inventory, walked to the door and out onto the porch. It was the delivery truck from Black Hills Feed. Looked like my hay, straw and feed had arrived.

"Hi, Martha," Leslie said as she jumped out of the passenger side of the truck. "I want you to meet Jack Byron."

A tall, maybe six-foot, young man with sandy hair and a ton of freckles unfolded himself from the front seat of the truck. As he put out his hand, a smile spread across his face. He had the clearest green eyes that I think I had ever seen.

"Good to meet you, Martha," he said.

"Jack has been working for Dad and me for about two weeks now," Leslie said. "We've been feeling a need for an extra hand ever since the first of the year."

Leslie's father, Ted Larson, was second generation in oper-
ating Black Hills Feed and Leslie has every intention of being
the third generation. Her brother wanted no part of the business and headed to Seattle and the U to get a law degree. He
settled in the big city up north and was very happy with the
change. Leslie, on the other hand, really loved working with
her father and helping to run their all-purpose country supply
store and greenhouse. Many of her ideas enlarged its scope and
business, so I could see how they might need some extra help.

"It's good to meet you, Jack," I said. "How do you like Black
Hills?"

"I like it a lot. My Aunt Jo says it's a great place and that has
been my experience so far."

"Jack is Jo Duncan's nephew," Leslie added.

Jo is an elementary school teacher in town and an infre-
quent customer of mine.

"It is a great place, Jack," I said. "I'm sure you will enjoy living here."

"Well, I suppose we should get this stuff unloaded, Martha," Leslie said. "We still have two more places to go before
lunch."

"OK, let me get the dogs corralled and I'll open the gate
for you."

I stopped by the back porch and gathered up a couple of
leashes. After going through the gate and shutting it behind
me, I collected both dogs, who were vigilantly watching the
activities on the other side of the gate. With the dogs shut se-
curely in the tack room, I opened the gate. A Pyr owner learns
quickly that you never let your dog see an open gate and wide
open territory beyond it. That is the way to have a walkabout
Pyr for some time.

Jack climbed back into the truck and expertly backed it up to my barn doors. Leslie was quickly moving bales of hay and straw to the edge of the truck for Jack to lift onto the dolly and move into the barn. Her lithe frame belied her strength and she soon had all of my order except the grain, chicken feed and dog food out of the truck. It took her no time to get those fifty-pound bags moved too.

Jumping off the tailgate, she wiped her hands on her jeans and then ran her fingers through her short blonde hair.

"Hey, Big Guy," she teased Jack, "don't you have that stuff taken care of in the barn yet?"

"Hey yourself," he answered, "one more bag and I'm done."

I laughed as I watched the byplay between the two of them. You'd think they'd been working together for a long time and not just two weeks. Looked to me like Jack had clicked with Leslie in more ways than one.

"Well, that's the last of it," Leslie said. "Dad will send you the bill as always."

"Want to come into the shop for a quick cup of coffee or tea?" I asked.

"I'd love to but we really do need to finish delivering this stuff," Leslie said. "I'll be here tomorrow though," she added.

Thursdays were Leslie's day off.

"OK, I'll let you go then," I said, "and talk to you tomorrow. Looks to me like we have some catching up to do."

Leslie just laughed and climbed into the cab of the truck next to Jack.

"OK, mister," she said. "Let's get this show on the road again."

"Yes, ma'am," he answered with a grin.

They both waved as Jack drove the truck out of my driveway and onto the road. I closed the gate and wandered into the barn thinking of those first weeks after I had met John. Were we as obvious to those around us? Probably so.

As I opened the tack room door, the dogs pushed past me and circled the barn, sniffing where Jack and Leslie had walked. They surveyed the new supplies and then loped outside to check out any changes there.

Nali came back toward me and then snorted as she marched off to check on her sheep. She obviously did not approve of my letting these people onto her property when she wasn't there to supervise.

As I started out the gate, I noticed that it had started to mist and the temperature had dropped some. Seemed like a good time to find some soup for lunch. As the last of my lunch disappeared, a horn blew and a familiar brown truck drove into the driveway. I ran out to sign for the package.

"Just one for you today, Martha," George said.

"That's fine with me," I answered. "I just finished putting the things away that you brought me on Monday."

"You don't order them, I don't deliver them," he said with a rather lopsided grin.

"I don't order them, I don't have anything to sell," I answered back.

George had been delivering to my business for the last three years. We have one of those easy acquaintances you often get with people that you deal with often for business.

"Well, I must keep up the reputation for quick and efficient delivery so I'll see you next time," he said as he started the truck. He turned around and was soon out of the driveway and on his way.

Denali, who had come running up to the fence when she

heard the truck arrive, sent him off with a woof. I picked up the box and walked into the shop.

My spindle maker had outdone herself this time. The spindles were absolutely beautiful, and the wood was wonderful, with a variety of choices. I'd probably call a couple of regular customers to let them know about the new shipment. After cataloging each one, I took them to where the spindles were displayed. With leaders attached and a little roving in a basket nearby, people could give each a test spin before buying. A spindle was a very personal choice.

I looked around the shop. The new fiber and yarn were now in place and added to the color palette of the large room, and the new spindles gave a great selection from which customers could choose. I did enjoy owning the shop and helping others with their spinning and weaving needs. I also carried a good selection of knitting and crochet products and lots of books. I couldn't imagine taking up a hobby and not reading all you could about it, so I just assumed that others felt the same way. By and large that seemed to be true, as I sold a lot of books.

I heard a dog shake and looked over to see Falcor standing in the dog area looking a mite wet, with a very wet and disgruntled-looking Sable next to him. Looking outside, I saw the reason why. The mist, that was falling when I walked over after lunch, had turned into a downpour, and the wind was coming up. It looked like it meant to stay that way for awhile too. Falcor and Sable seemed to think so as they made no attempt to go back outside. He lay down in his part of the shop for a snooze and Sable walked through the pickets and settled down in front of the stove. In the meantime, I decided to spin some more of the Samoyed.

There was something almost trance-inducing about spinning. Especially if you had some favorite music playing in the background. Once you were comfortable with the task, there was no need to concentrate on the spinning itself. The fiber just slipped between your fingers while your feet treadled the wheel. Meanwhile your head could be off wherever it wanted to be. As I listened to the rain on the roof and the wind, I thought of tropical torrents and green jungles on the north shore of Oahu. John and I had some of our finest times during our station in Hawai`i. One of these days, I would go back for a vacation, but not to where we were. You really can't go home again and I wasn't sure I wanted to see those places without him. I would go to the Big Island and see the land of Pele. For some reason, we never made it over there when we were together.

Wheels crunched on the driveway and both dogs barked. I looked up to see Jane blown in by the wind and followed by a spat of rain.

"My, you're out on a nasty day. What brings you here?"

Jane was a new teacher at Black Hills Elementary this year and a good one from what I'd heard. She looked like a little elf and couldn't have been more than five feet tall—petite in every way. Her dark curls ringed her face and bounced when she almost danced into any place she went.

"I ran out of the Brown Sheep Violet Fields and wanted to get some more before you ran out," Jane answered. "I'm knitting a sweater for my mom for her birthday."

"You're in luck then," I said. "I think I've three or four skeins left and they should be the same dye lot that you purchased. How much are you going to need?"

"I think I'll take four, if you have them, just to be safe," Jane answered. "If I have too much, I can knit a hat to go with it or something. I'd rather have too much than run out again since the next time you may not have the same dye lot."

"That's possible. I almost always have the Violet Fields because it is so popular but I do notice subtle differences in the shading between dye lots. They might show up in the middle of the back of a sweater. Can I get you anything else? I just got some of that great sock yarn that puts in the design for you as you knit. It should be on the shelf to the right of your Brown Sheep."

"I'll have to look at them. There is something about a day like today that calls out for handknit socks. By the way do you have the book, *Folk Socks*, by Nancy Bush?" Jane asked. "One of the other teachers at school says it's great."

"Sure do, it's on the second shelf of the books on the right-hand side. It is a wonderful book—lots of good information on knitting socks in general as well as some great patterns."

"I hear you discovered a robbery yesterday," Jane said as she walked to the counter. "I hope that doesn't mean that our quiet town's becoming dangerous."

"My, news does spread in this town. I just noticed an open door. I can't imagine Black Hills as dangerous. I can't remember the last time we had a major crime here—the kind with injuries. Hopefully this was just a transient passing through."

"Maybe," Jane said but she didn't sound convinced. "Still I worry about something worse happening."

"You've spent too much time in the big city," I said. "Need anything else?"

Jane laughed. "Nope," she said. "You've already managed to get me to buy two items that I didn't come in for. But I'm sure I'll enjoy both of them. I'm ready to get home before this rain gets any worse. It will be a good night to knit by the fire."

"I can't agree with you more on that assessment. OK, here are your packages and the charge slip for your signature. By the way, are you still planning on taking the spinning class starting Friday?"

"Yes, I am and I'm really looking forward to it. It will be great fun to learn how to spin my own yarn for knitting. Plus, I want to be able to teach my fifth graders how to do it. I think they'll have a great time and maybe we can manage a bookmark or something like that for a finished project before the end of the school year."

"Sounds like a grand plan to me," I responded. "Well, I'll see you Friday then."

I realized as Jane walked out the door that it was past four and time for me to close up shop. I shooed Falcor out his door and locked it. I went through my evening lockup ritual, gathered Sable into my arms, pulled the hood of my coat up over my head and dashed to the house to change into my barn clothes.

With my clothes changed and a rain slicker and boots on, I walked out to shut the outside gate. The dogs were waiting for me when I got to the inside one.

"Come on, guys. Let's get your charges fed and shut in for the night. Then we can settle in too."

They followed along as if they completely understood my chatter, and on some level, I was certain that they did. All the barn critters had already moved into their respective stall areas. They didn't like this weather either and they had supper on their minds. It didn't take long to feed and water them.

My white shadows and I decided to run for the back porch. As usual they beat me by a large margin. These dogs look slow as they do their usual amble but they can be incredibly quick when they want to be. I arrived at the porch just in time to get a good shower as both dogs shook hard.

"Here guys, let me towel you off. If I don't, you will shake even more water in my kitchen when we go in."

As I opened the door to let the toweled dogs and me into the house, I heard the phone ringing and then my machine come on. I grabbed it just before the person could leave their message.

"Hello."

"Martha, this is Tom. Does that offer still stand for wine and cheese?"

"Sure does. Are you planning on coming out on this nasty night?"

"No, I still have two appointments this evening. How about late tomorrow afternoon? I'm scheduled light because I have to give a talk at the Rotary meeting at seven o'clock. Thought maybe I could drop over to your house about five for an appetizer before boring myself to tears talking about the need for medical student scholarships."

"Sounds good to me," I answered. "I close the shop at four o'clock so anytime after that would work just fine."

"Well, Angie says my next appointment is here. So I'll see you tomorrow afternoon."

I hung up smiling. Tom was always great fun to talk to. I also wanted to ask him about his trip to New Mexico. I loved that country. My father was stationed at Kirtland Air Force Base and I went to high school there. The last time I was there was for my tenth high school reunion. I wondered if Tom was in Albuquerque at that time and why he left. He was always very silent about his decision to move up here.

Chapter 4

Metal shrieked as the truck tore into the small car and careened it into the cement center barrier. There was a flash and the flames started to roar through the car. I screamed and fought my way through the flames just as a cold nose pushed hard on my shoulder and a sloppy kiss pulled me out of my nightmare. I grabbed Denali and hugged her hard as I panted and tried to catch my breath. Gradually my pounding heart began to slow and my body stopped shaking. This nightmare was recurrent during the first year after John's death and then happened less frequently over the next couple of years. I hadn't suffered from it for over a year now. Why did it happen this morning? What was triggering those fears? I wasn't sure I wanted to find out.

"Thanks, big girl. You haven't had to do this duty for awhile. I'm so glad you were here to wake me."

It was still early, but there was no way I was going to go

back to sleep. A hot shower helped pull me back into my body and the current part of my life. It was too early to feed the animals so I settled on the window seat with my coffee. Sable curled up beside me and both dogs lay nearby to make sure that I really was OK.

As I sipped my coffee and gazed out the window, the morning dawned bright and clear. That was one thing about the weather in the Pacific Northwest—wait a short while and it will change. In the spring, it seemed even more erratic. I could wake up to a snow storm tomorrow.

Having recovered from my morning scare, the dogs and I walked out to the barn to take care of the animals. With all of them fed and the water troughs filled, I opened the doors to the lovely day. The dogs followed me out and as far as their inside gate. They knew they had to stay back and didn't bother to come through with me. I closed their gate and then walked to the front and opened my gate to the road.

As I turned to walk to the back door, I heard the squealing of tires way out on the highway. I flashed to my dream and once again wondered why it had come back at this time. I couldn't think of any reason so I gave myself a shake and went on into the house to fix my own breakfast.

After finishing my breakfast and taking care of some work around the house, I walked over to open the shop. I planned on preparing the classroom section for the spinning class before the Ewephoric group arrived at twelve-thirty. Each Thursday, somewhere between five and ten women brought their brown bag lunches and showed up for a couple of hours of spinning, knitting and chatting. They had a good time and I often sold fiber, patterns, books, needles or yarn to them so it worked well for me too.

Even with a few interruptions to make sales, the job went quickly and I soon had the things I would need for class tomorrow assembled. Just as I stood back to look at my work and see what else might be needed, Denali barked and I heard the sound of wheels on the driveway. The first of the women had arrived.

As Linda walked in the door, I saw another car pull up with Mary and Elizabeth. Leslie and Kerry were close behind. Jeevana was the last to arrive. Tiny and slim, she looked loaded down with her spinning wheel and basket of fiber.

"Hi, everybody," I said. "Make yourselves at home. The coffee should be ready any minute and the hot water is there. I think I even have some cocoa mix next to the tea if you want some."

The women began to settle into their favorite spots. Mary pulled one of the chairs from the classroom area over to where we were sitting and pulled her spindle from her bag. Kerry settled on one of the cushions on the floor with her knitting in hand. I marveled at how she could stay in that position for long periods. Just goes to show what yoga can do for you. Leslie curled up in one of the overstuffed chairs and Elizabeth and Linda settled on the couch. Jeevana and I pulled spinning chairs over and set up our wheels.

"Hey, Elizabeth, how is Martin doing since he was changed to Jane's class?" Linda asked.

"He's doing great," Elizabeth answered. "I can't tell you what a change it has made in the kid. He's actually looking forward to going to school in the mornings now. What a relief it is to not have to fight with him every morning of the week."

"My Darcy loves her too," Linda said. "She is so creative. She really helps the kids to see how everything they are learning is important to them as individuals. They were all writing poetry the other day and doing a pretty good job of it. She now has them researching on the Internet how a book is put together. They are going to produce their own book of their poetry. In the meantime, they are learning a lot about research, the art of book making, and anything else she can manage to place in the project. I really like the way she pulls all the subjects into whatever project they are working on. It helps the kids to see that this stuff is for real life and not just for grades."

"We're real lucky to have her decide to teach here this year," Elizabeth commented. "Does anyone know why she made the move? It's not as if we're some big school district that pays a bunch. We are a pretty small pond for such a talented teacher."

"She told me that she was tired of fighting big school politics and traffic jams while getting to work," I joined in. "She was here getting some yarn last night and she's going to take the spinning class that I'm starting tomorrow so she can teach the children to spin. Don't be surprised if you get an end-of-the-year present from your kids that has something to do with handspun. She really does seem creative in her approach to teaching. The kids are lucky to have her. By the way," I added, "I have a new supply of Brown Sheep yarn and Ashland Bay fiber in so you might want to check the shelves before you leave today."

"Notice how she just slips that in, girls," Elizabeth said. "Now we are going to have to check it out and for me that almost always means a purchase. Bad Martha. There goes my spending money for awhile."

I just chuckled.

"Martha," Mary said, "Walter tells me you had a bit of excitement on Tuesday."

"Not much," I answered. "He wouldn't let me stay around to see what was going on. Your husband is a stickler for police details."

"He is that. I guess Janelle accidentally left her door unlocked and the guy really trashed the place. Didn't take much except her TV, the computer and a small amount of change she had there. She had made a deposit the night before so didn't have a large amount of cash there, but he sure made a mess looking."

"I wonder if the insurance company will pay anything since she was negligent," Linda said.

"Good question," I commented. "I hope so, for her sake. Sean reminded me that we need to be extra vigilant in locking up right now. Dogs don't hurt either," I added.

"Especially dogs the size of yours," Jeevana quipped.

As if to underline that point, Denali came in to check on all of us and see what we were up to.

"Making sure we are behaving, big girl?" I said.

She answered with a soft woof and settled down to keep an eye on us for awhile.

"Hey, gang, have you seen the new guy who's working at the feed store?" Jeevana asked with a quick grin in Leslie's direction. Jeevana was Leslie's closest friend and didn't mind needling her a bit.

"Yep, met him last Friday when I went in for dog food for Blackie," Mary answered. "Come on, Leslie, tell us about him."

Leslie blushed, which of course caused all of us to laugh and prod her some more.

"Well, he comes from Portland and lives with Jo Duncan, who is his aunt. She was the one who told him about the job at the feed store. He has his degree from OSU and he was in the Air Force right out of high school. His mother is a legal secretary and she raised both him and his sister by herself. And that's about all I know except he is very nice, a hard worker and visits his mother on his days off."

"That's all?" Jeevana said and laughed again, which caused Leslie to blush again and all the rest of us to laugh.

The conversation then turned to what was happening in the legislative session and then to speculations on whether Sally was going to get married or not. Rumor had it that she and Jason were getting pretty serious. Jason Nordlund owned the lumber yard and hardware store in town and had been out there as a prime catch for quite some time. People in small towns do have a way of worrying about everyone's business in addition to their own.

"Oh my gosh, look at the time. I have a full house this week and need to stop at the grocery store before I pick up Darcy at school," Linda said. "I better get going."

Linda operated a bed-and-breakfast in her home called Lavender Nights. With her comment the others also realized that they needed to start packing things up and get ready to leave.

"Think I'll take a rain check on looking over that yarn today," Elizabeth commented as she packed up her things. "I really do need to finish up a few more things before I add to my stash. Though that seldom stops me for long," she added and laughed. "By the way, do you have room for a last-minute sign-up for the spinning class? I might try to make it. Need to check my calendar for the next few weeks and make sure the Fridays are free."

"Sure. I think we only have eight signed up and I can handle up to ten. You don't have to call me. Just show up at seven o'clock if you can make it."

"OK, I'll be here if I can. I would like to learn how to make some yarn from different fibers for my knitting."

"Great thing to do with handspun. And the spinning itself becomes addicting. You think you have a yarn stash," I added. "Wait until you add fiber to it. Just ask Jeevana. But then I better be careful, I may be talking myself out of a student."

Elizabeth laughed and followed Mary out the door. Linda, Leslie and Kerry were busy looking at the new yarn, and Jeevana was fondling the new Ashland Bay selection. "I also have some new patterns and the latest copy of *Interweave Knits* if you need something to do with that yarn." I commented to them. They just laughed.

"Okay, I'll take these," Kerry said as she piled her skeins of yarn on the counter. "Also a copy of *Interweave Knits*. One of these days I'll get me a subscription to it. Seems like I buy it every month anyway."

I rang up her purchases and those of Leslie.

"Anything for you, Linda?"

"Not today. But I do want some of the wonderful self-designing sock yarn. Just need the extra spending money," she answered.

"It should be here when you want it. I try to always have some on hand as it is quite popular."

"How about you, Jeevana, find anything tempting over there?"

"Lots but I'm saving my money for the fleece show in May. I want to buy some raw wool and try that. Are you going to be covering raw wool in the spinning class?"

"I am the second night. Do you want to come for just that night?"

"Maybe I'll come and just sit in on all of them. I might be

able to help you out with the rank beginners," she answered.
"That is if you would like me to."

"That would be great. As you know, the first night is very
hands on and an extra pair of experienced hands would be wonderful. I really appreciate the offer."

With that I walked them to the door and watched as they
left for their respective cars and lives. I straightened up the conversation area, totaled up my sales for today, closed up the shop
and headed to the house to get ready for Tom.

I decided that the farm animals could wait until after Tom's
visit since he would be leaving in time to get to the seven o'clock
meeting. However, Sable seemed to think that she couldn't wait
at all and was telling me about it in no uncertain terms.

"Okay, noisy face, we'll get you fed. Just give me a minute,
will you?" I was informed in a very strident Siamese voice that a
minute was longer than I should be allowed when her majesty
wanted attention.

Having fed the cat, I did a quick check of the house to make
sure it was in at least reasonable company order and started a
fire in the fireplace. Also ran a quick brush through my hair
and made sure I at least had some lipstick on. My slacks and
cashmere sweater from work would work for the evening too.

Just as I finished putting the cheese, along with some pear
and apple slices, onto a plate and back in the fridge, I heard
the dogs bark and wheels on the drive. I went to the door and
watched Tom unfold his large self from the front seat of his
Jeep. Like so many of us here, he went for utility in his vehicle.
If we don't drive pickups, we are in SUVs.

"Come in, Tom, you're all spiffed up. Not very often we see
you in a coat and tie."

"This monkey suit is my college professor and big city doctor uniform. I'm trying to impress people that I do know what I'm talking about when it comes to the need for scholarships. Think I'll fool them?" Tom said.

"I doubt that you'll have any problem convincing them. Anyone who knows the long hours that you work has to know that we need more family doctors. And with the cost of medical school, many worthy students won't make it without help."

I turned and led Tom into the kitchen. "I have a great Oregon gewürztraminer chilled in the fridge or a nice cabernet from eastern Washington," I said. "Which would you prefer?"

"If the gewürztraminer is dry, I'll take it."

"It is and has a wonderful bouquet and spice to it. If you like gewürztraminer, I think you'll like this one a lot," I answered.

I handed the wine to Tom along with the bottle opener and went back to the fridge for the cheese, pear and apple slices. Some crackers were already in a basket on the coffee table, along with some glasses, napkins, etc. Tom followed me with the open wine to the sitting area and we settled down by the fire.

"Now tell me about your trip. I haven't been back to New Mexico for years."

Tom grinned. "I didn't know that you had lived there."

"Yes, my father was an Air Force career officer and he was stationed there for my high school years. I loved the majesty of the area and the open spaciousness, but will have to admit that I longed for a little green."

"Well, Albuquerque has just grown bigger and sprawled further out in all directions, but the central area around the university is still much the same and quite nice. I actually didn't spend too much time there. I finally decided to sell my house and went down for the final signing of the paper. It had been my ace in the hole in case I wanted to move back, but I decided this past summer that I was here to stay so put it on the market. It took awhile to sell but I got a good price when it did go."

Tom shifted in his seat and reached for a slice of apple. "When I finished with the formal stuff, I headed up north. I still have a large ranch in northern New Mexico where I grew up. There is a great family living on the ranch and working it for me. I went up to see them and have a short vacation. The area hasn't developed yet though the growth from Taos is creeping in that direction. However as long as I own the ranch, it will stay rural."

That was more about Tom's history than I'd heard from him in the four years that I had known him. It is surprising how you think you know someone pretty well and then realize how little you do know. Tom is open and very friendly when it comes to his current life here in Black hills but he has always been pretty close-mouthed about his life in New Mexico.

"If you wanted to move to a more rural practice, why didn't you move up there when you left Albuquerque?" I asked.

"I was ready to leave New Mexico," Tom replied. For a moment he stared at the fire and then continued. "Things had changed for me there, including a divorce, and I was ready for new space and a new life."

"New Mexico's loss was our gain and I know people are very glad that you decided to settle here. Family physicians of your skill and old-fashioned practices are very hard to come by. Besides that, you've added one likable character to the town," I laughed.

"Enough about me," he said. "What has been happening in your world?"

"I'm getting ready for a spinning class that starts tomorrow night," I said. "Other than that, I'm just taking care of the shop and the animals. I need to start thinking about a small garden as soon as the chance of hard frost is pretty much gone. Like you, after a number of years living in large cities and working in various government or corporate jobs, I like this quiet lifestyle a lot."

Our conversation then drifted to what was happening around Black Hills and the latest cultural events that were coming up in Olympia and north and then back to Black Hills again.

"I appreciate your invitation," Tom said. "It's been a welcome breather in a much-too-busy schedule. Would you be willing to let me reciprocate with a dinner in the next couple of weeks?"

"That would be nice. Let me know when. Most of my evenings are unscheduled except for Fridays when I'll be teaching for the next couple of months."

"I will. I just need to check my schedule. And speaking of my schedule, I had better get a move on or I'm going to be late. I really did enjoy this break. Thanks again for having me over."

I walked Tom to the back porch and watched as he drove out. Denali and Falcor gave him their parting barks and then looked expectantly at me.

"Just a minute, guys. I have to change my clothes and I'll be out."

I looked across the pasture as I turned toward the door just in time to see the great horned owl glide across the face of the moon.

Chapter 5

I awoke to another clear, cold morning. Two in a row must be some kind of record. As I pulled on my barn clothes, Falcor walked into the room.

"You've decided it is time for me to be up and about, have you, big guy. OK, I'm coming. Let's go get everyone fed and ready for the day."

Just as I walked out onto the porch, Sean pulled up to my outside gate. I grabbed the dogs' leashes and yelled at him to come on in once they were secure. I had no idea why my brother was here this early in the morning. He drove inside and then shut the gate behind him. As he walked toward me, I noticed that he didn't have his usual grin for me. His eyes looked troubled and there was a slight line between his brows.

"What's wrong?" I called, as I once again released the dogs, who ran to him in glad abandon. He leaned down to give each one of them a pat and then looked up at me.

"Not good news," he said as he walked closer to me. "Tom was shot and killed last night."

"No, that's not possible," I said as Sean gathered me into his arms.

I just stood there for a minute in the comfort of his embrace as I tried to let the news sink in. I then pulled back and looked at him. I could feel tears welling up in my eyes and I brushed at them with the back of my hand.

"He was just here yesterday evening. What happened? How? Where?"

"I really don't know many details yet. The sheriff sent me over since I've been the lead deputy on the burglaries in our area. There might be a chance that this is related somehow."

"But Tom wouldn't have left his office open," I said.

"It appears it was open, though. There was no evidence of forced entry. From what I got on the phone, Jonathon is thinking that Tom surprised a burglar on his way home from the Rotary meeting and the guy panicked."

"I suppose, but that just doesn't seem to ring true. Why would someone who has done easy burglaries decide to kill? Why not just run?" I asked.

"I can't answer your questions, Sis. I wish I could."

Shaking my head, I moved back into the comfort of Sean's arms. I thought of Jane's comment: "I worry about something worse happening." It now seemed like prophecy. Tom and I had become good friends during the time when I was dealing with John's death. He was willing to listen as long as I needed him to as he dealt with my grief-induced health issues of sleeplessness and weight loss. Since then we had worked together on a couple of local committees, and just recently, our friendship had looked like it might move into something more. Now that was all put to an end by a violent death.

Sean gave me a squeeze and released me as he said, "I have to get to the scene, but I didn't want you to hear the news via the grapevine."

"I appreciate that," I replied. I was trying to stay calm but I could feel the tears near the surface again. "It will take a bit to assimilate your news. It still doesn't seem possible. Let me get the dogs behind their gate and I'll get the front gate for you."

"No need to do that. Just get the dogs under control, and I'll let myself out. Want me to leave the gate open?"

"Please," I replied. I gave him another big hug and turned toward the barn area.

"Come on Nali, Falcor. Time to go to the barn."

Once inside the closed inner gate, I turned and waved to Sean. He opened the outer gate and honked once as he drove out of the drive and on down the road.

As I walked into the barn, I tried to understand Tom's death, and there was no way to do it. Did he surprise the burglar? If he did see something on his way home from the Rotary meeting, why would he have decided to investigate it? He knew about the burglaries and a doctor's office is a prime target for drugs. Why didn't he just call Jonathon? Probably because he thought his size would protect him. After all, there was no indication that the burglar was really dangerous. But then, when cornered, many people do stupid things. Still the whole thing made no sense at all.

I finished the chores in the barn and started back toward the house. It was going to be a hard day to work but maybe it would help me keep my mind busy. Fat chance there, I had a feeling.

Back in the house, I saw that I had three new messages on my machine. Sean was right. The local news system was working overtime. Well, they could wait. I wanted to take a shower and see if it would help clear my head a little. Sometimes the feel of hot cascading water can help even the biggest hurt.

Standing in the shower crying, I realized one reason why Tom's death was hurting so bad. I was flashing back to the loss of John. Tom and I were good friends but I realized that my feelings were out of proportion to the loss of him. I was reliving that awful moment when I realized that John was not coming back again.

Showered and dressed, I went back to the kitchen. My machine delivered messages from Ellen, Elizabeth and Kerry, all with the same news in different variations. I took my coffee and decided to call Ellen back. Wasn't sure I would bother with the others this morning.

"Sean came by with the news early this morning," I said as soon as Ellen answered. "It doesn't seem real."

"It is, though," she responded. "I just got off the phone with Angie. She says the office is pure chaos with the phones ringing off the hook and the police there. So far they are guessing that Tom surprised the burglar that has hit before in the area."

"I'm assuming Angie didn't find him, though, since Sean was called so early this morning with the news. She wouldn't have been in the office yet."

"You're correct there," Ellen answered. "Bob Mitchell found him about four-thirty this morning when he went by on his way to open the gas station. The door was open, which Bob thought was rather odd, so he went in to check on it. Found Tom sprawled on the floor of the waiting room. When he went to check on him, Tom was already cold."

"The waiting room? That doesn't sound like the surprise of a burglar. Unless of course he was trying to get away just as Tom walked in."

"I know," Ellen said. "I promised Angie that I'd come down and help her inventory later this morning. Marlene is on vacation and Angie doesn't want to use the temporary nurses. Want to help? I think we could use some."

"Sounds like a good idea. I'll put a note on the door of the shop and leave a message on the shop machine saying we will have class tonight but that I'll be gone until late this afternoon."

"Good. Angie said to come about eleven. The crime scene team said they'd be done by then," Ellen said.

"OK, see you there. You can let Angie know that I'm coming to help too."

The police were just leaving when I got to Dr. Tom's office a little before eleven. Jonathon Green, our police chief, came over to me.

"Hi, Martha, I was going to call you. I wanted to show you this."

He handed me a plastic envelope.

"One of my business cards. Where did you find it, Jon?"

"Under Dr. Tom's body," Jon answered.

"Under his body? That means it was on the floor probably but how did it get there?" I asked.

"We are hoping that the murderer dropped it and that it might have fingerprints on it. Have you any idea who might frequent your shop and want to burglarize the office and kill Tom?" Jon asked.

"Jon, that's ridiculous. None of my customers would hurt Tom, but many of them are patients here and could have dropped it," I answered.

"Well, we'll see if it yields any clues for us. But I'm not optimistic," Jon said.

Jonathon stood there shaking his head. He appeared to have aged overnight. The gray in his dark hair seemed more prominent and his slumping shoulders made him appear even shorter than his 5'9". His usual crooked smile was missing and so was the twinkle in his eyes. It was obvious that our chief cop was taking this pretty hard.

"Hard job for you today, Jon. Hopefully Angie, Ellen and I can let you know by this afternoon what's missing," I said.

"Thanks. That will help," Jonathon answered. We've gotten what we can from here. Now, I need to head back to the office and see if I can make any sense of the evidence we have so far. It doesn't quite fit the other burglaries but that's our best guess so far. Walter had Blackie try to follow a trail but looks like the person got into a car very quickly and Bob Mitchell ran over the tracks that were off the road when he pulled in before he realized that there was a real problem. I have men going to all the neighbors to see if anyone saw a car here last night. It looks like it was pretty late, though, according to the first estimate of the coroner. Which makes it odd that he would surprise a burglar on his way home. The Rotary meeting was over at nine o'clock. I know because I was there."

"Take care. Hope you get a lucky break soon. It is not too comforting to know that someone who could kill Tom is loose in the area."

Jon turned to get into his car and I walked into the office. The waiting room wasn't in too bad a shape. Then I caught sight of the blood on the carpet where Dr. Tom had fallen. I just stood there a moment and stared at it. The tears started to surface again. How could that be all of Tom that remained in the office?

The sound of Angie setting upright a small table that had been knocked over brought me back from my thoughts. I walked over and hugged her. There were no words to say at a point like this. She had worked with Tom for almost eight years and I knew she was extremely fond of him. I knew this would be a double blow to her. Her much loved boss and friend was gone, and she would feel the pain of her community, which also lost him.

Angie gave me an extra squeeze. Even today she looked lovely and pulled together. Her gray hair was styled in a casual short cut that framed her face. Her lovely wool teal pants and her tunic top gave her slightly plump frame a sleek look. Her hazel eyes reflected her grief but she still smiled as she pulled back from me.

"Thanks so much for coming, Martha," she said. "It means a lot to have help that I can trust to be both efficient and discreet. I already have Ellen in the office cleaning up, and organizing and counting drugs. I'm going to put you to work in the storage closet," Angie said. "I'm still trying to locate Marlene to let her know what happened." Marlene was Tom's office nurse who had worked for him about a year. "She's on a ski vacation in Sun Valley with her family," she continued. "I'm going to encourage her to stay and finish her vacation, but I don't want her to hear the news from someone else. She would feel like I didn't care enough to call. After that, I'll be going through the files trying to make sense of them again. Whoever did this emptied the file cabinets, including Tom's personal ones, which seems very odd behavior for a drug burglar."

"I agree that does seem odd," I said. "Was Jonathon told about the files?"

"Yes. He said to let him know if anything was actually missing."

"Was the computer stolen?" I asked. "I don't see it on your desk."

"Yes, both computers are gone. I'm sure glad that I back up every night and that the backup drive was at my house. I'm not sure about Tom's laptop. It's missing but he often took it home with him. It didn't really have office information on it. Tom used it more for his own personal correspondence and email."

"Well," I said, "I'll just stick my head in the office to say 'hi' to Ellen and then head for the closet."

Ellen was on her knees in the office putting little bottles of pill samples into boxes and counting them as she went. She got up and gave me a big hug when I walked in.

"So far, I haven't found much missing. But most of the drugs were kept in the storage closet that you are going to be working on. Here is another copy of the drug inventory that Angie gave me. Thank goodness she had a hard copy of it as well as it being on the computer."

I gave Ellen another hug and headed to the storage closet. It was a disaster area. Everything had been swept off the shelves. A couple of bottles of Betadine had broken and made a real mess. I decided to clean that up first and then start organizing the drugs.

Y ou going to come up for air?"
      I looked up to see Ellen and Angie standing there and realized that it was almost two.

"Guess I should," I answered. "I have found a number of bottles of drugs missing. Mainly pain medication with codeine in it and other pain meds plus some antibiotics. But they didn't take all of the pain meds. It almost looks like whoever did it just grabbed whatever bottles were at hand quickly and then dumped the rest on the floor."

"We're going over to Angie's for a quick sandwich," Ellen said. "Then come back here for about another hour. At which point both Angie and I feel that we will have had it for the day."

"I'm with you," I said as we all grabbed our coats and headed out the door.

We started to get into Angie's car and then decided to walk the few blocks to her house. The exercise would help clear our heads.

It took no time for Angie to fix tuna salad for sandwiches. Ellen cut up some apples and oranges and I put the tea kettle on. I was surprised that I was hungry and then remembered that I had eaten no breakfast. I imagined that the others had also skipped it this morning.

"You know," Angie said, "although the files are a total mess, none of the patient files are missing or actually damaged. I'm not sure if something else might be missing. Tom may have had some personal files in his office, but I wouldn't miss those readily. That seems totally odd behavior for a burglar. I called Jonathon and let him know. He just went 'Hmmmm.' I think he is focused on it being a drug burglary. I'll give him the results of the inventory that you took as soon as we finish it."

I thought about what Angie had just said.

"Who is his next of kin, Angie?"

"He didn't have any that were real close," she answered. "There was an ex-wife, Lenore, who came up for a visit about a year after he moved here. They seemed to be amicable. His parents are dead. He was an only child, and he had no children."

"Do you have any idea who might profit from his death?" Ellen asked.

"I have no idea," Angie said. "Tom was pretty private about his life, especially the things that occurred before he moved up here. I always thought that something had happened down there that had hurt him deeply and I don't think it was the divorce. Could have been, though. A divorce, especially if you don't want it yourself, can be pretty gut wrenching."

Ellen and I nodded. We both knew that Angie's husband of twenty-six years had walked out on her one day and moved in with someone else.

We had started to clear up the dishes when the phone rang. Angie answered it and Ellen and I shamelessly listened in to her side of the conversation.

"Who? What's she doing in town? I have no idea. No, I don't. You might check at his home. OK. Goodbye."

"That was Jon. Lenore Walker is in his office. She claims to be Tom's heir and wants to see the will. Now what is she doing here at this time?"

"Her timing is a little mercenary, don't you think?" I answered. "I wonder if she is his heir."

We all puzzled over the latest news as we put on our coats and headed back to the office.

It took us just about an hour to finish up the inventory and give the results to Angie. Ellen and I gave her a hug and headed out after getting a promise from her that she would call either of us if she needed anything at all.

"Are you still coming tonight?" I asked Ellen as we headed for the cars.

"Yes, I think I will," she answered. "Stopping my activities won't bring Tom back. My guess is you will have a full house as everyone will want to gossip about the news."

"Bet you're right. Well, I better get home and ready for the students. Want to come for dinner before class?" I asked.

"I might as well. I've pretty much lost my day as far as progressing with any work that I need to do. I'll take care of my critters, answer some emails and come on over."

Chapter 6

The answering machine light in the shop was blinking. I had one cancellation but most of the calls were from students saying they would be there unless I called them to tell them that class was cancelled. It looked like Ellen had pegged the local attitude pretty well.

As long as I was in there, I double-checked things to make sure that I was ready for tonight. We would be working with spindles and prepared wool batts. Later classes would branch out to other equipment and fibers. I had made toy wheel spindles and CD spindles that were included in the cost of the class. I also had many other spindle choices for sale that students could purchase once they had some experience. The tea and coffee supplies were ample and I had plenty of cups. So it looked like all was set for class.

I was just checking on the Chicken Florentine in the oven when I heard the dogs bark and Ellen's truck pull into the driveway. I looked out to see her walk over to the fence to give Denali and Falcor a scratch before heading my way.

"Found a nice bottle of chardonnay at QFC the other day," Ellen said once she was in the kitchen. "Figured we might as well have a glass tonight."

"Great, it will go well with the chicken. I just need to fix a salad while it finishes. Why don't you open the wine?"

"Oh, by the way," Ellen added, "I heard at the gas station on my way over here that Jonathon is talking to the new guy at the feed store. It seems someone saw him out toward Dr. Tom's office late last night."

"Really? Odd. Well, maybe it doesn't mean anything. Doesn't he live out that way? If I remember correctly, his aunt Jo's house is only a few blocks from the office. It wouldn't be too unusual for him to be there if he had been into Olympia or somewhere for a late movie."

"Probably that was all it was. He seems like a very nice young man and I can't imagine him being on drugs. I think he is very strong on healthy living from what I heard—lots of exercise, good healthy food, that kind of thing."

Ellen finished setting the table and that sentence at the same time. The chicken was out of the oven and our conversation over dinner turned to other things. Ellen had me in stitches over the escapades of Shasta and we discussed our plans for the Black Hills Fiber Gathering in May. I would have a booth there for sales and Ellen would be helping out the Pyr club with their booth.

Just as we were finishing up, the phone rang.

"Hello. Oh hi, Elizabeth. Yes, I am still having the class tonight. Sure, come on. There's always room for one more. See you in about forty-five minutes." I hung up the phone and turned back to Ellen. "That was Elizabeth Swanson. She is coming for class tonight. Said she might when she was here on Thursday. Wonder if she would have come without the need to gossip. I think you were right, Ellen."

Ellen gave me a "told you so" glance as we started cleaning up the kitchen so we would be ready for the class.

I had a full class of ten when everyone had arrived and, to our surprise, Michael Green was one of them. Although there are many men who excel at fiber arts, I had not had many frequent my shop. Michael, a professor at Evergreen State College, was warmly welcomed by the women and seemed to enjoy his minority status.

I started by demonstrating fiber preparation and drafting. Soon everyone was spinning using the park-and-draft method, where you add twist to the yarn and then stop the spindle while you draft out more fiber to take up the twist. This allowed the new spinners to control just one item at a time, either their drafting or the spinning of the spindle.

At the end of the hour, we stopped for a break and the conversation quickly turned to the murder of Dr. Tom.

"I understand that the sheriff was interested in the new guy working at the feed store, Leslie," Allison said when everyone had settled down with their drinks.

"They wanted to know why he was out late and seen in the area of Dr. Tom's office. Jack was out of town for the evening and had just returned," Leslie replied. "I don't think there is any problem."

"I don't know," Allison said. "He still could have done it. After all, what do we know about him? He's new in town and no one knows much about his past."

"Hey, I'm new in town," Jane chimed in. "Does that automatically make me a suspect?"

"But you're a teacher. And anyway you're a woman," was Allison's reply.

"That's a pretty sexist remark from someone who earns her living as a timber cruiser," Leslie said. "Anyway, I like Jack. And I don't think you'd find anything untoward in his past. After all, his aunt Jo has lived here for years."

"It could also have been someone who came off the main highway. Anyone in the county would know that this town rolls up its sidewalks early in the evening."

This comment came from Theresa Sorenson. She's mayor of Black Hills and our town's greatest proponent.

"I bet it'll be a total stranger," Theresa continued.

"Speaking of strangers," Elizabeth spoke up. "Dr. Tom's ex-wife was in town today. Talked to Jonathon and then called David. She wanted to see his will. It seems that she thinks that she'll inherit some of his property."

"Boy that's interesting," Allison said. "Didn't take her long to show up, did it? I didn't even know that he had an ex-wife. Hmmmmm. Maybe we have another possible suspect."

"I don't know," I said, "but if we don't get back to spinning class, you all won't get out of here on time, for sure."

With that we returned to the classroom, and I started them spinning again. The hour passed quickly and it was soon time to hand out supplies for them to practice on and send them on their way. I walked out onto the porch with Ellen, who was the last to leave. It had been a good start to the class and a good ending to a day that started off badly.

I turned and went back inside the shop. I had thanked everyone, even Ellen, for offers to help clean up. Frankly, I needed a little time by myself for awhile. I decided to pour myself a cup of tea and sit for a bit before I got things picked up. There really wasn't that much to do and the shop was cozy. The dogs came back in and flopped on their rugs. They were ready for the day to end also.

I just let my mind wander as I sipped my tea. I thought about Allison's comments on both Jack and Dr. Tom's ex-wife. Was there really any reason to suspect either one of them? I couldn't see one, although I did have to admit that the timing for the ex seemed a little odd. Why did she show up the day that he died? How had she heard about it so quickly? Who told her? Few of us even knew that he had an ex-wife. Angie said that she'd been here only once before. And maybe most important of all, why did she think she would be his heir when they were divorced so long ago?

A short woof and a scramble as the dogs charged outside brought me out of my musings. I listened carefully and could also hear the coyote in the distance. The dogs would make sure he knew he wasn't welcome here.

I cleaned the classroom area and closed the shop. It was a cold, clear night and the stars were bright. I walked to the outer gate, savoring the chill and watching my breath on the night air. With the gate closed, I opened the inner gate for the dogs and went into the house. It was time for bed. I could sleep well knowing that all was watched over by my two shaggy protectors.

Chapter 7

A Pyr nose on my cheek woke me up the next morning.
"Okay, okay. It's breakfast time, is it? Don't you
know that it isn't even light out yet? OK, I'll be there
in a few minutes."

I hauled myself out of bed and dressed to take care of the
animals. I switched on the coffee pot on my way through the
kitchen to the back door.

It looked like it was going to be another beautiful winter
day. The sky was clear and I could see the morning star low on
the horizon. It would be a good day to take the dogs for a walk
before the shop opened up. They would enjoy it and I could sure
use the exercise. It didn't take me long to feed and water the
animals. The thought of hot coffee drew me back to the house
and the comfortable kitchen.

I had just settled down on the couch with my cup of coffee,
Sable on my lap, and NPR's "Weekend Edition" in the back-

ground when the phone rang. A glance at the clock as I reached for it indicated that it was a little early for just a morning chat.

"Hello, Martha, this is Angie."

"Hi, Angie. What's up?"

"I got a call from David last night. Given the circumstances, he wanted me to come in today to talk about Tom's will. Evidently Tom did change his will and I'm the executor. He had asked me if I would be willing to do it a couple of months ago, but I didn't know that he had made the changes. Would you be willing to go in with me? I'd like an extra pair of ears."

"I think I can, Angie. Let me get my calendar. It's upstairs in the office so you'll just have to walk up there with me. How are you doing today?"

"A little better but also quite overwhelmed with the work that will need to be done to close up the office and take care of Tom's affairs."

"Here it is. Let me see. Yes, I can do it, Angie," I said. "I'll need to close the shop but I don't have any special appointments today and most of my regulars were here for class last night so they probably wouldn't be coming in today anyway. What time do we need to go?"

"I told David that I'd be at his office about nine-thirty. Will that work for you?"

"I can do that. I'll just meet you at David's office if that's OK."

"Sounds good," Angie responded. I'll see you then. I really appreciate your help."

"No problem, see you in a bit."

I looked at the clock as I hung up and decided that I could get a few things done before I left to meet Angie. But it would mean that the dogs wouldn't get their walk today after all.

Having finished my tasks, I walked out onto the porch, calling the dogs as I descended the stairs. I handed each one a cookie, a token to replace the walk, as I shut them in their area. With them secure, I opened the outside gate before going to the shop. I quickly changed the message on the answering machine and made a sign for the shop door saying that I had an emergency and would be back later in the afternoon. Nali gave me one parting woof as I drove out of the driveway.

Angie was waiting for me outside of David's office when I drove up. "Hi, hope I'm not late," I said as I climbed out of the truck.

"No, I'm just early. Anxiety working, I think."

We headed into the office together.

"Hi, Angie. Oh hi, Martha, I didn't know you were coming." David's handshake was firm and his blue eyes had a smile in them as he greeted us. David Swanson was my attorney as well as that of probably three-fourths of the town. He had grown up in Black Hills and played an active part in the community.

"I asked her to come so that I would have an extra pair of ears," Angie explained.

"Probably a good idea, Angie. Anyone for coffee? I just made a pot."

Angie and I answered in the affirmative. David poured cups for both of us and refilled his own.

"Let's sit around the table here," he directed. "It will make it more comfortable. As I told Angie, I think that she needs to know what is in the will right away, given the circumstances of Tom's death and her responsibilities," David began. "Tom had planned on the three of us going over this early next week, Angie. However, now I'll have to help you understand what he had in mind and his reasoning for things. We talked a long time before he made the changes."

"Tom was very quiet about his personal life even with me," Angie responded. "I do wish that he had been able to discuss these things. But I guess if wishes were horses and all that...."

"The people of Black Hills really had no idea that Tom worked only because he loved medicine and his patients," David began. "He came from a very old New Mexico family and had more money than he could possibly need even if he never worked a day. There are a number of organizations and a few people who will profit nicely from Tom's death."

"Does that include Lenore, his ex-wife?" Angie asked.

"No. It did up until the will changed because his previous will had been written a good number of years ago. I haven't returned her call yet, but I'm sure she won't be happy with the news that I have to give to her. It does include you, though, Angie. You'll be able to retire comfortably now if you want to."

Angie's eyes filled with tears. "I didn't know," she said. "When he asked me to be executor, I figured it was because I was a disinterested party."

"Tom knew that you thought that," David continued. "He figured he would let you in on the rest of his ideas during our meeting. So shall we go over the basics of the will?" He reached for and opened a large file folder. "Tom put the ranch in northern New Mexico into a trust. The Hernandez family will be able to continue living there as long as a member of that family chooses to use it as a working ranch. There is to be no development of the land beyond what would make sense for a ranch. The trust will pay all property taxes and necessary repairs or improvements to the buildings, fences, etc. The family must make their personal living off the ranch activities. If at any time the family members choose to no longer live there and work the ranch, it will become a wildlife preserve. A board of trustees has been set up. It includes me, James Hernandez, and Tom Garcia, who is a banker and old family friend of Tom's. There are provisions for replacements to the board when necessary. Basically you won't have to deal with the ranch at all, Angie. The trustees will take care of all the details there as the trust was in force before Tom's death."

"Thank goodness for that," Angie said. "But then what do I need to handle?"

"The disbursement of the rest of Tom's estate, which amounts to a little over ten million dollars."

"Ten million dollars," Angie echoed in disbelief. "But I've been lucky to see ten thousand dollars at one time in one place during my lifetime. What do I know about dealing with that kind of money?"

"Tom has left you a paid accountant and me to help you with the details. What he knew was that you had basic honesty and a desire to see that his wishes were fulfilled even if there were pressures for you to do something else," David replied. "Tom has spelled out pretty clearly what he wants done in the will and he left you a letter, Angie. I have no idea of the contents of that letter. He brought it to me sealed and said to place it with the will."

"Now, here are the basics of the rest of the will. A scholarship fund is to be set up at the University of New Mexico Medical School in Albuquerque for low-income students. Another similar one is to be set up at the University of Washington Medical School. Money has been left to a family planning clinic in Albuquerque that Tom founded just before he moved here. There are bequests to a number of theater groups, two environmental groups, a medical clinic on the Navajo reservation, and the Evergreen State College. He lists gifts to a couple of cousins whom I think were Tom's only living relatives and for Marilyn Davis, his nurse in Albuquerque. And you, Angie, are left three hundred thousand dollars and Tom's office and house here in Black Hills, plus all their contents and his cars."

Angie gasped and looked like she would faint for a minute. Then, she did start to cry. I put my arms around her and just held her for a bit while David had the good sense to just sit quietly. In a few minutes, Angie gained control and started to hiccup. I handed her the box of tissues that David had slid toward me earlier.

"I don't understand," she said softly. "Why would Tom leave me so much?"

"Because, to quote Tom, 'you made each day enjoyable with your good common sense, your love of people and your wonderful sense of humor.' Tom said that you were the person that held his practice together. All he did was come in and do the fun part—making people well or helping them be more comfortable if he couldn't make them well. You, according to Tom, did all the difficult things in the office. And he said that your company was gentle and companionable without being intrusive. As you can see, Angie, he valued you a great deal."

"I'm still overwhelmed with it all," she replied, turned her head and quietly blew her nose. Then with a little shake that seemed to bring our competent Angie back front and center, she added, "OK, David what do I need to do next? If Tom trusted me with all of this responsibility, I guess I need to start moving forward."

"First you need to make arrangements for the cremation of Tom's body. He has asked that the final disbursement of the ashes take place on the ranch in New Mexico. I have the paperwork giving you the authority to make these decisions and I'll give that to you when we're done here. And you'll need to decide what, if anything, you want to do about a memorial service. Tom left that up to you completely. He just had one request. Don't make it dreary. Then I would say that you need to start making an inventory of the contents of the two properties, but I can see this is overwhelming you today. We'll talk about the details later. Okay? I'll talk to the bank on Monday about setting up an estate account and will let you know when you need to sign papers. In the meantime, I'll be available to you if you have any questions. Tom trusted you, Angie, and I trust you."

"Well, then I guess I need to get busy. Do you have any idea when the police will be able to release Tom's body?" Angie's eyes still glistened with tears but her voice remained calm and steady.

"No, I don't, but I can call Jonathon and ask him for you. Where can I reach you when I find out?"

"I think I'll get lunch someplace and go to the mortuary. Then I'll probably go back to the office for a bit. Why don't you call there? If I'm not there, just leave a message on the machine. I guess we'll be talking a lot over the next few months," Angie added as she rose to leave. I followed her toward the door.

"We will," David responded as he walked with us. "And you take care. Don't worry, you can handle it and you'll have help. Here are your authorizations to give to the mortuary, and here is your letter. It was good to see you, Martha, and I know that Angie will have a lot of help coming from her many friends."

"Yes she will," I replied. "I'm glad that she has your help, David."

"Thanks, David," Angie said as she placed the envelopes in her purse and we headed down the steps and into the parking lot.

We walked to our cars in silence and then Angie turned to look at me.

"Oh, Martha, what am I going to do? I had no idea that we were talking this kind of responsibility when I told Tom yes. Besides, I figured he would outlive me. After all he was 20 years younger than I am. And all that money, I can't believe that he left that much to me."

"You're going to handle it one task at a time just like you always do things," I told her. "To start with, we're going to lunch. Then, I'll go with you to the mortuary. Do you want to use one in Shelton or Olympia?" There were none in Black Hills.

Angie thought for a minute. "Olympia, I think. I'll use the one that I used when my father died a couple of years ago. Let's eat in Olympia too. That way, I don't have to face questions from locals. At least the possibility is less. Why don't we leave your truck here and I can drive?"

"That suits me fine. Let me just check the shop phone for messages before we leave and I'm ready to go." I had a message from Ellen wondering what I was up to and another from Leslie asking me to call her. Both had tried the house first and then left a message on the shop machine. "Nothing I can't deal with later," I told Angie as I relayed the messages.

"Why don't we call Ellen and see if she'd like to go with us?" Angie asked. "I wouldn't mind another head in on all of this and Ellen has a good one."

"Fine by me. I'll give her a quick call."

After calling Ellen, Angie and I drove out to her place. She lived to the east of Black Hills a couple of miles off Black Hills Road so it wasn't too far out of our way to get her. As we drove into Ellen's yard, a white tornado came barking from behind the house with Ellen in hot pursuit.

"Come here, you little monster," Ellen gasped as she grabbed for Shasta.

Angie and I were laughing as we watched the pup evade Ellen's grasp again. I stepped out of the car and she came over and stood a few feet from me barking like mad. My diversion let Ellen hook a leash on her collar.

"Meet the terror of the Pyr world," Ellen said as she panted to catch her breath. "Actually I'm glad you showed up when you did because I'm not sure I would have caught her before she really took off. She is a real shape shifter and slipped out the gate just as I was shutting it."

I crouched down and reached out my hand for Shasta to sniff.

"How are you, young lady? Ready to go on a walkabout, are you?"

I got a wiggle and a sloppy puppy kiss for my efforts.

"Looks like you have your hands full with this one." I laughed as I got up.

"You've got that right. Just let me put her back in a secure spot and wash my hands and I'll be ready to go," Ellen responded.

We were soon on our way.

"Let's go to the Fall's Terrace," Angie said when we were on the highway. "We are past the lunch rush and the falls should be lovely. I always find them calming. We've got a lot to fill you in on, Ellen."

"The Falls's Terrace is fine with me," I responded and Ellen nodded.

The restaurant has been a landmark in the area for many years. It's actually in Tumwater rather than Olympia. Located right on the Deschutes River, its windows look out over a small but often very active set of falls and the grounds of the Tumwater Falls Park.

We soon were seated at a table with a great view of the falls and had our orders placed. Ellen was as surprised as Angie and I had been with the news of both the amount of money in Tom's estate and the fact that he had left so much to Angie.

"Where do you go from here, Angie?" Ellen asked.

"Well after we're done with the mortuary, I thought I would go back to the office. I want to look for a couple of books of poetry that Tom kept there. He had some favorites and I'm hoping he marked something in a way that I can know it was special. You know, like some people do in books they love."

We both nodded.

"Anyway," Angie continued, "I want to find something to have read at the memorial service. Then I'll need to make arrangements for the memorial service. Would you both help me on that?"

We both agreed.

"Thanks. I didn't want to impose on you but I could really use the help. Well, I guess we're ready to go to the mortuary," Angie said as she reached for the bill. "My treat."

It didn't take us too long at the mortuary. Angie made the necessary decisions and signed the papers. As she reached into her purse for the authorization to give the mortuary, she realized that she still had Tom's letter and hadn't opened it.

She looked at me; but since we were still in the mortuary office, she just smiled and put it back in the purse.

When we walked out to the car Angie turned to me. "I had forgotten about the letter with all that has followed. I'm almost afraid to open it."

"You may want to do it in private," I commented.

"No, I don't think so," she said. "I think I'll read it after we get back to the office."

Ellen was waiting for us in the car as she hadn't gone into the mortuary. Angie and I climbed in and we headed back to Black Hills.

The light was blinking on the office answering machine when the three of us entered. The first message was David saying that the police thought they would be able to release Tom's body toward the middle of next week. The autopsy still had to be completed and they needed to receive the coroner's report. The second message was a hang-up.

"Let me fix us a cup of tea," Angie said. "And then I guess I need to read the letter."

"I'll fix the tea," I commented. "You read."

Angie sat down and pulled the letter out of her purse. She just held it a moment in her hand and then opened it. She scanned it quickly and then handed it to me and said, "You read it out loud. I'll just become a sobbing idiot if I try to."

" 'Dear Angie,' " I started.

" 'I am writing this in case something happens to me before you and I can get together with David. I can't tell you why but I have a feeling that something might. Nothing that I can put my finger on, just a vague feeling that when looked upon in the light of day seems silly. Anyway, just in case, I want you to have this information.

" 'I know the responsibility for an estate the size of mine may be overwhelming, but I am totally confident that you will rise to the challenge. You may rely on David completely. As I'm sure David will tell you, you will also have the services of Michael Albritton. He is my accountant and has helped me greatly over the years. I know he will do the same for you.

" 'I can also hear you saying that I should not have left you the inheritance that I did. And I reply to you that it was exactly what I wanted to do. Your presence has made going to the office a time of pleasure. You have mothered me and made sure that I took care of myself. You have worried over me and my lack of social life. And you have made sure that I knew that someone out there cared for me from the first day I walked into the practice that I purchased from Dr. Breck. In short, you most of all made my transition to Black Hills one of peace and contentment. Mere financial gifts can never repay you enough.

" 'As you begin working on my estate, you may be hit with tales from my past. You can find some of the details of them in the personal files that are marked "Albuquerque" in both the file cabinet at the office and on my computer. Believe me when I say that I have never in my life nor in my career done anything that was illegal. Although I often wonder if I could have done things differently, I can tell you that I have never willfully done anything to harm a patient. The allegations made about me in Albuquerque were totally false, and the courts found them to be so. However, they may raise their ugly head again as you deal with my affairs.

" 'Know, Angie, that I have total faith in your ability to ac-complish the tasks I have laid before you. Enjoy my gifts. They are given with my love, Tom.'"

We all just looked at each other when I had finished read-ing the letter.

"What could Tom mean about things from his past?" Ellen broke the silence. "Looks like we need to find those files."

"It does," Angie replied. "I don't remember files that matched that description when I cleaned up the mess yesterday. I'll start looking in Tom's desk. Ellen, you start on the file cabinet in Tom's office. Martha, would you look at the files in my office? I can't do much about the computer until I get it replaced and the backup files in place. And Tom may have been talking about his personal computer, which I didn't backup. I'll have to see if he had a backup stored someplace."

We all set to our assigned tasks. I searched the files in Angie's office. There was no mention of Albuquerque in any of the file names. Ellen went through all the files in the office with the same luck, and Angie came up just as empty.

"I guess I'll check Tom's house tomorrow," Angie said. "I'm emotionally and physically exhausted and not up to it tonight. Right now, a hot bath and an early bedtime sound wonderful. I just hope I can sleep."

I looked at the clock and realized that it was well after five o'clock.

"Looks like we should all head home," I commented. "Ellen and I both have livestock to take care of."

"Let us help you close up, Angie," Ellen added. "Then you can take Martha and me to her truck and she can run me home."

"I'll take Martha to her truck, but I'll take you home, Ellen. It's less out of my way."

"OK, it's a deal," Ellen replied.

We made sure that the office was all locked up and headed out the door together. It had been a long day and one with not a few surprises.

I was just getting out of Angie's car at David's office when a very attractive red-headed woman stormed out of his door. She was dressed to the nines, which is unusual in Black

Hills and obviously extremely angry. She also looked slightly familiar.

"Like hell will he get away with that," she yelled back at the open door where David was standing. "That ranch was to be mine and you'll be hearing from my attorney."

She rushed passed me without even glancing in my direction.

"That," commented David from the open door, "is the ex-Mrs. Tom Walker."

"Doesn't seem happy, does she?" I responded.

"Not a bit," David replied. "I'll talk to you all later. Right now I'm ready to go home. It's time for a drink."

We told him good night and all of us went our separate ways. As I drove home, I remembered once again that I needed to call Leslie as soon as I got there.

Chapter 8

I was greeted by Pyr barks as I pulled into my driveway. I stopped and shut the outside gate as I went in. I wasn't expecting anyone and I was very much ready for a quiet evening. The animals all let me know that it was past feeding time as I entered the barn.

"Sorry, guys. Sometimes other things just get in the way."

I quickly fed all the fiber critters and shut the doors to the pasture. By the time I had checked on the chickens, the Pyrs had finished their food and were ready to follow me into the house.

Just as I opened the back door, the phone started to ring. I made a dash for it and caught it just before the answering machine cut in. "Good eve—," I started to say.

"Oh, Martha," Leslie cut me off. "I'm so glad I caught you. I've been trying to get you all day."

"I'm sorry, Leslie. I spent the day helping Angie. She has

been made executor of Tom's estate and there were quite a few tasks to do. But what's wrong? You sound terribly upset."

"I may be jumping to conclusions, Martha, but I'm so worried about Jack. Jonathon was out questioning him again today. I don't understand it. It's almost as if the town has decided that it would be easy to pin this horrible murder on someone from outside and be done with it."

"Why would they think it was Jack, Leslie?"

"I don't know. Jonathon doesn't say. He hasn't even told Jack why he keeps coming back asking more questions. But it has me really spooked. I have to confess that I really like Jack, and I can't believe that he'd do such a terrible thing."

"I don't think Jonathon would just jump to conclusions, Leslie," I said slowly. I was trying to comfort her and yet lots of questions were running through my head. "It sounds to me like he's just following up on every lead. I wonder if he's talked to Tom's ex-wife. I still find it odd that she turned up just after Tom was murdered, especially since she expected to inherit his ranch in New Mexico."

"Maybe you're right, Martha," Leslie sighed. "I can be a real worry wart. Jack isn't terribly concerned. He says that he didn't do anything wrong and it will all work out. I just know this town, and it can be hard on outsiders. You heard Allison last night."

"Yes, I did. But you also saw how she backed down when Jane showed her the inconsistency of her thinking. I imagine the town will rally if they think any kind of injustice is being done."

"I hope so. Well, talking to you has helped. I needed to air my worries to someone that I knew wouldn't blab my feelings all over town. Thanks for listening."

"Anytime, Leslie. Now try to stop those runaway demons, enjoy the rest of the evening and get a good night's sleep. I'm sure tomorrow will look a little brighter."

"OK, I'll try. Talk to you soon."

"Good night, Leslie. Take care."

I hung up and thought about Leslie and Jack. She loved working at the feed store and had no desire to leave Black Hills. However, there weren't many eligible, young men in town. I could see why she would find Jack interesting. His red hair and freckles along with his cheery countenance and ready smile invited people to like him. He was about her age and from all accounts appeared to like the work at the feed store. But the burglaries started here about the time he arrived. Could he possibly be involved? It didn't feel right. However …

I was just opening the refrigerator to look for something to eat when the phone rang again. I realized that I hadn't checked my messages yet and wondered if this was another person who had been trying to reach me.

"Good evening," I answered.

"Hi, Martha. This is Jane. I came by the store today but noticed that you were closed. Hope it wasn't anything too serious."

"No, I just needed to help Angie. She's somewhat overwhelmed with her responsibilities right now."

"I can understand that," Jane answered. "I wanted to pick up some knitting needles. I need some Brittany double points. Do you have any?"

"Yes, I do and I think I have some in all sizes. What size did you need?"

"I need size two. I'm looking at a sock pattern in *Folk Socks* that I want to try. I have the yarn but no needles that size."

"I have them. Can I drop them off for you tomorrow? I

hate to have you make another trip since the one today was unfruitful."

"I'll be at the school tomorrow morning. That might be easier for you. My room is the one with the Valentine decoration on the door."

"OK, I'll drop them off about ten if that will work for you. They are six dollars plus tax."

"Sounds good. I'll bring the book and show you the pattern that I'm considering."

"I'd like to see it," I answered. "I'll see you tomorrow."

I hung up and once again went to the refrigerator. The leftover chicken from last night seemed like a good choice. I sure didn't feel like cooking anything. I put the chicken in the microwave and checked out the answering machine. The only messages were those from Ellen and Leslie earlier in the day. I called over and checked the shop machine. It had one additional message along with theirs. Michael had called to say that he enjoyed the class the night before and that he would be stopping by next week to get some additional fiber.

As I hung up, it dawned on me why Tom's ex-wife looked familiar. She had been in my shop the week before. She commented that she liked to stop at fiber shops on her trips. We talked for awhile and she bought some of my handspun yarn. I stopped and thought about it for a minute and I remembered that she also picked up one of my business cards and slipped it into her pocket. She would have also gotten another one in her package because I always slip a business card in the packages of new customers.

I reached for the phone to call Jonathon.

"Black Hills Police. How may I help you?" Jonathon said.

"Hi, Jonathon. It's Martha. I thought you might like to

know that the ex-Mrs. Tom Walker had one of my business cards."

"And you are just telling me this now?" Jonathon responded.

"I didn't know her name. Last week, she was just a pleasant customer on her vacation shopping in my store. When I saw her storming out of David's office today, she looked familiar. Then a few minutes ago, I realized why."

"Looks like I may need to talk to her again," Jonathon answered. "She didn't mention that she had been in town earlier. She's staying in Olympia until after the memorial service so I can call her. I wonder if she still has that business card."

"I'll leave all of that in your good hands," I replied. "I just wanted you to have the information."

"Thanks for calling. I'll take care of it. You have a good night, Martha."

"You too, Jonathon."

I hung up the phone and returned to the kitchen to get my dinner from the microwave. With Jeff Peterson's slack key guitar playing in the background, I settled down on the couch with my warmed-over dinner and a glass of wine. With luck, the rest of the evening would be uneventful.

Chapter 9

I woke up Sunday morning to the sound of steady rain. I turned on the coffee on my way through the kitchen and headed to the barn with both Pyrs leading the way. Unless the weather changed, Falcor and Denali would not get their walk today and I wouldn't get my peas planted as planned. Oh well, maybe tomorrow.

The smell of coffee greeted me as I returned to the kitchen. I poured a cup and settled down with the Sunday paper. It looked like a good day to do some spinning when I got back from delivering the needles to Jane. Maybe Ellen would like to join me for a private lesson and dinner afterward. I'd give her a call in awhile. She was not an early riser if she could help it and there was no need for me to be her alarm clock. In the meantime, I needed to do some light housecleaning. It looked like it might be a busy week coming up.

I had just finished vacuuming when the phone rang.

"Good morning," I said.

"Hey, Sis." Sean's tone of voice said something exciting had happened. "Blackie caught the burglar."

"He did? That's great!"

"This isn't for publication and that means to anyone yet. At least I don't want it to have come from me. Who knows what the rest of the grapevine may find?"

"But where and how?" I asked.

"Last night. Walter was taking Blackie for his last walk of the evening. They had just turned the corner onto the next street when Blackie began to let Walter know that he'd picked up a scent. Walter decided to let Blackie check it out and turned him loose with a command to find it. Blackie made a beeline for a house two doors down. He had just gotten to the front door when a woman walked out carrying a TV. She looked at Blackie, then at Walter, who was following Blackie to the door, and did a very stupid thing. She dropped the TV and started to run. Blackie had her on the ground in about two seconds and held her there until Walter caught up. Didn't help that Walter knew the neighbor, and he was a single male. So the gal is now cooling her heels in the Black Hills jail and I'm about ready to head over there to talk to her about our burglaries. It seems her fingerprints match those found at a couple of the sites, including Tom's."

"Tom's killer is a woman?" I asked, disbelief clearly showing in my voice.

"Possibly, although I haven't talked to either Jonathon or Walter. I got my information from the sheriff when he called and asked me to go over and talk to her."

"Well, I hope they have the right person," I responded. "I don't like the idea of having a murderer loose in the area."

"None of us do," Sean said. "I'll let you know when I know more. In the meantime, I need to get to the jail. I told Jonathon I'd be there by nine-thirty."

"I'm glad you called. Talk to you later and love ya," I responded.

"Love ya too," Sean said as he hung up.

That was exciting news. I hoped that Blackie had caught Tom's murderer as well as a burglar. Everyone would sleep easier if that were true. What a twist that the burglar was a woman. Well, I guessed crime had always been an equal opportunity career area. Still, it surprised me for some reason.

An hour later found me turning into the parking lot at Black Hills Elementary. I pulled the hood of my coat up over my head and walked to Jane's classroom. She must have seen me coming as she was standing at the door waiting for me.

"Come in. Isn't it a miserable day out?" she greeted me.

"Pretty typical for February," I answered. "You came from southern California, right?"

"I was raised there," Jane answered. "I went to college in Arizona so I've never lived in an area that got quite so much rain or was quite so dreary during the winter. I love the kids and the school here but I don't know if I want to spend another winter here. I'll have to make up my mind by the end of next month, though, when contracts will come up again."

"I hope you'll stay. I've heard nothing but raves from the parents of your students. We need quality teachers like you. Here are the needles you wanted."

"Oh good," Jane said. "Come over to the desk and I'll show you the pattern."

As Jane and I walked over to her desk, I couldn't help but notice how delightful her classroom was. She obviously put a lot of thought into the decorations that she used. There was a colorful heart made from multiple pieces of paper that was halfway completed on one bulletin board.

"What's the heart all about?" I asked.

"Oh, we are building the heart by reading. Each time a student finishes a book, they get to fill in one section of the heart. We started it in January. It takes a hundred and fifty books to complete it. Each student has already contributed, so even my less-than-enthusiastic readers have been caught up in the project. They are well over halfway; I think they're going to make it. If it's all done by Valentine's Day, we'll have a special treat at our party."

"What a great way to get them reading. Like I said; I sure hope you decide to stay on."

Jane pulled out her book and showed me the pattern. It was the Highland Schottische Kilt Hose and looked to be a fairly challenging pattern. I usually stayed with a fairly basic sock pattern so I was impressed.

"They'll be beautiful, Jane," I said.

"I'm making them for my father. His mother was from Scotland. She married my grandfather when he was stationed in England just after World War II. It makes for a crazy heritage for me. My grandfather's parents came from Mexico. My mother's heritage is not so clear. Like many whose families have been in this country a long time, she is a mixture but basically British Isles and northern European. My father, however, is very proud of his Scottish heritage and I know he'll be delighted with the socks."

"And well he should be." As I said that, a picture on Jane's desk caught my eye. It was of a young girl and an older one. Both looked like Jane. "Is one of these attractive girls you?" I asked.

"I'm the younger one. The other is my older sister."

"I notice that you both have on sweaters that look handknit. Did your mother knit?" I asked.

"No, but my Scottish grandmother did. She taught all of us, even the boys, to knit. However, I hadn't done much in years until I moved here. The winter here seems to encourage that kind of indoor activity."

"It does that," I said. "I actually enjoy the long winter evenings with a fire and my handwork."

"I'd like it better if it wasn't quite so gray so often, but maybe I'll adjust," Jane said. "How much do I owe you for the needles?"

I told her and she paid me. I knew Jane needed to get back to her work and I had plans for the day too.

"Call me if you need help with those socks, Jane," I said. "And I'll see you on Friday."

"Will do, Martha. Thanks for bringing me the needles. I really appreciate it."

"No problem," I said as I let myself out the door of Jane's room and walked through the rain to my pickup.

We were really very lucky to have a teacher of Jane's excellence in our school. I did hope that she would decide that she could tolerate our gray winters and stay another year.

Chapter 10

I stopped at the local market on my way home and picked up a small ham and some yams for dinner. I had called Ellen earlier and she was coming over about two-thirty to spin for awhile and then stay for dinner.

I also grabbed a couple sprays of dendrobriums. They would add some color to the table. Flowers in the house were an important part of my life. John loved to arrange flowers, and he always made sure that I had some. Our time in Hawai`i was a great joy for him because beautiful cut flowers were so plentiful and so inexpensive. Keeping up the tradition was a small way of acknowledging him in my life today.

Pyr barks welcomed me home as always. As soon as I put the groceries away, I called Angie to see if she wanted to join us for dinner. She was happy to get the invitation and would come over about five o'clock. That gave Ellen and me about two hours to spin before Angie arrived.

I had decided to work on the Samoyed yarn. I really didn't have much left to spin and I would be finished with it. A quick trip to the shop let me retrieve the Samoyed fiber, the nice spindle that I was going to give Ellen, and some lovely batts that I had made from her last year's lamb fleece.

I brought the fiber back to the house and placed it in a covered basket where Sable wouldn't be tempted to play with it. Cats and fiber don't mix. Then I arranged the flowers, set a fire in the fireplace, and readied the ham for the oven. Just as I'd decided to give my email a quick check, the phone rang.

"Martha." It was Leslie and it sounded like she was crying. "Can I come over and talk to you? They have arrested Jack for Tom's murder."

"They what?" I asked. Now I was confused. What happened to the burglar that Blackie caught?

"I know. It just isn't possible that he'd do it. But Jonathon said something about someone seeing him leaving the area. I don't know much more but I'm trying to find out. However, I need someone to talk to. My folks are in Seattle for the weekend and Jeevana is in Oregon."

"Of course you're welcome to come over, but I have Ellen arriving at any moment and Angie coming at five o'clock for dinner. If you don't mind them hearing what you have to say, come along."

I wasn't sure that she would want to have the other women in on her conversation.

"I guess it doesn't matter if they know," she answered. "I screamed at Jonathon when he came to arrest Jack so the whole town probably is talking about it by now."

"Come along then."

"OK, I must stay at the store until four o'clock even though

I would like to run out now. With the folks gone and Jack in jail, I'm the only one left to keep the place open. I'll come over as soon as I can after I close up."

"Sounds good. Plan on dinner here."

"I don't know if I'll be able to eat, but I'll be there. Thanks for being willing to listen."

Just as I hung up, I heard Pyr barks and tires in the driveway. Ellen had arrived. As she was letting herself in, the phone rang again.

"Hey, Sis," Sean said. "Sorry to be so long in getting back with you. Things have been crazy and events have happened quickly."

I signaled Ellen to make herself comfortable while I answered Sean.

"I guess. Can you tell me at all why Jonathon arrested Jack today?"

Ellen raised her eyebrow and I knew she was listening to my half of the conversation.

"I don't have all of Jonathon's information because I had to leave as soon as I talked to the burglar about our burglaries in the county. I got called out on a domestic violence issue that erupted at your end of the county. The burglar was adamant that Tom was dead when she arrived at the office. She saw the office door open and, following her usual mode of operation, she decided to check it out. The computers were in plain sight and it wasn't until she actually walked in the door that she realized that Tom was on the floor and the office trashed. She claims that she grabbed the computers and got the hell out of there."

"OK, so Tom was dead," I interrupted, "but why say it was Jack?"

"At least two of the neighbors saw Jack's truck go by late Thursday night. One was walking his dog and the other had a case of insomnia and had glanced out the window while fixing some warm milk."

"Is that all Jonathon is going on? Some neighbors saw him drive by. That doesn't seem like much for a murder arrest." I was finding this very hard to believe.

"Jonathon rarely does anything without good reason. He is an excellent cop and has a reputation for thoroughness. I'm sure he has something stronger, Martha. I just don't know what it is. I haven't talked to Jonathon since I was there this morning. I'll see if I can find out why he is so certain that Jack is guilty."

"Well, I can tell you that Leslie is very upset," I said. "Jonathon arrested Jack at the store this afternoon. She is coming over here this evening, along with Angie, and Ellen is here now. Can I tell them any of this?"

"Well, I haven't told you much more than Leslie already knows. The rest of the info will probably hit the grapevine soon. You can't have something like this murder in Black Hills without everyone talking about it. So, yes, I think you can talk about it. You all might think of something new. I don't know what else Jonathon knows, but the burglar could be just trying to save her own skin. I'm sure that thought has gone through Jonathon's mind too."

"I doubt we can trump the pros," I said, "but I must admit that Jack as a murderer doesn't sit well with my instincts. Do keep me up to date if you can."

"If there's anything more that I can share, I will. I have the afternoon off tomorrow and your shop's closed. Maybe I could drive over."

"Why don't you come late afternoon and plan on dinner?"

"Will do. Give my love to Ellen and the rest. Talk to you tomorrow."

I hung up and Ellen immediately wanted to know about Jack. I filled her in and also let her know that Leslie was coming around five o'clock along with Angie.

"Why don't you put on a pot of tea for us? And I'll get the fire started," I said as I went to the fireplace.

"Sounds good. These rainy winter afternoons really do call for both tea and fires. If I were home, I'd be curling up with a good book. I have the new J.A. Jance started."

"Well, we will substitute fiber and conversation for J.P. Beaumont and his adventures," I answered. "And when everyone gets here maybe we can put our heads together on our own mystery. Here, I have something for you," I said as I pulled Ellen's spindle out of the basket. It was made of curly Koa and had beautiful figure in it.

"Oooo, how lovely. I was looking at that one Friday during class. Did you spot me doing it?"

"No. It was just my favorite of the new ones that came in last week and it looked like you. And this," I added as I pulled out her fiber, "is the fiber from Boy's lamb fleece. I thought you would like to spin it."

Boy was one of the few sheep Ellen had that wasn't Navajo Churro. He was a Jacob and I had decided to blend the colors of his fleece together in these batts so it was sort of a tweed color even in the batts.

"My first chance to spin the fiber I raised. Thank you so much. But now what do I do with all these wonderful toys?"

I set the basket with the Samoyed next to my spinning wheel and helped Ellen get started on her spinning. Learning the basic techniques of spinning is relatively simple. Then it is practice that brings about even yarn of a weight and texture that you want. Before I settled down to my own spinning, I poured our tea and set the mugs on the coffee table. For awhile we just sat there spinning in the companionable silence that good friends can enjoy.

"You know," Ellen broke the silence. "I keep coming back to those Albuquerque files in my mind. Did Angie say if she had looked for them and if she had found them?"

"When I talked to her, she hadn't looked for them yet. But she was going to check for them at Tom's on her way here. We should know whether she found them after she gets here."

"The fact that Tom said they should be there and then they aren't makes me think that they might have something to do with his death. And if they do," Ellen continued, "it doesn't make sense that the murder was just a simple robbery gone wrong."

"I agree. Well, we will have to see if Angie has found them at the house."

With that, I looked at the clock and realized that I needed to stop spinning long enough to put the ham and yams in the oven. "Want some more tea?" I asked.

"Sure but let me get it. I need to stretch my legs a bit. I seem to have been sitting pretty stiffly while concentrating on the spinning."

"That's not unusual. Soon it will become very natural and you'll find that you can even spin while standing in line or walking or whatever. A lot of women spin and walk as a form of meditation."

"Maybe so," Ellen said. "but right now I can't imagine spinning and walking."

"Oh you will be able to. No problem. It just takes some more practice."

With the dinner in the oven, Ellen and I settled down with our second cup of tea and our spinning.

"I keep coming back to the ex-wife too," I commented as I started verbalizing the thoughts that had been going on in my head. "Why is she here now? To my knowledge she was only up here to see Tom once before. Why now? Or maybe she wasn't up here to see Tom. She just keeps ringing as a false note."

"I know, and she sure was angry yesterday at David's. I wonder if she'll come to the memorial service. Did Angie say when she planned on having it?"

"She didn't say on the phone, but it is one of the things that she wants to discuss with us tonight."

"Sounds like we will have a busy conversation around dinner."

"Speaking of which," I said. "We should probably put this stuff away from kitty paws and get ready for the rest to arrive. Ellen, you want to get some more wood for the fire and set the table? I need to run out and take care of the barn critters." It was nice to have friends that were family.

"No problem. I need to move again after all that sitting."

We proceeded with our tasks, and just as we finished, I heard Angie and Leslie arriving at the same time. I went to the back door to greet them as the Pyrs ran to the fence to warn me that they had arrived. I wonder, does anyone really use their front door? It seems to me that we've used the kitchen entrance on most houses that I've lived in.

Angie and Leslie both made a dash for the house as it was still raining pretty steadily.

"OK, shake," I said as they came up on the porch. They both laughed at my doggie comment.

"Here," Angie said as she walked into the mud room area and handed me a pie. "I'll take this wet coat off out here." Leslie had set the bottle of wine she was carrying onto the washing machine and was in the process of also divesting herself of her wet coat.

"I picked this up at Jeevana's last week," Leslie said. Jeevana owned the local natural foods store and carried a wonderful supply of nice wines. "She thought I'd like this French Provencal rose."

"Thanks, Leslie," I said. "It is one I haven't tried, but it should go great with the ham. There's just time for a glass of wine before we eat. You guys find a seat by the fire and I'll get the wine. I think Ellen already has the cheese and crackers on the coffee table."

"I'm one ahead of you," Ellen commented. "The wine and wine glasses are out there too. I assumed that you wanted to use the bottle of sparkling for before dinner."

"You know me well."

"To good friends," I toasted once we each had our wine glasses in hand. "Now Leslie, fill us in on what happened this afternoon."

"Jack and I were working in the store today. Dad and Mom had decided to go to Seattle for the weekend. I think it was about one o'clock when Jonathon showed up. I thought it was a little weird that he had Jordan with him. He had always come by himself before. I guess he thought Jack might give him some trouble. Anyway, he didn't waste any time in getting straight to the point. He walked up to Jack and said that he was arresting him for the murder of Dr. Tom Walker." She paused and looked like she might start crying again but continued.

"At that point, I lost it. I screamed at Jonathon that he was out of his mind. That Jack would never do such a thing. Jonathon just looked at me with this look that parents get for wayward children and said, 'What do you really know about this man, Leslie?' I yelled back at him that I knew what I needed to know. Jack was a kind and gentle man and he wouldn't hurt a flea let alone someone as good as Dr. Tom. All Jack said was, 'Leslie, would you please call my Aunt Jo and let her know what happened? It will be all right,' and he let Jonathon take him off in the police car."

Leslie did start to cry now. Angie was sitting closest to her and she wrapped Leslie in her arms. Ellen got up to find a box of tissues. All of us hurt with her. At the same time, I wondered what we really did know about Jack.

When Leslie had gained control and was ready to talk again, I asked her "Leslie, how much do you know about Jack and his past?"

"Not a whole lot. He was raised in Portland by his single mother, Jo's younger sister. He went to school there and then into the Air Force. After two tours of duty, he went to Oregon State. His degree is in agribusiness and with a minor in biology. He's a hard worker."

Leslie's eyes started to fill again. "He wants to have a small farm one day and he loves working at the feed store. He likes the mix of agricultural things and people. He really is a people person." She shifted on the couch, pulling her knees up to her chest and hugging them before she continued. "He goes home to see his mother on almost all of his days off and really doesn't like it if something keeps him from making that trip. That is the only thing that I've found rather odd about him. Most adult men aren't that connected to their mothers." She grabbed for a tissue as tears started down her cheeks unbidden.

We all sat there for a few minutes while Leslie fought for control and we considered what she had told us.

"Visiting his mother is somewhat unusual but not something one could fault him for," Ellen said.

"Did you call David for him?" Angie asked.

"I did call. David wasn't comfortable representing him because he is Tom's and now your attorney, Angie. He gave me the name of another attorney that he said was good, and he offered to call him at home since it was Sunday. I got a call from the attorney just before I left. He had been in to see Jack and he'll be representing him. But none of it makes sense." Leslie's voice rose with this last sentence. "I just don't understand why Jonathon thinks it could be Jack," she wailed.

"I got a call from Sean earlier today," I added. "He gave me a few more details. However, I think the ham is ready. So let's move to the table and I'll fill you in on them over food."

After we had managed all the logistics of sitting down to eat, I filled Angie and Leslie in on the information that Sean had given me.

"You mean Jonathon arrested Jack because some neighbors saw his truck? And he did this even though a burglar has been arrested whose fingerprints are in Tom's office?" Leslie sounded incredulous.

"It seems to me that our burglar was really very lucky to have someone spot Jack and that Jack's timing was just bad luck," Angie said.

"I kind of think so too," I said. "But then, is the burglar telling the truth about Tom being dead when she got there?"

"Would she have killed Tom if she were surprised?" Ellen

asked. "Her other burglaries were non-violent. But then she wasn't surprised either except for the one where she was caught. Was she armed when Blackie caught her?"

"I don't know," I responded. "I can ask Sean when I see him. He is to come over tomorrow and promised to give me any more details that he could. If the burglar wasn't armed there, I guess one might make an assumption that she didn't go armed to these burglaries. And if she wasn't armed, she couldn't have shot Dr. Tom."

"But just because she didn't shoot Dr. Tom doesn't mean that Jack did," Leslie jumped in.

"I agree, Leslie," I said. "Angie, did you find the files at Tom's house?"

"No, and my gut reaction is that they have something to do with Tom's death. I think Jonathon may be barking up the wrong tree with Jack. But since we can't find the files and don't know what's in them, I'm sure we will have a hard time convincing him."

"I wonder if they have searched the burglar's home. Could she have them there?" Ellen asked.

"I can ask Sean tomorrow," I responded. "We know that the files have to do with his life in Albuquerque. I wonder who could tell us more about things down there. The ex-wife could if she would talk to us, but who else goes back that far with Tom that we know about?"

"Maybe the people that live on the ranch," Ellen added. "David would know how to get in touch with them. And maybe some of these people will come to the memorial service. What plans have you made for it, Angie?"

"Nothing concrete. I do know I want it to be here in Black Hills, not at the mortuary chapel. I'd like it to be timed so as many people as possible can come, so I'm thinking next Saturday afternoon. Where is a problem. We could have a large group. There aren't too many places in town that handle large groups, and it is still too cold to do something outside."

"How about the high school?" Leslie asked. "Tom was a great booster. He came to almost all the home games for a number of the sports and was there for many of the concerts and plays. I bet that Marian would be quite amenable to having it there."

"That's a good idea, Leslie. We could use the multipurpose room. Set up chairs at one end for the service and food at the other end," Ellen responded.

"I hadn't thought of the high school," Angie said. "You are correct, though; Tom was a great supporter, and it's quite centrally located. I'll call Marian tomorrow and see if she'll agree. If she does, I'll call the mortuary and make sure that a notice goes into the Albuquerque paper as well as *The Olympian*, and I'll get it into the *Black Hills Weekly* myself."

"Now that we have the easy part figured out," I said, "have you thought about who will speak?"

"Well," Angie said. "I was hoping you would officiate, Martha. Tom didn't attend any of the churches in town and I hate it when a minister is pulled into a memorial service just to have one there. You handle yourself well in front of a group. Would you be willing to do it?"

Angie caught me by surprise. I paused a moment before answering.

"I guess I could. I'm assuming that we plan on keeping this pretty informal. Just a sharing of memories by Tom's friends."

"Yes," Angie said. "I'm still looking for some favorite poems of Tom's for someone to read and I need to figure out some music. Any of you have ideas of who might be willing to sing or play something?"

"Not right at the moment. However if we could clean up in here and move to the fire for Angie's homemade pie and ice cream—I peeked and Martha does have some ice cream—we might think of someone in the process."

This last came from Ellen and we all laughed. Ellen was known for her sweet tooth and we all marveled at how she could stay so slim and still eat like that.

"OK, everyone grab their plate and we will help Ellen out before she dies of sugar deprivation," I said.

Soon we were settled again near the fire with our pie, ice cream and tea.

"Our church has a group that plays bagpipes and drums." Leslie brought us back to the topic at hand. "I realize that Tom wasn't a member but he touched every family in this town just about. I bet they'd be willing to play. And there is nothing like 'Amazing Grace' on bagpipes."

"And my church has a great handbell choir," Angie added. "I bet they would be willing to play also."

"Ellen, would you be willing to dance?" This came from me. "I know that you still perform from time to time, and I can see your modern dance as a beautiful interpretation of our feelings for Tom."

Ellen looked like I'd asked her to walk on stage naked. "I haven't danced in front of a large group in almost fifteen years," she said. "Let me think about that one."

"And people might not know it but David and Elizabeth both have beautiful voices and they often sing duets at church," Angie added. "They might be willing to sing."

"I bet the Black Hills Garden Club would be willing to help with the decorations," Ellen said.

"Looks like we've got a good start on this," Angie said. "Martha, I'll get the biographical information on Tom to you. Leslie, would you contact the people from your church? I'll contact the people from mine, Marian, and the garden club. Ellen, you let us know your decision."

That was our organized Angie getting us all lined up for our tasks. I could see why Tom chose her to handle his affairs.

"Oh, my goodness." This was from Leslie. "I just looked at my watch. I really do have to be leaving. I promised Dad that I'd open up the store tomorrow."

We all looked at the clock. It was after nine and everyone realized that we needed to bring the evening to a close.

"Don't worry about the dessert dishes," I said. "We have everything else cleaned up and I can take care of them."

I walked my guests to the door and gave everyone a hug as they left. "I'll talk to each of you sometime tomorrow," I added. "Ellen would you close the outside gate?"

"No problem."

I watched as they drove off and grabbed my rain slicker to walk to the inside gate. The Pyrs gave one joyful bark as they bounded out and proceeded to check out all the smells left by the guests. They would soon join me inside.

Chapter 11

I awoke to another gray, damp morning. My mood seemed to echo the dreary skies as I climbed out of bed and got ready for barn duty. Maybe the coffee that would be waiting for me when I came back in would help brighten things a bit. Then as I walked out the door, I had to laugh. Denali greeted me with a happy dance then whirled around and flattened the surprised Falcor with one joyous leap. How could I stay grumpy with that kind of joy for life staring me in the face?

I laughed again as I started toward the barn and she made a bound toward me with Falcor in hot pursuit. I realized again as I started feeding and watering my friends in the barn that we did have to grab the small joys that permeate every day even when the circumstances surrounding us want to pull us down. This was what brought me through the days after John's death, and I knew that it would be what would bring me and my friends through the next few days and weeks. We needed to celebrate Tom and his life with us, not darken our days.

The smell of the hot coffee was a wonderful greeting as I walked in the back door, and I felt like something totally sinful for breakfast. I had a few cinnamon rolls in the freezer. For some reason, today felt like a cinnamon roll day. I pulled one out and popped it in the microwave to thaw and poured myself that first fragrant cup of coffee. I love tea later in the day; but first thing in the morning, only coffee hits the spot.

With breakfast in hand, I curled up on the couch to think about my tasks for the day. I had my usual Monday morning errands to run. I'd call Angie and see if I could meet her for lunch and pick up the items she needed to give me, and I had a few things I wanted to do in the shop before Sean arrived for dinner. So I needed to get busy.

I called Angie and we decided to meet at Black Hills Café for lunch.

"We might as well hear the gossip while we eat," Angie had said. "I'd like to know what the town is saying about Jonathon arresting Jack."

I finished my errands in good time and found a parking place in front of Black Hills Café just before noon.

"Hey, Martha."

I was hailed from about three directions as I walked into the door of the café. I gave people a wave and looked around for Angie. I had arrived ahead of her so I started toward a table in the corner and by the window. By the time I actually made it to the table because of stops at almost every table along the way, Angie was walking in the door. I smiled when she looked my way and sat down. Angie had the same interruptions on her way to the table so I had time to read the menu. I have no idea why I did because I was in a total rut when it came to eating here. Sally makes the best Portuguese bean soup and I love it.

Sally was right behind Angie when she finally sat down. "What can I get you both? Any surprises from either one of you?"

"Not me," I answered. "I'll have the Portuguese bean soup, a roll and hot tea."

"Me either," responded Angie. "I'll have your clam chowder, a roll and coffee."

"Figured as much." Sally laughed and then her face became serious. "Have you both heard about Jack? Ted says that Leslie is just devastated, and I didn't even know that she was sweet on the guy. I must be slipping as the font of all Black Hills gossip," she added with her ever-present grin back in place.

"We know Jonathon arrested him. Haven't heard any more," I said.

"Guess David got him a good attorney," Sally added. "At least that is what the scuttlebutt is. Well, I'll get your order ready. Good food helps, I always say."

Angie and I smiled at the effervescent café owner as we watched her make her way across the café. She added more than good food to the atmosphere here. It was like coming into the large kitchen of a good friend.

"Well," I asked Angie as we turned toward each other, "did you bring the items that you wanted me to have?"

"Yes, I did. Here is the information that I thought might help. It is mainly biographical stuff like where he was born, went to school, degrees, that sort of thing."

"Thanks, all of that will help," I said.

"I also called Marian and we can hold it at the high school on Saturday. I contacted the garden club and the people in my church. They were thrilled to be asked to help. Ellen hasn't called me back but I expect her to say yes. And I'm sure that people will want to talk about Tom and what he meant to them. It should be a celebratory occasion," Angie said, her voice shaking slightly. "That's what he wanted."

"Oh," Angie added. "I also received a call from Jonathon. The coroner's report has come in from the autopsy and the cause of death was what everyone thought it was—Tom was shot to death at close range."

"That seems to say that he either knew the person or had no reason to fear them," I said. "I still think the robbery or robberies, if we have a drug robbery before the captured burglar came in, is barking up the wrong tree. Wish I could come up with something other than my gut instinct to back that up."

"I know. I feel the same way, but I can't think of any reason why anyone who knew Tom would want to kill him."

Angie's eyes filled with tears and she looked out the window for a minute while she regained control. I knew this was hitting my friend a lot harder than she was letting on even to those who were close to her.

"Well, maybe Sean will have some information when he comes by this afternoon. Although my little brother can be pretty close-mouthed if he feels that it will jeopardize a case to talk to me."

"Can't blame him for that," Angie said. "After all, it's his job and he's good at it; and I sure wouldn't want to be the one who was responsible for messing up an investigation. Sometimes those of us outside can give something away without even realizing we are doing it."

"True. Thanks, Sally, that looks and smells wonderful as always," I added as Sally placed our bowls of soup in front of us.

"Enjoy and let me know if you want anything else."

Angie and I curtailed our conversation as we followed Sally's admonition and did enjoy our first spoonfuls of the fragrant soup.

"I love the fact that Sally's soup is always hot," Angie said. "So many times soup in restaurants is just kind of warm, but never here."

"I know. Sally's smart. She doesn't try to maintain a huge menu. She sticks to a few things that she knows her customers really enjoy and then she does them superbly. That and the fact that it is the friendliest place in town keep all of us coming back. Now, what can I help you with over the next few days?"

"I actually think I have things pretty well in hand for the moment. I'm not going to even consider doing anything about Tom's house and the office until after the memorial service. I'm watering the plants and taking care of Tom's cat but leaving him in his home for the time being. I think I might advertise the practice for sale," Angie continued. "We really do need a doctor in this town and I helped Dr. Breck when he retired and sold out to Tom so I think I can handle that. I have no idea what I'm going to do with the house. I have an appointment with David this afternoon to talk about some of the other financial matters. He has been a lifesaver. And speaking of that appointment, I need to finish my soup if I'm going to get to the post office before I go to David's."

We both turned our attention back to our soup. The café was filled with the chatter of other diners around us. It was obvious that Jack's arrest and Leslie's interest in him were the two main topics for the town's gossip mill.

"You go ahead and run your errands," I told Angie as she finished her coffee and looked around for Sally. "My treat today.

I'm going to finish my tea and check my list of errands to make sure I haven't forgotten anything."

"Okay. Thanks for the lunch and the help. I'll call you in the next day or so to touch base for Saturday."

Angie got up and worked her way through the tables and greetings from friends again on her way out. As she walked out, Tom's ex-wife walked in and found a table on the other side of the room. There was a lady who might have a motive for wanting Tom dead. It didn't seem like she had known about the will change. Had she hoped to stop that from happening? Now what was she doing back in town? Maybe Jonathon had asked her to come here to talk about my business card. I thought about walking over and reintroducing myself but then decided against it. She might not be too pleased with me at the moment.

I finished my tea and turned down the offer of homemade pie from Sally. My mental recount of my errands said that I had finished the things I needed to do in town and it was time to go tend to the shop. It had been pretty well ignored the last few days.

I arrived home to find a box on the porch of the shop. My mohair had arrived. Sheila had some of the most beautiful mohair around and the colors were extremely popular with my customers. Her results from dye were inspired. I was glad that the box had gotten here in time for the spinning class this next Friday. I opened the shop and hauled the box inside.

There was a message on the shop machine saying that Sean would be over around four o'clock. That gave me a couple of hours to get some work done in the shop. The mohair fulfilled all my expectations as I unwrapped it—lustrous and soft with beautiful colors. I especially loved the one called Beautiful Waves. It was a lovely soft green with just hints of white and blue and yellow to give it a richness that a single color wouldn't have provided. I bagged the different colors and tagged them. Then I set them up in a series of baskets near the cash register area. That would ensure that my customers noticed them as new items. Later, I would move them back to the regular shelves for fiber.

I completed the few other tasks that I wanted to do and realized that I probably had just enough time to take care of the barn chores and start dinner before Sean arrived. It was still getting dark well before five o'clock and the fiber critters never minded coming in a bit early on damp, chilly days like today. Speaking of chilly, I realized that the temperature was dropping as I left the snug warm shop. With the amount of moisture around, it could be a nasty night for black ice. I was glad I was home and didn't need to go out again. Hopefully it wouldn't drop to freezing before Sean got home. However, it was part of his job to be on the roads on nights like this. Not a part I liked but part of it none the less.

Just as I finished the barn tasks, I heard the crunch of tires on the drive and my four-footed alarms let out a bark. Then they barked again with a bark that said that it wasn't Sean who had arrived. I walked out of the barn to see that Jane had arrived. Since the shop was closed, I was a little surprised to see her. I like the young teacher but we hadn't become the kind of friends that socialize together.

"Hi, Jane, what's up?"

"Hi, Martha. I'm sorry to bother you on your day off but I'm having a terrible time with one part of the pattern on these socks. I really wanted to work on them tonight so was hoping that you might give me some quick help. Your place is on my way home so I figured if you were too busy, I wouldn't have lost anything by stopping."

"I've got time. Why don't you come in the house? I want to put a scalloped potato and ham casserole in the oven for dinner. If you can wait the few minutes for me to get that done, I'll be glad to look at it."

"Thanks. I really appreciate your time."

Jane and I walked toward the house together. I marveled again at how petite she was. I'm five-foot-seven and she made me feel like a giant.

"Here, let me take your coat. Can I get you something to drink? I think I have leftover coffee in a carafe—I can fix a pot of tea quickly—or I have wine or beer."

"Actually, tea sounds nice," Jane answered.

"Tea it is then. It's also my favorite for this time of after-noon. How are things going at school?"

"It's going well. We have added more books to the valentine heart, and they will have it done in time for the valentine party. Our next project is going to be covering colonial days on the East Coast. I'm hoping that you might come demonstrate spin-ning for the class, Martha. Elizabeth will teach soap making, and Kerry is coming to demonstrate candle making. We really do have some talented people in this town."

She said that last sentence with a tone that said she was surprised to find that out. I had a feeling that Jane thought she had moved to the end of the earth when she came to Black Hills. It made me wonder again why she had made the move.

"I'd love to demonstrate spinning, Jane. It sounds like you have a very creative unit planned out. I'm sure it'll keep the children interested and they'll learn a lot in the process."

I finished putting the casserole in the oven as I spoke the last sentence. "Let me get my hands washed and we'll look at that pattern."

Jane got out her knitting and showed me where she was having problems. She had picked a somewhat complicated pattern, and she didn't understand the directions where she needed to turn the sock inside out. I soon had her started again and on her way to working the pattern on the calf.

"Thanks, Martha. I can now spend my evening knitting and know that I'm on the right track."

Jane gathered up her knitting and got ready to leave.

"No problem. I love to help anytime I can," I said as I walked her to the door.

I walked out on the porch with her and saw that Sean was getting ready to pull into the driveway. We walked to the driveway as he parked and got out of his truck.

"Hey, Sis," Sean said, but I noticed that his eyes were on the attractive young teacher.

"Hi, I'm Sean," he introduced himself, and I couldn't help but note how handsome he was in his sheriff's uniform.

"Sean, this is Jane. She teaches at Black Hills Elementary."

"Glad to meet you, Jane."

"It's good to meet you, Sean. Well, I don't want to interrupt your visit, so I'll be running. You both have a good visit. Martha, thanks again for your help."

With that, Jane moved quickly to her car.

"Hey, Bro, I think you might have scared her with your official status. Do you have that effect on every young woman you meet?"

"It happens with some. Normally I wouldn't be in uniform, but my afternoon off kind of disappeared. I've been in court on an old assault case that all of a sudden needed my testimony."

We watched Jane leave. She honked as she drove out of the driveway and we waved back.

"Come on in. I have some scalloped potatoes and ham in the oven. I'll let you build the fire and I'll fix our salad and then we can sit with a glass of wine and catch up for a few minutes before we eat."

"However," I added as a cacophony of barking erupted from the fenced area. "I think you need to say hello to your furry kin before you come in."

"Did I forget you?" Sean said as he walked over to give the dogs a scratch through the fence. "Sis, are expecting anyone else?" He turned to me.

"No. You want to shut the outside gate and let the dogs loose?"

"Yep, I was thinking about doing just that. Wait a minute, guys, and I'll let you come out for a good pet."

Sean shut the outside gate and was greeted with many sniffs, Pyr snuffles and loves as soon as he opened the inside one. Then with a business-like bark, the dogs went to check out their territory before following us inside on their own schedule.

"OK, now that they are happy," I said, "let's go in and take care of ourselves."

Each of us finished our chores quickly and soon we were sitting in front of the fire with our glasses of wine.

"So can you tell me anything about why Jonathon arrested Jack?"

"I can, but this isn't for public information. Jonathon did have more information than just the neighbor's statement that they saw Jack. Jonathon had found a record of a drug arrest for Jack just after he graduated from high school and information that he had drug problems in the Air Force. Jack's fingerprints were in Tom's office. Jon also found some drugs from Tom's office in Jack's car. You know the sample kind that all doctors give out. He figures that Jack broke into Tom's office and Tom surprised him."

"What does Jack say about all this?" I asked. I had real problems thinking of Jack as a drug user, especially at a level that he needed to rob for the drugs. "Surely he has an explanation."

"He says that he stopped in to see Tom on Wednesday night just as Tom was closing the office. Angie had already gone home for the day. He had a sore throat and wanted Tom to check him out because he's prone to strep. Tom said that it looked like he did have an infection and gave him some antibiotic samples. The problem is he won't say where he was on Thursday evening and Angie has no knowledge of him being in the office."

"Did he say anything about the accusations of drug problems?" I asked.

"Jack says that he has been totally clean since he was in college. Something happened while he was at Oregon State that caused him to get clean and stay clean."

"Did Jon find anything other than antibiotics in Jack's car?"

"No. Jack's story does hang together there. If you want my personal opinion, Sis, I think that Jonathon may be grasping at straws a little bit. He is under a lot of pressure from the town to solve this one. On the other hand, Jack isn't helping himself at all by not saying where he was on Thursday. He just says that he had some personal business to attend to and that he didn't get home until late."

"I wonder if Leslie could get Jack to tell the sheriff where he was." I asked.

"I don't think so," Sean answered. "Jack is kind of clamming up around her, and of course that is making her even more miserable."

"Poor Leslie. I haven't seen her quite so taken with anyone since I moved here. For her sake, I sure hope that this doesn't turn out as bad it appears. But what about the burglar? Her statement that Tom was already dead seems a bit far-fetched. Why would she go in or at least stay in, if she found him dead on the floor?"

"Can't answer that, Sis. I am never surprised at some of the things crooks do, and yes, she could be lying. I'm sure Jonathon is still considering that."

"Was she armed when Blackie caught her?" I asked.

"No. If you had just killed someone, would you be running around with the murder weapon on you?"

"I guess you're right. I was hoping that it might give a clue to whether she was armed when she did the burglaries and thus could have had the means to shoot Tom."

"I'm afraid that it doesn't help one way or the other," Sean said. "Well, that is the end of my information. What did you do today?"

"Mainly ran errands but before I fill you in, let's go get some of that casserole and salad. It smells pretty good and I'm getting hungry."

In less than a minute, we were seated at the table with our food.

"Hmmm this is one of my favorites, Sis. You do as good a job with it as Grandma used to do."

"I use her recipe pretty much, but do modify it a bit to cut down on the fat. People in Grandma's day didn't worry about the amount of fat that was in their food. They worked it off with hard physical labor."

I filled Sean in on the information that I had from Angie on the memorial service and on the fact that Tom's ex-wife was still in the area. Then our conversation turned to other topics of interest. He caught me up on his current case. He also let me in on his plans to go to Vancouver, British Columbia, over the President's Day weekend and invited me to join him.

"I have some ice cream if you want some dessert," I commented when we came to a lull in the conversation and our plates were empty.

"Nope, I'd better pass. And looking at the time, I think I should help you clean up and take myself home. I need to be on the job early tomorrow. My penance for the afternoon off that I didn't get."

We quickly got the food put away and the dishes into the dishwasher. The dogs were waiting on the back porch to greet us as Sean and I walked out. I took the opportunity that their greetings for him gave me to slip leashes on both of them. I didn't want them deciding that it was a good night for a walkabout as soon as he opened the gate.

"Drive carefully. It feels quite a bit colder than when you got here. You could hit black ice easily. I don't want to hear that you spent the night in a ditch somewhere."

"I will. Thanks for the supper, Sis."

"It was good to have your company. And thanks for the information on Jack. I hope he changes his mind and says where he was Thursday. If he's innocent, it might clear him. Maybe he has another lady friend and doesn't want to hurt Leslie."

"Could be, but he is hurting Leslie by not talking to her too," Sean responded.

"That's true," I said. "Well, take care and be safe. I love ya."

"You too."

The last was said as Sean closed the door to his pickup and started to turn around to go out of the driveway. He stopped, opened the gate, drove through and closed it behind him. I love guests that are gate savvy. We were always taught that you leave a gate the way you found it. If it is open, you leave it open. If it is closed, you leave it closed.

I watched as Sean's taillights receded in the distance and thought about the information he had given me.

"Jack's just making more trouble for himself," I said to the dogs as I unleashed them and turned to go back into the house. They decided to follow for some quiet time with me.

I still had my spinning supplies at the house so decided to sit by the fire and spin. Maybe my mind would come up with something while I did the comforting and so-routine work. I had forgotten to ask Sean the burglar's name. I wondered if she was a local person who had been in the county a long time or if she was a newcomer like Jack. Was Tom dead when she arrived? I was brought out of my reverie by the phone ringing.

"Have you looked outside recently?" Ellen asked.

"No, why?" I asked as I looked out the window. "Oh my gosh, it's snowing."

And it was: big soft fluffy flakes. We get very little snow in the Puget Sound area and a snow storm almost always means that life is going to come to at least a partial standstill. "I didn't even listen to the weather this evening. Is this supposed to last?"

"They say no. But then we know how well they forecast the weather around here," Ellen responded. "I'm glad I'm stocked up. And I have lots of programming to do so have no real reason to go out. Let it snow."

"I wouldn't mind the snow either, but it sure does make a mess of lots of people's days. Have you decided if you are going to dance at Tom's service?"

"I called Angie today and told her I would."

"I'm glad that you did. I love to watch you dance and it will add just the right note of the sacred and the celebratory with it."

"Well, I just called you to see if you'd noticed the weather, and it's your bedtime, so I'd better get off here."

With Ellen's comment, I noticed that it was indeed after ten o'clock. "You are right. I think I'll head there as soon as we hang up. Don't stay up too late. I'll talk to you in the morning."

"Oh, you know me. I'll be working for a couple more hours. I do my best work late at night."

I knew that was true. Ellen and I were exact opposites when it came to our energy habits and when we thought one should go to bed.

"Well, good luck on the programming then. I'll talk to you later."

I hung up and made sure that the fire was safely contained. After turning out the lights, I paused at the window and watched the lazy snowflakes floating down in the light of the moon. It was going to be a good night for sleeping.

Chapter 12

I awoke Tuesday morning to the quiet that only comes from a heavy fresh snowfall. It looked like the weather forces had miscalled this one. I grabbed my warm wool robe and pulled it on as I walked toward the window. Everything was coated in a garment of white. It was a lovely pristine, unbroken landscape except for a few places where I could see that the Pyrs had plowed through to get to their fence lines. Guard duty had to be done even if there was snow, or maybe because there was snow. And speaking of the white monsters, a wet head poked its way into the bedroom.

"Hello, Nali. Are you ready for breakfast? You have to wait for me to get clothes on and I'll be out."

I bundled up for the weather, turned on the coffee on my way through the kitchen, stuck my feet in my boots and broke a trail to the barn. The snow was about eight inches, which is a lot for us. The local news would have all kinds of messages on school closures, meeting cancellations and traffic accidents. I was glad I could just stay home. The odds were that no one would come to the shop so my day would be fairly lazy and slow.

After I fed the livestock and grabbed the snow shovel from the barn, the dogs and I had a great game of dumping snow on them as they charged me in mock battle. I shoveled a path to the barn and cleared enough of the driveway and parking lot to allow for at least one car at the shop. Then, feeling like a kid, I threw myself backward into an unblemished section of snow, created a snow angel and lay there enjoying the view of the clear blue sky with big fluffy clouds. Falcor, wondering what Mom was doing on the ground, flopped down beside me and poked his nose under my arm.

"Want to go for a walk today?" I asked the dogs. "You got cheated the other morning but I doubt that anyone will bother us today."

My question was met with Pyr snuffles and one quick kiss from Nali. Pyr kisses are seldom given once they leave puppy-hood but evidently she was feeling a bit like a puppy with this unusual weather.

It did not take me long to change into dry clothes and eat breakfast. Soon I was walking out the back door with leashes in hand. At the sight of the Flexi leads, Falcor raced to the gate and back and Nali whirled in place and leaped up to meet me on the steps. They loved a chance to explore their neighborhood with the freedom of a Flexi lead.

With the dogs leashed, I opened the front gate and we plowed through the snow to the road. I would have to shovel the outside drive when we got home. The heavy snow pulled the lower evergreen limbs down to where they met the snow on the ground. This kind of snow meant broken tree limbs and broken tree limbs meant broken power lines. Puget Power would be busy today.

I could see their breath as the dogs moved ahead of me, plunging into the deeper snow in low areas and then shoving it ahead of them with their noses. Nali would bite great mouthfuls of it and then scoop some up on the end of her nose and toss it in the air. Falcor decided that, leash or no leash, he needed to roll in one wonderful spot and then race on ahead of Nali and me. By the time we had slogged the distance from my gate to where the county trail started up into Capitol Forrest, I was warm and the dogs were slowing down to their normal sedate walk.

Because of the heavy tree cover, the snow on the path was a little less deep, but it still made for great exercise for me. We were only a few yards up the trail when the deep silence of the woods and the snow enveloped us. Pine and Douglas fir branches had a layer of meringue that glistened in the morning sun. A Steller's jay broke the peace with his raucous call and sent a shower of snow on my head as he flew off the branch above me. Off to the side, I heard the chit, chit, chit of a bushy-tailed gray squirrel as he sat on a limb and worked on the fir cone he was holding. Alerted by Nali's low woof, I noticed a white-tailed doe just as she whirled to go back up the hillside away from the large monsters. As we moved up the trail, the Jay followed us, scolding as he went. They are one of my favorite local birds, the clowns of the area who keep me entertained all year round.

Falcor was in the lead, looking back every once in awhile to see if Nali and I were following him. As we made a turn around the bend in the trail, Falcor decided to check out the hole near the base of a large Douglas fir tree. He stuck his head down in it and snorted at the snow that got up his nose. Then his head dove down into it further and it was obvious that he was sniffing at something, or at least he thought he had found something.

"What did you find, big guy?" I asked as Nali and I caught up. We were answered with Falcor starting to dig. As this was not particularly normal behavior for him, Nali and I looked closer. I could see the edge of a cloth of some sort and that seemed to be what had his interest.

"Come on, Falcor. You don't need that old thing. Nali and I want to continue our walk."

Nali indicated her agreement by starting to go further up the trail. But Falcor was not to be deterred. He was going to find out what this thing was so I decided that I might as well help. I started scraping the snow away from the edge that he wasn't working on and then I saw something metallic on my side. What had Falcor found? I moved a little more snow on my side and realized that it was a gun.

"Whoa, big boy. I think we need to stop our digging and call Jonathon. It may be nothing or you may have found something very important. Time to move away from your hole."

I pulled Falcor away and locked his leash as he still thought that he should uncover his prize completely. Once he was secure, I used my cell phone to call Jonathon.

"Black Hills Police," Tammie answered. A fixture with the force, she acted as dispatcher during the day, answered people's questions, kept track of Jonathon and just generally made sure the office ran smoothly.

"Hi, Tammie. This is Martha Williamson. I think I've, or rather Falcor, has found something important. Is Jonathon there?"

"He just headed for Black Hills Café, Martha. May I have him call you right back?"

"Yes, I'm on my cell phone."

"Thanks. I'll have him get right back to you."

I looked again at the base of the tree. Was it the murder weapon? And why place it here? A shiver ran up my spine and it wasn't caused by the cold. The murderer had to go right by my home to get here. And he was walking very close to my fence lines. Had I ignored a warning bark that I should have paid attention to? Had the dogs alerted me to his presence?

My head was whirling with questions, but I decided to let the dogs go ahead and walk a little further up the trail. Just standing when we were on a walk was not their idea of fun.

"Come on, Falcor. You did a good job, now let's walk some more."

I let the brake off on his leash and we started up the trail. Falcor decided that new areas to explore were maybe better than worrying about his old hole and his nose went down to the snow to see what messages it could retrieve.

We hadn't walked far when my phone rang.

"Hello, Jonathon."

"What's up? Tammie said that Falcor found something."

"Yes, he found a gun next to a big Douglas Fir tree on the county trail that is just beyond my property line. We haven't disturbed it. I thought you might want to come get it."

"You bet I do. I'll be there in about ten minutes."

"We'll stay in the area. I'm going to let the dogs walk a little further up the trail but will try to time it so we're back at the tree when you get here. I doubt anyone else will be on the trail this morning. I'll keep my phone on in case you need to call me again."

"OK, I'll see you soon. I may bring Walter and Blackie. Although between the snow and the things you and the white monsters have done, it probably won't do much good, but it'll give Blackie some experience."

"I'll see you when you get here. Warn Walter that Falcor and Nali don't like strange dogs. I'll make sure they are on short leashes."

I hung up and turned to see two questioning faces.

"All right, all right. We will continue our walk. Sorry but Mom had business to take care of."

I glanced at my watch so I could keep track of the time and started to follow the dogs up the trail but the peace of the morning had been pretty well disrupted by Falcor's find.

"Falcor, Nali, it's time for us to turn around. Let's go."

This brought looks that said volumes. Obviously the Pyrs had planned on a much longer walk.

"I know, but we have to meet Jonathon back at Falcor's tree. Can't help it, big guys."

The dogs turned around and led me back down the trail. Just before we turned a bend that would allow us to see the tree, I shortened their leashes to six feet. This brought another look about humans who broke the rules of walks. I was glad that I did, though, because Jonathon, Walter and Blackie were just reaching the tree when we were in a position to see it, and the Pyrs immediately let Blackie know that he was on their territory.

"OK, monsters, enough already." I walked to within about fifteen feet of the tree which kept the dogs separated.

"Nali, Falcor, down. No, down. Good dogs. Stay."

Pyrs are notorious about ignoring obedience commands, but this time they seemed to sense that it was important and

I meant it. With both dogs down and settled, I turned to Jonathon.

"You can see where Falcor and I removed snow there by the tree. Neither of us actually touched the gun."

"Thanks, Martha. I'll just clear it away and we'll see what you found."

Jonathon began to methodically remove the snow and soon we could see a black revolver. He reached down using plastic gloves to keep from damaging any of the evidence and picked it up.

"It's the right caliber," he said. "We'll have to send it to the lab to see if it's the right gun."

"Hopefully it is. Maybe it can give some more clues to what happened to Tom."

"I think I have my killer, Martha. But this might just seal it."

"I'm sorry, Jonathon, but I have problems with it being Jack. Maybe this will give us a clue to who it really was."

"Well, we'll see what it tells us. I'll have Walter and Blackie search around but between the snow and you three, I don't hold out much hope of finding anything. We will check out this towel too. It appears to have some blood on it. I wonder if it came from Tom's office."

"Angie could probably tell you if it came from there, and she'll be glad to know that the gun has been found. I wonder if Tom had any guns in his office. I never thought to ask her."

"She said that he didn't, to her knowledge. But that doesn't mean that he couldn't have had one. Well, I need to get back into town. Thanks again, Martha. Give Falcor a nice treat for his find today."

"I will, Jonathon. And speaking of the dogs, I'm sure they

are ready to start walking again. Although I think it'll just be back to the house. I still have a driveway to dig out."

Jonathon drove off. Walter and Blackie began their search of the area, and the monster dogs and I began our walk home.

"That was a good find, Falcor. You were a good boy. And I think this may be the piece that will unravel the case against Jack. I hope so."

Chapter 13

Walking back to the house was easier; we could stay in the path that we had made on our way to the trail. As we came within sight of my buildings, the dogs alerted and started to move quickly toward the house. With excited barks, they let me know that we had a trespasser. However, that trespasser was shoveling my drive, so I figured it was pretty benign. Soon the tenor of the dogs' bark changed as they realized it was Ellen.

"Hey, lady, you can visit my house anytime if you're willing to shovel snow," I yelled when we were within earshot.

"I figured you wouldn't be gone too long and it was good exercise," Ellen answered. "My neighbor cleared mine with his tractor so I didn't have to do any work there. The main streets in town are cleared so getting here wasn't too bad. You might have some customers from people who don't have to go to work today and want something cozy to do with their time. I brought my spinning. We're celebrating. I finished the beta version of the program from hell and it has been shipped off to the buyer. It will be a few days before they get back to me with changes and bugs."

Just then Nali had had enough of these long-winded people conversations and she gave Ellen a nudge that caught her off balance. Down they both went into the snow with Nali wagging her tail and snuffling Ellen all over.

"OK, girl. So I ignored you. Did you have to push me down?"

Laughing, Ellen got up and gave Nali a good love. Then she turned to Falcor, ever the gentleman, and petted him also.

"Come on, guys, you've had your walk and a chance to greet Ellen. Now it is back into your space for the day."

I walked the dogs to the inner gate where I let them off leash and closed the gate to secure them. They would sleep in the barn where it was warm or in the snow. Either one suited them just fine.

"Come inside and let's get dried off and have a cup of tea. I even have some cinnamon rolls in the freezer if you want to celebrate with mucho calories."

"Sounds good to me."

"Looks like the dogs have both of us soaked. Here is a towel. I'll get us something dry to change into. I can toss our wet things into the washer and we can get them clean and dry while we visit."

Ellen proceeded to get out of her wet clothes while I went into the bedroom to get a couple of warm mu`u mu`us for us to wear. I love the Hawaiian dress and I've adapted it to this cooler climate by making them out of warmer material.

"Here, you can put this on. Why don't you start the tea water and get the rolls from the freezer? I'll get this load of wash going."

With the tea water on the stove, the rolls ready to nuke as soon as the water was boiling, and the washing machine started, Ellen and I sat down at the kitchen table.

"Now catch me up," Ellen said.

I proceeded to tell her about Falcor's find this morning and Jonathon's take on it.

"But I'm hoping that it'll be the clue that starts to unravel the case against Jack. I just don't think he did it," I continued. "However, that is all instinct and has nothing to do with any evidence that I can put forth."

"I feel the same way," Ellen replied. "I don't know Jack very well but I do know Leslie. I don't think she is being swayed by her love for the man when she says that he is innocent. I just wish he would tell someone where he was that night."

"Has anyone talked to his mother?" I asked.

"I don't know. I wonder if she knows where he was, and would she tell us if she did?"

The tea kettle interrupted our conversation, letting us know that it was ready. Ellen poured the tea and I stuck the rolls into the microwave to heat. Soon we were seated again with our tea and well earned calories.

"Now your turn," I said. "You finished the program and put it in the mail. Did you find out any gossip while you were at the post office?"

"Not at the post office but I did talk to Angie. The plans for the memorial service this Saturday are coming together just fine. She'd like to get together with us this week to go over things and make sure we have all the ends pulled together."

"That's good. Did she say whether anyone from New Mexico is coming up?" I asked.

"Yes, they are," Ellen answered. "Lenore Walker will be there, which we pretty much figured already. Marilyn Davis, Tom's nurse when he was in Albuquerque, is coming and James Hernandez, the man who lives on Tom's ranch. There may be others but we know about these for sure."

"Maybe some of these people can enlighten us a little bit on what happened in New Mexico," I said. "Tom did infer problems in his letter to Angie, and the missing Albuquerque files say to me that there is a connection. Could Lenore have confronted him for some reason? It wouldn't be the first time that someone killed an ex-spouse in a fit of anger."

"That's true," Ellen responded as I headed for the washer to shift our clothes to the dryer

"Come on, let's see if a pair of my jeans will fit you at all," I said. "If they do, we can go over to the shop and spin while the clothes are drying."

"They may be a little short," Ellen said and laughed. At five-foot-eleven, Ellen was about four inches taller than I was. "But other than that, they should fit."

They did fit, other than being high water. I handed her a sweater. By the time I had dressed, Ellen had cleaned up our dishes and was ready to go next door. I picked up my basket of Samoyed fiber and we stopped at Ellen's truck so she could gather up her spinning on our way to the shop.

"Yikes, it's cold in here. You turn up the thermostat and I'll start a fire. It will be cozy in no time. If you want more tea, run some water through the pot."

"I'll pass on the tea right now but I'll run some water through so we can have some later if we want."

With the fire started, I unlocked the dog's door so they could visit if they wanted to. Sable immediately came through the door looking indignant and shaking one snowy paw. Evidently she felt that the snow was a personal insult. With another shake, she sauntered through the fence and curled up in front of the fire for a snooze.

"Now let me see your spinning," I said. Ellen pulled out the work she had done and it was really quite lovely. "This is looking great. You are gaining consistency and it looks like you are being fairly productive too."

"It's addicting," Ellen said. "And I find that it's a great break from programming. I try to get away from the computer for about ten minutes every hour and the spindle is just the thing to pick up. I still have to concentrate enough that it takes my mind off the program. And the hand motion is different than my computer work. And—drum roll, please—I can walk and spin so it gets that part of me moving too."

"You have come a long way in a very few days if you are walking while you spin. Just keep up the good work. You are going to be accomplished in no time."

I pulled out the Samoyed hair to start spinning on it. It looked like I had enough hair left for about one more skein. Just as Ellen and I sat down to start spinning, the dogs barked and I heard a car pull into the parking lot. It was Jane. She paused when she noticed Ellen's truck but came on up to the shop. She kicked her boots off on the porch as Ellen and I had done and came into the shop just as Nali made a dive through the doggy door, barking her head off.

"Hi. With school closed, I thought I'd take advantage of my time off and come over here to spin for awhile. I figured that way you could answer any questions I had along the way. Am I interrupting something?"

"Not at all, Jane; the shop is open. Ellen and I had the same idea that it was a perfect day for spinning. So grab a place to sit and come join us. There is tea water over there if you want some."

"Not right now, thanks."

Jane decided to sit on one of the pillows on the floor and Nali lay down in her corner with a bit of a grumble. She preferred guests that at least acknowledged her presence, but I had noticed that Jane appeared to have some fear of the dogs.

"Let me see how you are doing, Jane."

She handed me her spindle and a small skein of yarn. It was obvious that Jane was a perfectionist. She had very little inconsistency even in the beginning. The yarn was lovely and well spun. She obviously had a talent for it.

"That is lovely, Jane. You are doing a beautiful job. You will be ready to pick some fiber to spin for a project real soon."

"Thank you. Actually, I was thinking about doing that today. I'd like to try a scarf for my brother for a first project. I figure that it won't take very much yarn and the knitting is simple."

"That is a great first project. Do you want to look at what's available now so you can start spinning on it here?"

"Yes. That way, if it spins differently, I'll have you to answer questions right away."

"OK, let's go over here and I'll show you what I have. I began to pull out fiber that I thought she might like.

"Oh, I like these with the silver thread in them. What are they?"

"Those are Ashland Bay's merino and tencel. I have it in a number of colors and I believe that we might find one that would be perfect."

"I like this one."

"That's Honey," I said. Jane had picked out a cream color that was just slightly on the beige side. "It is a pretty color and would go with anything."

"It isn't quite what I had in mind when I came in," Jane said, "but I like it a lot. And you're right: It will go with anything he might want to wear. I think I'll take it."

Jane started toward the sitting area and then paused at the spindles.

"You know, maybe I'll get a real spindle too. Which would you recommend?"

"Well, my personal preference is a top whorl. I think you'd like one just under a couple of ounces."

I pulled out three that I thought she might like.

"Try each of these; they have leaders on them so you can spin them."

Jane worked with each one, using some of the fiber that I had placed next to the spindles to help with the testing.

"I like this one," she said as she handed me one of the spindles with a llama design that was made by a spindle maker in Colorado.

After I weighed out Jane's fiber and completed her purchase, we moved back to join Ellen.

"This is a little different to spin, but the spindle is sure easier to use," Jane commented.

"Yes, merino is a little slicker than the wool you were using and the tencel adds to that. It may take a little more twist than the fiber you started with."

"Hey," Ellen broke in. "Did I tell you that I heard from Barret yesterday? He's my ex," she added, to Jane's questioning look.

"No, you didn't. How is he and why the call?"

"He just wanted to chat. He's going to be in Portland for a medical conference the first of next month and wanted to know if I wanted a visit on his way in either direction."

"You want a visit from your ex?" Jane asked, rather incredulously. "I wouldn't want mine in the same state with me."

"Oh, Barret and I are still good friends. We just discovered that we like each other a whole lot more if we aren't living together. Neither of us has remarried. I think we are happier when we have control of our own lives with no interference. A couple of control freaks if I ever knew any. But I didn't know that you had been married, Jane."

"Yes, I got married during my sophomore year of college, much to the anger of my parents. And they were even angrier when I got divorced. As far as they were concerned, good Catholic girls do not marry without their parents' permission; and if they were stupid enough to do it, they sure don't get a divorce later. However, when they realized that he had been beating me, they at least relaxed on the anger about the divorce. I think they figured I could get an annulment from the church when I wanted to get married again. In their minds, there was no 'if.' We have since worked through it and have a good relationship again."

"I'm glad you and your parents managed to work things out. Our relationship with our parents and family is so important," I added.

"I was glad we could too. I was the youngest and the most protected of the children. There were six of us. We do have a close-knit family and I always enjoy it when we can get together."

"Where was the sister whose picture I saw in the lineup of children?"

A little cloud flashed through Jane's eyes but she answered. "She was number two and the only other girl."

I noticed the past tense.

"Is she no longer living?" I asked.

"She died twelve years ago. I had just started high school."

"How did she die?" Ellen asked.

"She got a terrible infection that wasn't controlled," Jane answered. "She was only twenty-four and had her whole life ahead of her."

"I'm terribly sorry," I said and then decided that maybe I should change the subject because this seemed to distress Jane some. "Your yarn is looking great, Jane. You really are a natural when it comes to fiber arts."

"Thanks, Martha. I do enjoy them. And I want to get good enough to teach the children in a month or so. I have a project planned to go with the lesson you will give them on spinning history."

"That's great. I'll be glad to help on the day that you decide to teach them to spin. That way there will be more than one person to help with questions."

"I could use the help. I'll let you know the exact days so that you can schedule them."

"Good. I'll look forward to it. Anyone want tea?"

"I'll get it." This was from Ellen. "I need to move. Jane, do you want some?"

"Yes, please. Peppermint."

"Peppermint it is. Martha?"

"I think I'd like some Earl Gray."

"OK, and I see you have some Jasmine, which I love. Tea coming right up."

"Have you planted your peas yet, Martha?" Ellen asked as she came back with the tea.

"No. I had planned on doing it this past weekend but then things got kind of out of hand with Tom's death. And with this snow, looks like it will be a bit before I can do it."

"Isn't it a little early?" Jane asked.

"Nope. The old saw around here is that you put peas in the ground around Washington's birthday. It is a few days before but at the rate I'm going, it will probably be after before I get it done. I also want to get some pansies and primroses to put in the window boxes too. They can be put out this time of year and they add so much color."

"I thought I noticed something coming up in the garden where I'm living," Jane said. "Any idea what that might be?"

"Probably crocus," Ellen answered, "although, it could be the very beginnings of the daffodils coming up. The crocus will bloom well before the daffodils. Some of my most protected ones are in bloom. But the daffodils will start putting out their leaves about now. Cold weather slows down both of them but doesn't stop them."

"Everything is so different here," Jane said. "I'm not used to the cold, and the variety of plants that seem to grow easily is quite different from where I was in school in Arizona."

"Puget Sound is a great place to garden," I said. "It is warm enough to handle some of the more delicate plants, if they are sheltered, and cool enough for those that like a bit of a cold spell in the winter."

"I've never been much of a gardener but you two make me feel like I should try it."

"Oh you should, Jane," Ellen joined in. I find that it is a very welcome break from my programming. I will often just take ten minutes after an hour at the computer and go out. Getting my hands in the dirt for that short period of time clears my head and helps my body."

I was about to add something when Nali went racing out the dog door, barking. All three of us got up to see what had caused her to react that way and saw Sean's truck coming to a stop in the driveway close to the inside gate and Nali and Falcor standing there barking and jumping up and down like puppies.

"Well, I guess it's obvious that the dogs like Sean." I commented.

"He works for the police?" Jane asked.

"Actually, the Thurston County sheriff's office. He's been with them about seven years. He went through the State Patrol Academy but didn't like working highways exclusively. He likes the variety at the sheriff's office—some burglary, some domestic violence which no one likes, some murder, and a whole lot of other things. Keeps him busy."

"Murder? Is he working on Dr. Walker's murder?"

"No, that is being handled by our local chief of police because it happened within the city limits. But my guess is that Sean is keeping up with the investigation as much as he can. Like all of us, he liked Tom."

"I didn't know him," Jane commented. "I prefer a woman doctor so I go into Olympia to Group Health."

This last was said as Sean walked in the door and the dogs raced in through their door.

"Looks like I'm breaking up a party, Sis," Sean said as he walked over to give the dogs a pet and slip them a treat he had in his pocket. He often came treat-laden.

"Not really. We were just sitting here spinning. Want to join us in a cup of tea?"

"Will do and I've got a little news for you."

I noticed that Jane was gathering up her things.

"I just noticed the time. I really need to get into town for a couple of errands. Thanks for the help, Martha. It was good to spend some time with you, Ellen, and to see you again, Sean."

I walked Jane to the door.

"Drive carefully. Most of us are idiots here when we get snow and it will get really slick when it cools down enough to freeze hard tonight."

"Don't worry. That is one reason that I want to run my errands and get home. I have no desire to be out when the roads could get worse."

"I'll see you Friday if not before," I said as I shut the door and joined Sean and Ellen with my cup of tea. "You said you had news."

"I do. I stopped in at the police station on my way here. I was curious to see if they had found anything new on Tom's death. It turns out that Walter and Blackie did find something besides the towel and gun. There was a small piece of cloth caught on one of the branches of a blackberry vine. The print is rather distinctive and it looks like it may have blood on it. They have sent it to the lab along with the towel which Angie does think came from Tom's office."

"That is great news, Sean. I keep hoping for something that will clear Jack and find out who really did it."

"That makes two of us," Ellen added.

"Well, for Leslie's sake, I hope you two are correct. You haven't convinced Jonathon yet, however." Looking into his empty cup, Sean added, "Do you women only drink tea? Or could a guy maybe bum a late lunch while he's here?"

I looked at the clock and realized that it was close to two and Ellen and I hadn't eaten much either.

"I think we could all do with some food. Let's go over to the house and see what there is to eat."

Chapter 14

S ean, why don't you build us a fire while Ellen and I see if there is anything worth eating in this house," I said.

"OK," Sean said, "looks like I need to bring in some wood."

"You know where it is."

"We've got some frozen chicken breast and some fresh veggies. I can build a stir fry if that suits everyone or I can do a quick pasta sauce. You two choose."

"I'm for pasta," Sean said, as he walked in with his arms full of wood.

"That's OK by me too," Ellen added.

"Linguini it is then."

While the pasta was cooking, I made a quick sauce with the chicken and tomatoes. Meanwhile, Ellen fixed a green salad and some garlic bread. In no time we were ready to eat.

"OK, everyone, food is ready. Let's eat," I said.

"Now, Sean, tell us a little bit more about that piece of material that Walter and Blackie found," I said as soon as we were seated at the table.

"Well, I've only seen pictures because the fabric was sent to the state lab. But it has a small print that has southwest characters in it. You know that flute dancer. I can't remember the name of it."

"Kokopelli?" I asked as I reached for a piece of garlic bread. "He was an ancient fertility symbol among other things with the Southwest Native Americans."

"That's the one," Sean answered. "Anyway, the fabric is blue and it has a small yellow design with him in it. Also some suns. There may be other pieces to the design but this piece was only a little over an inch in size. So you can see that the print is quite small."

"Doesn't sound like something a man would have," Ellen added to the conversation.

"I don't know. It could have been a print shirt. I've been known to be given crazier things by a sister of mine."

"Yes, but those were aloha shirts. They were supposed to be crazy," I said and laughed.

"Still someone may have given a shirt to Jack that he thought he should wear once in awhile." Sean had a wry look that said it had happened to him before.

I thought about this for a minute; but from Sean's description, it didn't ring true for me.

"Hmmm, I think I'll go down tomorrow and see if Jonathon will let me look at the pictures. Who knows? I might have seen it on someone. I'll have to go early though so I can be back to open the shop at ten."

"How about I meet you for breakfast at Black Hills Café?" Ellen said. "Then we can both go."

"Sounds good, Ellen. Let's plan on seven-thirty at the café. That should put us at the police station about the time Jonathon gets there. I'll call him this afternoon and let him know that we will be coming. About how long do you think it'll take the lab to do the ballistics on that gun and the work on the fabric?" I directed this last to Sean.

"They should get the ballistics back by tomorrow. The blood samples may take a little longer but that mainly depends on how busy they are. Murder always takes a higher priority than other items. Now, enough about business. What have you got for dessert, Sis?"

I laughed. Sean always had his priorities straight. With the dishes in the dishwasher and a couple of scoops of ice cream each, we moved to the living room and the welcoming glow of the fire. However, just before I could settle into my favorite corner of the couch, the phone rang.

"Martha." Angie was so excited she didn't even let me say hello. "I just found a folder at Tom's that might help us know what happened in Albuquerque."

"The folders that we were looking for?" I asked.

"I don't think so. This one contains letters from Tom to James Hernandez, the ranch manager. I've just scanned them but they seem to have been written about the time of Tom's divorce. Do you want to look at them?"

"You bet I do. But the roads are getting slick. How about coming over by the shop tomorrow at ten and we can go through them there?"

"Sounds good," Angie answered. "I'll meet you then. In the meantime, I'll keep looking. I might find something else. Earlier I was just looking at labels. Now I'm actually looking at the contents of the folders."

I turned to questioning looks from Ellen and Sean.

"Angie found a folder at Tom's with some letters in it that she thinks might help us know what happened in Albuquerque."

"It is the folder we were looking for?" Ellen asked.

"No, it's some correspondence but she says it covers the time period we are interested in."

"Has she told Jonathon?" Sean asked.

"I doubt it," I said. "Tom had mentioned some folders in his letter to Angie. They are missing. She did tell Jonathon that. This isn't the same thing but covers the same period. I doubt that Jonathon would be interested. He didn't seem very interested in the fact that the files were missing."

"Well, she should probably tell him anyway," Sean said.

"She's going to bring it over in the morning so we can go through it. If we find anything more other than comments about the ranch management, I promise we will call Jonathon."

"OK," Sean said. "But don't play detective. Jonathon's the pro; and if you are correct and Jack isn't the murderer, the murderer may still be loose."

"Promise. We'll not do anything stupid," I said to Sean and then turned to Ellen. "Want to come back here after we go to the police station?"

"Absolutely. I still think Albuquerque is a big clue."

Sean just shook his head in a way that said that he thought his sister and her best friend had lost their marbles.

"Well, Sis, I have to run some errands before I head home, so I better be on my way."

"I better go too," Ellen chimed in. "I have animals to feed and would just as soon do that before it gets too dark and colder. By the way, did anyone hear a weather report? I wonder if this is going to hang around or if it will be gone in the morning."

"The radio said that it might rain tonight," Sean said. "I was listening on my way over here. But that could be just wishful thinking on the part of the weather forecasters."

"Wishful thinking or not, I hope they are correct," I said. "I love the snow for about one day. Then it just gets sloppy and dirty and in the way. Well, if the two of you are going to desert me, I guess I might have to give in and do some financial work on the computer this evening after I feed my critters."

I followed Sean to the back door while Ellen got her clothes out of the dryer and headed for my bedroom to change.

"Take care, little brother, and drive carefully. Talk to you later."

"Will do. Let me know if you all find anything interesting in those files."

I sent Sean off with a hug and came back into the kitchen as Ellen was coming out dressed in her own clothes.

"I must say that those do look a little better on you than mine do."

"A better fit at least. Style is about the same—jeans are jeans. Thanks for a great day. Let's see. I think I left my spinning in the shop so guess I should go over there and pick it up."

"I'll go with you. I have to shut it up for the day and may do a little work over there before I feed the livestock."

We walked over to the shop and Ellen packed up her spinning.

"Will you close the outside gate on the way out? I doubt very much that I'll have any more customers today," I said, giving Ellen a goodbye hug.

"Will do. See you in the morning bright and early. Too early for me but I'll manage," she added with a grin.

I watched Ellen until she had closed the gate and pulled out onto the road then turned back into the shop.

As I walked in, two white streaks came bounding through the dog door. "Hi, you two. Want to come into the shop?" I opened their gate and let them in with me. "You have to wait until I pick up a little bit in here and call Jonathon. Then we can go out and take care of your charges and feed you."

I called Jonathon and made the appointment for the next morning. He wasn't real excited about showing me the pictures but decided that it couldn't hurt anything. With that done, it was a quick sweep through the shop and I was ready to lock it up for the night.

"Come on, guys. Let's go get some feeding and watering done."

The dogs bounded out the front door of the shop ahead of me and raced each other to the fence line. Then they turned and followed me back to the barn where I fed and watered everyone and shut the livestock inside.

With that task done, I headed inside to see what I needed to do in there and hopefully to a quiet evening. I felt the need for one and tomorrow looked like it was going to be a busy day.

Chapter 15

The phone was ringing as I walked in the door. I caught it just before my message cut in.

"Martha," Ellen's voice sounded frantic. "Shasta is gone. I've looked everywhere and I can't find her. There's a hole where she dug under the fence but no sign of her. It's getting dark and I heard the coyotes last night. She is so small. She'll be no match for a coyote."

"I'm on my way," I said. "Why don't you put Tahoma on a leash and walk with him? He may find her or she may see him and come out of wherever she is hiding."

"Good idea. And thank you for coming. I am so scared for my little fluff ball."

"Come on, guys," I said, "back into your part of the yard with you. I need to go help Ellen find Shasta."

I pulled on my jacket, gloves and hat and plunged my feet into my boots. The dogs and I walked out to their part of the yard. I tethered them while I backed my truck out into my driveway and then let them loose and shut the gate, leaving them behind the inside gate. I didn't need to come home to find out that my two were missing.

I hate driving in the snow and ice. Doing so after dark just makes it worse. Because John and I spent most of our married life in the south or the tropics, I have very little experience with bad winter roads. John's death had made me even more tentative in nasty road situations. One of the advantages of working from home and living in a relatively mild climate was that I seldom had to do it. But my friend's agony took precedence over my fears.

The roads in town had been cleared of snow but it was obvious that the wet had now turned to ice. I slowed down and tried to remember all that John had taught me about driving in these conditions. As I pulled off Black Hills Road, I once again encountered packed snow on the road. I slowed down even more as I started to scan the sides of the road for any sign of Shasta. If she were here, her white body against the snow was not going to make her easy to see in the light provided by my headlights. Even though it was freezing out, I rolled down my window so that I might hear anything out of the usual along the way.

At one point, I thought I saw something so I stopped and climbed out of the truck to take a closer look. It turned out to be an old garbage bag huddled up against the base of a tree and covered with snow. Disappointed, I climbed back into the truck and proceeded down the road.

Once more, I thought I saw something and climbed out of the truck only to slip and land solidly on my backside. Damn! The snow had developed a nice ice crust on top of it in this area. Gingerly getting back onto my feet, I carefully walked over to what I wanted to examine, which turned out to be a "puppy"-shaped bush. Obviously my desires to find her were placing Shasta in all kinds of unlikely spots. As I turned carefully and slowly started back to my pickup, my flashlight caught another item near the edge of the road. My curiosity got the best of me and I moved over to check it out.

A plastic grocery bag was lying by the side of the road. I leaned over to get a closer look and the edge of a file folder showed in the light. Opening the bag, I was surprised to see the name Albuquerque on the label tab of one of the files. Could these be the files we were looking for? My hands shook as I checked them out a little more closely. They seemed to contain newspaper clippings from New Mexico newspapers. I still wasn't sure but it looked like I'd found the Albuquerque files. They were damp but the plastic bag had kept them from being totally destroyed and the bag did not have snow over it. Why? Had it just recently been dumped? And why here? All questions that came to mind with no ready answers. I wanted to look at them more closely but standing on the side of a snowy road wasn't the place, and I still had a small white dog to look for.

I started to move toward my truck when headlights seemed to come out of nowhere. I hadn't heard the vehicle. Where did it come from? It was coming much too fast and seemed to be very close to the edge of the road. Just as it became parallel with me it started to slide. I leaped back and slipped. As I fought to keep from falling, the driver appeared to regain control of the car, but he didn't slow down. Had he seen me? Did he know how close he came to hitting me? I watched as it sped down the road. I had caught just a glimpse of the license plate and it wasn't from Washington. I wasn't sure but I thought it might have been red and yellow. Those were colors that New Mexico and Hawai`i used for some of their plates. But who would be racing down this back road with a plate from there? Had they tried to run me down, or was I just unlucky in my position when they lost control?

Shaken, I made my way slowly and carefully back across the road to my truck. I placed the bag with the files on the seat beside me and just sat there for a few minutes. The near miss at the side of the road had spooked me. I took a deep breath and tried to center myself. Once again, I started down the road. My hands were clenched onto the wheel in a death grip and my breath was shallow as I tried to concentrate on my driving and still keep my eyes open for Shasta.

I heard her before I saw her. Shasta was barking her head off at something and then she tore across the road directly in front of me. I slammed on my brakes.

"Oh, shit." The expletive was out of my mouth as the back end of the truck started to slide. Frantically I fought to control the truck in the slide, all the time wondering if I had hit the subject of my search. In spite of my efforts, the back end continued to slide toward the side of the road. As I felt it go over the edge, I remembered a fairly deep ditch on this side of Ellen's road. Praying that the truck wouldn't turn over, I finally gave up and let it go where it wanted to. With a thunk, I felt it come to rest with its rear end down a few feet but the truck still upright.

"Shasta," I called as I threw open the door of the truck and climbed out onto the ground. "Shasta."

I heard a joyful bark and a very happy, wiggling puppy raced toward me. I braced myself as she jumped up, but the footing was treacherous, and we landed in the snow with me on my back and Shasta giving me puppy kisses all over my face. I sunk my fingers deep into her long fur and held on tight. There was no way that I was going to give her a chance to take off again.

"OK, you little monster, let me get into a position where I can reach into my pocket."

I received another kiss for my efforts, as I moved to my knees, still keeping a solid hold on her. I reached into my pocket with my free hand and pulled out the collar and leash that I had brought from home. The collar slipped easily over her head and I breathed easily for the first time since I'd left home.

Then I looked at my truck. As far as I could see, I hadn't done any major damage to it but it was very firmly stuck in the ditch. I was going to need help. I reached into the cab for my cell phone to call Ellen. No cell phone.

"Shasta, any idea where my cell phone is?"

She cocked her head, but of course, I got no answer. I thought back to when I had left the house. I had grabbed my billfold and stuck it in my jeans pocket, but I realized that the cell phone was still sitting on the shelf where I had placed it when Ellen and I came in much earlier in the day. Shit!

Well, Shasta and I had a choice. We could sit here in the truck and freeze or we could start walking toward Ellen's. I figured that I still had about a mile to her house. I've never been one to just sit and it would be warmer walking. I started to lock up the truck. As I was rolling up my window, I saw lights coming from the direction of Ellen's farm. Maybe help was coming.

However, thinking of my earlier encounter, I pulled Shasta fully off the road and waited for the vehicle to come even with us.

"Martha, are you all right?" It was the voice of my veterinarian, Mark Begay.

"I'm fine and I've found Ellen's wayward puppy but obviously this truck is not moving on its own," I answered.

Mark pulled over to the side of the road and climbed out of his van. He walked over and stooped down to say hello to Shasta.

"Hey, big girl, what are you doing out here on your own on a night like this?" Shasta answered with major tail wags and a snuffle. "Pretty proud of yourself are you? Did you cause your aunt Martha to do this to her truck?"

"Well, it was probably my inept driving in this kind of weather," I answered for her, "but she didn't help by running across the road right in front of me. As the truck was sliding out of control, I was a whole lot more worried about whether I had hit her than about what was happening to me."

"Well, let's see how bad it is," Mark said as he stood up. He pulled a large flashlight out of his van and walked toward the rear of my truck. "I don't see any damage. I think you are just off the road and obviously in this snow it isn't going to come out on its own. I'm not sure that my van would be able to pull it out from this position. We may need help."

"I have Triple A," I said. "I just managed to go off without my cell phone in my haste to get here."

"I have mine."

"Good," I said, "but let's call Ellen before we call them. I know she is frantic with worry about this girl."

I took Mark's phone and called Ellen's house. I was not surprised when I got her machine. I left a message and then tried her cell phone.

"Hello?" I could hear the worry in Ellen's voice.

"Want me to kill her or would you like to do it when I get her home?" I said.

"You have her? Really? Thank God." Ellen's words all tumbled together. "Where are you?"

"In the ditch about a mile from your house," I said.

"In a ditch?"

"Yep, she ran across the road in front of me, barking her head off at something she saw on the other side of the road. I think the sight of the truck careening around on the road stopped her. She came as soon as I called her. She is fully leashed and safe and sound."

"But how are you?" Ellen asked.

"I'm fine. Mark just came by and lent me his cell phone. As soon as I hang up, I'll call Triple A."

"Maybe we can get it with my truck," Ellen responded.

"Nope. This is what I pay Triple A for and we don't need both of us in the ditch. Just stay put. I'll be there after I get out of here."

"OK, I won't try to pull you out but I'm coming down there anyway."

"You might want to bring a crate for Little Miss Runaway too," I said.

"On my way as soon as I get back to the house. Tahoma and I are back by the stream so it will take me a bit."

"Ellen is coming," I said to Mark as I hung up.

"I figured she would. Why don't you and your shaggy friend climb into my van? We might as well be warm while we wait for Triple A."

We climbed into Mark's van and I contacted Triple A. They would be out within the next forty-five minutes. Actually I expected them sooner. The Triple A agent in Black Hills was Bob Mitchell. I didn't expect him to leave me sitting in a ditch for anywhere near that amount of time.

"What were you doing out here on a night like this?" I finally asked Mark as we settled in to wait in the warm van. Shasta was sitting between the seats and thoroughly enjoying the pets that she was getting from both of us.

"I got a call from Norma Welsh. Her mare was having trouble giving birth. Turned out to mainly be an overanxious owner with her first birthing but I stayed until the little filly was born. She's a pretty one. Norma was pleased as punch."

I looked at Mark in the dim light of the van. He was tall and slim. His Navajo heritage gave him high cheek bones, strong facial features, thick black hair and black eyes that snapped when he was angry and sparkled when something tickled him. I watched as his slim strong fingers stroked Shasta's ears absently while his mouth smiled at the thought of the new baby girl. Mark was one of the few large animal vets in the area and always willing to make house and barn calls when necessary. Our town was very lucky to have him just as we had been so lucky to have Tom.

"Well, I'm glad she called you," I said. "I wasn't looking forward to the walk to Ellen's."

"Glad to be of service, madam," he said. "How are my clients at your place?"

"All fine and hopefully they won't be in need of your services for awhile. I see lights ahead," I added. "I didn't think it would take Bob long to get here, and it looks like we have lights coming up from behind too. Help in all varieties is on the way."

As I said that, Bob Mitchell pulled up with his tow truck behind my truck and Ellen pulled her truck behind Mark's van. I noticed that she had put a crate in the back of her truck and she also had some heavy pieces of wood in there too—something that I should have done before I left home. It might have helped me to control the back end of my truck.

"Martha, are you all right?" Bob asked as he climbed out of the tow truck.

"I'm fine. Just a little embarrassed," I answered.

"Just as long as you are OK, we can handle the truck problems. Why were you out here to begin with?"

"This monster," I said as I let Shasta out of Mark's van, "decided to go on a walkabout in the snow this evening. I was coming over to help Ellen look for her. She ran across the road in front of me and, well, you can see the rest of the story."

"Come here, you," Ellen said as she walked up and took Shasta's leash. She gave me a big hug. "I'm so thankful that both of you are safe. I would have had trouble forgiving myself if you'd been hurt trying to find her."

"No injuries other than to my pride," I said. "I think the truck is fine too."

"That is the way it looks to me," Bob said. "But why don't I pull it out and tow it to Ellen's? Then we can get a better look at it in the light from her barn floods. In the meantime, you can go back to Ellen's with Shasta and get warm."

"That sounds like a good idea," Mark said. "I'll stay here and help Bob in any way that I can and then I'll follow him to Ellen's. I want to make sure that you are safe and have transportation home before I leave."

"Thanks, Mark," I said. "You don't have to do that, though, you know."

"But I want to," he responded. "It'll give me a chance to take a look at that young lady in some decent light too. I want to make sure she didn't manage to get any significant scrapes while she was out running around."

"Thank you for that too," Ellen said. "Well, I think we've been ordered home, Martha. Let's go. I'll have a fire in the fireplace and something hot to drink when the two of you arrive." This last was for Bob and Mark.

"Thanks," Bob said. "This shouldn't take us long."

Ellen and I walked carefully back to her truck and put Shasta in the crate. We made sure the crate was tied down well in the back of the truck and climbed in the cab. It took some careful maneuvering but Ellen soon had us turned around and on our way back to her house.

"Thanks again for being there when I needed you," Ellen said.

"Hey, no problem. You'd have done the same for me. It just added a little more excitement to my evening than I'd planned on."

"Shasta'll go back into the barn as soon as we get her home. I don't want her to think that misbehaving gets her a chance to stay in the house at night."

"Good plan. I assume that the hole will be fixed before she is let out into the pasture again."

"She'll be in a kennel tomorrow since I don't have time to fix it in the morning. Are we meeting with Jonathon?"

"Yep. He wasn't terribly happy that we knew about the fabric but he said he would show us the pictures."

Ellen turned into her driveway and parked by her barn so there would be room for the other three vehicles. Tahoma greeted us with his deep Pyr bark and then gave another one that seemed to be meant just for Shasta. I walked over and gave him an ear scratch through the fence.

"You glad to have her back, big guy?" I asked him. He just pressed his head against the fence to get a better look at her and gave us a tail wag.

"She'll be there in a little bit, Tahoma," Ellen said. "You get back to your work and we'll take care of this end."

He seemed to understand and wandered off to where a group of the sheep was huddled in a sheltered area out of the wind. Ellen and I walked into the barn with Shasta and locked her in a stall area with a gentle old ewe.

"I have wood inside already if you want to start the fire," Ellen said as we walked into her house and pulled off our coats. The warmth of the kitchen felt especially good. "I'll just get hot chocolate going and put some of these frozen cookies in the oven to warm up. I imagine we'll be able to tempt the guys with them."

Ellen lived in a lovely large cedar home that made me think of a mountain lodge. It had a huge stone fireplace that dominated the living and kitchen area. The two bedrooms and the bath were off to the side and there was a large loft area upstairs where she had her office. I soon had a good fire going and wandered over to the stove to help myself to a cup of the hot chocolate.

"Hmmm. This must be homemade," I said. "It doesn't taste like Nestle's."

"It's not. I started with some pure cocoa powder and then added whole milk, sugar, cinnamon and just a touch of ground chili."

"I think it's the chili that makes it so unusual. You don't actually taste it but you know that it is somehow better than normal. Of course, the whole milk doesn't hurt either. So much for watching one's weight or cholesterol."

It wasn't long before I heard the sound of automobile engines. Bob and Mark were pulling into the driveway. Ellen and I pulled on our coats and walked out to see if my truck had survived its evening spin in the snow.

"Looks fine to me, Martha," Bob said as he finished walking around the truck.

"Can't see any problems under here either," Mark's voice came from under the truck. He had crawled under it while it was still winched up on one end.

"Great," I said. "I can't thank the two of you enough for all your help."

"I'll just get this thing back on its own wheels and it will be ready to go," Bob said.

"There is a fire and hot chocolate inside," Ellen said. "Come on inside as soon as you get done, Bob. Mark, you want to come look at Shasta. She's in the barn. We can do that while they are getting Martha's truck ready to drive again."

We were soon walking back into Ellen's welcoming kitchen. Mark's examination had shown Shasta to be no worse off for her adventure.

"Here's some hot chocolate and cookies," Ellen said. We helped ourselves and settled down near the fire. "I can't tell you how much I appreciate the help that each of you have given this evening. Martha can tell you that I was one scared woman when I called her earlier."

"Glad to be of help, and I even get paid for my part in it." Bob laughed.

"I'm just glad I was on the road when I was needed," Mark said. "And this is the best hot chocolate I think I've ever had. Thanks for fixing it, Ellen."

"You know, something odd happened when I was out looking for Shasta," I said and then continued to tell them about my adventures with the car.

"Do you think it was deliberate?" Bob asked.

"I don't know," I said. "It happened right after I found a

grocery bag with some files in it and was returning to my truck."

"Files?" Ellen responded. "The files."

"I think so, but I haven't had a chance to look at them. Some files were missing from Tom's office," I said to Bob and Mark in answer to their questioning looks.

"But what would they have been doing on my out-of-the-way road?" Ellen continued her thoughts.

"I have no idea," I said.

"More important," Mark chimed in, "is why was the car there and why did it try to run you down?"

"You didn't get the license plate?" This was from Bob.

"No, it went by too fast and part of it was covered with snow but I'd swear that it was red and yellow, not a Washington plate," I answered. "It may all be a coincidence and I just happened to be in a bad place when they started to slip, but it makes me nervous."

"I think you two should just turn those files over to Jonathon and stop this curiosity business," Bob said. "After all, he is paid to get in trouble and you aren't."

"I'll give them to him tomorrow, Bob," I said. "But I'll ask for copies. I still think that events in Albuquerque have something to do with Tom's death. We can go over them tomorrow with Angie, Ellen."

"And I agree with Bob," Mark said. "I think you two should be very careful. Tonight may have been deliberate."

"Deliberate or not, Mark, I can't let fear control my life. I'll do what seems right and be as cautious as I can, but I need answers," I said.

"Anyone for a second cup?" Ellen asked as Bob drained his.

"Not me," I said. "I'm nearing my bedtime and I still have to get that truck home."

"I'll follow you home," Mark said.

"You don't have to do that," I said. "I'm sure I won't have a big problem."

"I'll do it anyway," Mark answered. "I'll sleep much better if I know that you are home safe."

"Thank you," I said as I stood and gathered up a couple of cups to take to the dishwasher on my way to the back door.

"Leave the dishes," Ellen said. "I'll get them. All of you should get home so that you do get some sleep tonight."

Ellen walked us out to her drive and we all said our good-byes and walked to our vehicles. My drive home was uneventful and I was soon pulling into my own yard. I parked, picked up the bag with the files, and climbed out of my pickup and walked over to Mark's van where he had pulled into the parking area.

"Thanks so much, Mark. I really appreciate all of your help this evening."

"No problem. I'm glad that I was there when you needed help. With your healthy animals, I seldom see you. That is good but that is bad," he grinned.

"Well, thanks again," I said, wondering at his last phrase. "I'm sure I'll see you soon."

I didn't realize how soon or how much I would need his services in the days to come. I watched as he drove out, then walked over and closed the gate.

Chapter 16

I awoke to the sound of rain on the roof. Not the lovely loud rain on the tin roof of Hawai`i but the more muffled north-west sound where I had an attic and insulation between me and the roof. It was very soothing and I was tempted to just roll over and go back to sleep. Then I remembered I was to meet Ellen in town. A glance at the clock told me that I would have to move quickly to get my morning chores done before I needed to leave.

I quickly pulled on some clothes to go out to the barn and was walking through the kitchen when my white alarm clock came in through the doggy door.

"Beat you this morning, Nali. You were sleeping on the job."

I was answered with a gentle tail wag and a spin as she turned around to go back out the door with me.

The coffee was ready and smelling wonderful as I walked back into the kitchen after feeding and watering the critters.

I poured a cup of coffee and walked over to the table where I had spread out the contents of the files last night. Mainly newspaper clippings, they were now dry and most of them were quite readable. I picked up one that talked about a new wing at an Albuquerque hospital and wondered why Tom had thought that was eventful. They would need to be read carefully to see what clues they might hold. I gathered them together in a clean file folder to take to Jonathon this morning. Hopefully, he would let us keep copies.

I wondered if I should give Ellen a call to make sure she was up. She was notorious for sleeping through early morning appointments. I decided against it. It wasn't critical that she be with me, and if she needed the sleep after our eventful evening before, I'd let her have it.

The roads were clear when I drove out of my driveway. The warmer temperatures and the rain had done their job. That was one of the things I liked about the Pacific Northwest. The snow could be lovely once in awhile but usually before you were terribly tired of it, the weather warmed up and the rain washed away all the ugly dirty snow and the ice. I decided to park in front of the police station and walk back to Black Hills Café. It looked like Ellen had decided the same thing because her truck was parked just in front of where I stopped.

"There's that sleepy head," Ellen's voice came across the café as I walked in the door.

I looked at my watch and it was exactly seven-thirty.

"You're just feeling smug because you beat me here. How much earlier than me was she, Sally?"

"About three minutes. Long enough for me to pour her a cup of coffee and that was all. By the way, I heard you had quite an adventure last night."

"Oops, my driving precedes me." I laughed. "Bob Mitchell must have been in for his early morning coffee."

"Yep. He said that you were soundly stuck."

"I was," I said. "It was great to have his help and that of Mark Begay. They pulled my truck out and made sure I got home safe and sound. And I managed to not run over the barking white ball of fluff that caused the whole thing."

"Well, I'm glad both you and Ellen's puppy came out of it fine," Sally said as she poured my coffee. "Our omelet special today is Spanish," Sally added. "The sauce is quite spicy and has a great flavor if I do say so myself." She moved on to take another order, leaving Ellen and I to make our decision.

"You two decided?" Sally asked, returning with the ever-present coffee pot in her hand.

"I'm going to have the special with sausage and hash browns," Ellen said.

"I think I'll have the special but would you substitute some kind of fruit for the hash browns and meat? I don't know where Ellen puts all that food."

"I can do that. How about some orange and grapefruit pieces?"

"That sounds good. Thanks for doing the substitutions."

I took a sip of my hot coffee and turned to Ellen as Sally walked off to place our orders and refill coffee cups along her way.

"Well, how is our escape artist today?" I asked.

"Great. She didn't like the fact that she was confined in the kennel but she'll survive. It won't take me too long to repair and fill her hole. I'll probably add a hot wire too. That should help her learn that fences are there for a reason."

"Well, she did help out our mystery a little bit," I said. "I've brought the files for Jonathon this morning."

"Did you look at them? Any chance they will help?"

"I spread them out to dry last night. They are newspaper clippings, but with a quick glance this morning, I couldn't tell if they were pertinent."

"If Jonathon will let us, we can check them out at the same time that we look at the files that Angie is bringing," Ellen said. "By the way, I got a call from Angie late last night. She didn't call you because she figured you would be in bed already. Anyway, she'll be meeting us at ten o'clock at your shop. She just said that the files were interesting."

"Interesting. I wonder what she means by that."

"I don't know. I'm also wondering how Leslie is doing. Think we should stop by the feed store before we leave town?"

"Sounds good to me. We can at least offer a hug if nothing else. Well, here comes our breakfast. How are you going to get around all of that?"

"Easy-peasy, lady. Obviously you have never been a dancer. We have prodigious appetites."

"Nope, I never have and neither are you anymore. I never have understood how you manage to stay so slim."

"Probably metabolism as much as anything, although I do try to do a dance workout every day at the house. It is good exercise and keeps me supple even if I'm not performing any more. And this last week I've been practicing for the memorial service."

"What music are you using?"

"A Native American flute piece by R. Carlos Nakai. I know that Tom liked his music and this one is quite haunting. It is called 'Death Song—Lament.' Seemed quite appropriate to me. I've choreographed a dance that includes birds riding the thermals and other moves that I thought might be evocative of the southwest."

"Sounds perfect. Tom was never far from his roots. I wonder what did cause him to move up here. Maybe we will learn a bit from the people who are coming to the memorial service."

We finished our omelets in silence. As always, Sally's recommendations were excellent.

"Well, we had better get over to the station," I said as I swallowed the last of my coffee. "Sally, want to bring us our check?"

"On my way, Martha. Sure I can't interest you in a malasada for the road."

"Actually, I think you can. Why don't you give me a dozen? Might appease a friend of ours if we took them with us."

"OK, just take me a minute to box them up."

Ellen and I were soon out the door, into the rain, and up the street to the police station. There were still some mounds of dirty snow taking up parking places where the snow plow had piled them up along the road and lots of slush in areas of low traffic, but basically the snow was gone. I stopped and got the files from my truck where I had left them.

"We come bearing gifts from afar," I said, as I walked into the police station. Jonathon grinned.

"You do know how to make peace, lady. Come into my office and I'll show you the pictures. Better bring those with you or there will be none left for the chief by the time we come out."

"Ah, Chief, how could you malign us so?" Tammie said.

"Because I know you," Jonathon said and laughed. "I'll share when I come back out and can make sure I get at least one." With that he led us into his office.

"Well, here are the pictures. By the way, we have not let it out to the world that we have this, so I'm trusting you two to keep your mouths shut."

"Will do, Jonathon, and I'm sure Sean knew that we would be totally discreet or he wouldn't have mentioned it to us."

"I know that, Martha, or I would have had your brother's hide and his badge for talking out of school. I still gave him a lecture last night on the phone. He had to admit that maybe he had been a little too free with information. However when it comes to you, I have a feeling he'll make the same mistake again. Sort of like cops who talk to their wives about their cases. So I have to trust that you know to keep your mouth shut."

"I do, Jonathon. You can't have spent as much time as a military wife as I did and not know when things are not for public disclosure. Let's look at that fabric print closer. Do you have a magnifying glass, Jonathon?"

"Here's one."

"It is Kokopelli; Sean was correct about that. There is a sun and it looks like a piece of what was probably a cactus. Very southwest, that is for sure. And what would you call the color, Ellen, teal? I sure wouldn't call it blue, which is what Sean said."

"I'd call it aqua," Ellen said. "It is a little lighter than what I think of when I think of teal. And the print is definitely yellow. A pretty feminine piece of fabric if you ask me, Jonathon."

"Have you reconsidered the burglar's statement that Tom was already dead in light of this feminine fabric?" I asked.

"I have," Jon answered, "and Brenda may have lied."

"Brenda?" I asked. "The burglar's name is Brenda?"

"Yes, Brenda O'Brien," Jon answered.

"Hmmm. I wonder. This seems like way too big a stretch, Jon, but I knew a Brenda O'Brien in Charleston, South Carolina. She was an airman in John's unit. I didn't know her well and probably wouldn't even recognize her today. But I do remember that John complained a number of times about her. Her favorite role was that of victim. No matter what went wrong, it was never her fault. Someone else was always to blame. If this is the same person, I would look at that self-rescuing statement again."

"Well she was in the Air Force. I don't know where she was stationed, but I can find out," Jonathon answered. "I'll take that information under advisement. I have to admit that a couple of things have happened in the last few days that seem to weaken my case against Jack. However, right now he is still my best candidate, and I think I'll keep him where he is for a bit more. His attorney has requested a bail hearing. That is set for next Monday so he may be out of here then.

" Actually, I like the guy," Jonathon continued. "I would just as soon have myself proved wrong. However, then we might find that the true killer is also someone we wouldn't suspect and that we like. I've found over the years that the person who murders is often a very complex human being and many times can be very likable under most circumstances."

"Now I have something else to show you," I said as I pulled out the files.

"Where did you get these?" Jonathon asked as he looked through the files.

I went through the events of the evening before finishing with a question. "Would it be possible for us to get copies of the information? Angie is coming over this morning to go over some letters she has found. I thought it might be good if we could look at these too."

"I don't like it, Martha. You could have been killed last night. That person could have well been coming after you because they saw you pick up those files. I don't want you women putting yourselves in danger."

"I don't know how reading those files can change that, Jonathon," I answered. "The driver already knows that I have the files. They will assume that I've read them. So if I'm in danger because of them, that scenario is already in place. Therefore, we might as well have the knowledge that they think I have."

"I'm not sure your reasoning is sound, Martha. On the other hand, you could be right. OK, I'll have Tammie make copies for you," Jonathon said. "Angie did let me know about the file that she found. I doubt it will help anything, but you women are bound and determined to check them out, so go ahead."

"When do you expect to hear back on the gun and the lab work on the cloth?" I asked.

"I should hear on the gun today. I'll let you know what I find out since you were the one who found it, but I want you to slow down on this detective business."

"Tom was my friend," I said. "He helped keep me sane during a very bad time and I take his murder very personally. If I can help you find his murderer, I will. I won't do anything stupid, but I'm not going to turn my brain off either."

"OK, a functioning brain is acceptable, but no more. If you think of something or either of you remember seeing this fabric on someone, let me know. But don't go trying any heroics on your own. Whoever killed Tom has done it at least once and might be quite willing to kill again, especially if they think they are cornered."

"Thanks, Jonathon. We promise we won't do anything stupid. Right, Ellen?"

"No heroics, Jonathon," Ellen responded. "I like living too well to put my neck out there for someone to chop off. But I'll let you know if the fabric rings any bells in my subconscious over the next few days."

"Well, I had better get these malasadas out to the troops before I have mutiny out there. I'm sure that Tammie has spread the word that they entered the building."

""We want to stop and see Leslie for a minute. Maybe Tammie can make those copies while we are there," I said as we all left Jonathon's office for the main reception area of the station.

"About time you came out with those," Walter said. "Tammie must have called me twenty minutes ago to say they were being held captive. I was trying to decide if I needed to go on a rescue mission. I did make sure we had some fresh coffee, though."

"See, I told you, Martha. They would grant me no mercy if I didn't get out with these. OK, here they are but make sure you save me at least one."

"Enjoy, everyone," I added as Ellen and I headed out the door, "and don't be too hard on Jonathon. It was our fault."

"Oh, we'll just hang him instead of drawing and quartering him first," Tammie said, as we headed out the door and she reached for a malasada.

I looked at my watch. It was just a little before nine so we did have time to drop in on Leslie for a couple of minutes.

"Let's walk down rather than move the cars," Ellen said. "I do need to walk off some of that breakfast."

"I told you that you would regret it."

"Not regretting it, but still, exercise is good for the body and soul. Right?"

"Yep, and we won't melt," I said as I pulled up my hood for some protection from the light rain that was still falling. I rarely used umbrellas here—partially because it was usually cool enough to have on some kind of jacket if it was raining and partially because it seldom rained great torrential buckets like it did in the tropics.

"Hi. What brings you two out this morning?" Leslie greeted us as we walked into the feed store.

"Had some business with Jonathon so we decided to come by and check on you before we headed back to my place," I said.

"I'm doing pretty well, although I'll do better if we can get Jack out on bail. Did Jonathon tell you that he has a bail hearing set for Monday?"

"Yes, he did," I said.

"Leslie, has he ever said where he was that night?" Ellen asked.

"No, and that does bother me. I'm sticking by him and it seems like he should trust me enough to let me know where he was. I even talked to his mother. Her answer was that Jack would have to tell me, but I think she does know where he was. Her tone of voice seemed to say that she thought Jack should tell me but she wasn't going to break his confidence. I can respect her for that, but it is frustrating when it might clear him altogether. If he were with another woman, I might not like it, but it would clear him. I just don't understand why he is being so close-mouthed on the subject."

"It has seemed odd from the beginning," I said, "and of course raises questions about Jack. Maybe if we can find out that someone else killed Tom, we can convince him to trust us with his secret. My guess is that it is something that you can live with, Leslie."

At the same time, I was wondering. We all liked what we knew of Jack, but could he be keeping his mouth shut because he had murdered Tom?

"I hope so, Martha. I really hope so." Just as she finished her sentence, a customer drove into the lot. "Well, looks like I have to return to work but let me give both of you a hug. Thanks for coming by and thanks for your support. I'll keep you informed if I hear anything new."

"We'll do the same," I said and Ellen and I hugged her goodbye and turned back up the street to where our cars were parked.

"I'll meet you back at my place," I said to Ellen as we reached her truck.

"OK. I need to get gas. Want me to pick up anything for lunch?"

"Why don't you get one of the deli-roasted chickens? We can add to it with stuff I have. That should feed all three of us just fine since I imagine Angie will stay too."

"Will do. See you in a few," Ellen said as she climbed into her truck.

I turned and entered the police station to pick up the copies that Jonathon had promised us.

Chapter 17

It was just a few minutes before ten when I drove into my driveway. Angie hadn't arrived yet, which was fine. It gave me time to check my phone messages in the house and get the shop opened up. There were no blinking lights on the phone so I had managed to escape phone calls unless they all ended up on the shop machine. I gave the house a quick glance over to make sure that it was decent for guests and then went back outside and across the drive to the shop. That phone was blinking with a message from Angie saying I could expect her by ten-thirty.

As I turned from the machine, I heard a muffled bark. I hadn't opened the dog door yet and I was getting protests.

"All right," I said as I let the dogs in. 'Don't you know that patience is a virtue?"

I was answered with a large white head pushing over the fence to get pets. I gave each of the dogs a scratch and a cookie, which they promptly took back outside to eat.

"Shows how much you really want my company," I commented after their disappearing tails.

I started a fire against the morning dampness and got tea water going. Just as I finished the dogs raced back into the shop, barking joyously. That could only mean that Ellen had arrived.

"I put the chicken in your oven on warm so it would stay hot," she said as she entered. However, after that breakfast, I may never eat again."

"Want to take any bets?"

"Nope. I'll probably have a marvelous appetite by lunch time. Where is Angie?"

"I had a phone message. She said that she would be a few minutes late."

I was interrupted by a low woof of an ignored Pyr.

"Hi, guys," Ellen said. "You think that I need to come see you, but what makes you think that I want to pet such dirty dogs. Did your mom lock you out of the nice, dry, clean barn?"

"Are you kidding? They choose to look this way. Dry covered shelter would be too sensible for these two."

"OK, you've been petted; now go lie down. I need to talk to your mom about my spinning."

"You brought it? Good. It will make our waiting time more productive. What is your problem?"

"It is getting fairly even as you can see, but how do I make it the size that I want it?" Ellen said as she pulled out her spindle with a good cop of yarn on it.

"A lot of that is practice. The easiest way is to use your pre-drafting to your advantage. Do you want it thinner or thicker than what you have here?"

"I'd like it a little thinner so that the final yarn would be good for socks."

"Then you need to make your predrafted fiber thinner. To do this, I usually pull it out once and then go back the opposite direction and make it thinner. What you want is roving that is just slightly heavier than you want your final single to be. You will do the final drafting as you spin."

"I think I understand it," Ellen said. "Let me try a small amount while we wait."

I watched as she began to pull the fiber apart.

"Be a little gentler with it, and you need to have your hands just a little further apart. You are running into places where you have both hands on the same fiber. It won't draft that way."

Ellen continued to work the fiber while laughing at herself.

"That's it. You have the idea now."

Just then the dogs barked and I heard a car door slam. It was Angie. Ellen and I had been concentrating on her spinning and hadn't heard her drive in.

"Come in out of the rain, lady," I greeted Angie.

"Sorry I'm late but David called and he had some paperwork that I needed to go over before I came out."

"Not a problem. We were just working on Ellen's spinning. She is doing very well. When are we going to get you addicted, Angie?"

"Not me. Quilting takes up enough of my time. I don't need another major fiber habit."

Ellen interrupted us. "Angie, can I get you some tea or coffee and Martha, do you want a warm up?"

"Coffee please, Ellen, with some cream if Martha has it."

"She usually does. Martha?"

"It's in the small refrigerator, Ellen. And yes, I'll take a warm up. Angie, why don't we sit at the table? That way we can spread the papers out."

While saying that, I pulled up some chairs to the table in the classroom area and Ellen came over carrying our cups.

"Well, here is what we have," Angie said. "They are copies of letters from Tom to James Hernandez. I think he kept copies because most of it has to do with the management of the ranch. I stopped by the office and made additional copies so each of us would have a set. I don't know if any of it will help us but it's worth going over, I think."

"And I have something to add to this," I said. I proceeded to catch Angie up on the discovery of the files the night before.

"We just have one copy of the clippings," I said. "Why don't I read through those and you can read the letters?"

I arranged the clippings in date order, mixing the two papers together. They covered a period of about four years from 1990 to 1994. As I began to read, I noticed date gaps between articles, even those with the same subject matter. Sometimes it was weeks, sometimes just a day or so. It appeared that particular articles had been removed. But why?

The earliest articles were about Tom opening his practice after leaving a partnership. Then there was an article about a bill that his father-in-law had put forward in the state senate that would make it easier for young women to get family planning information without parental consent. Tom seemed to have been following this bill rather closely because there were a number of articles pertaining to it. Then there was a big gap and then some articles on the Family Planning and Women's Health Clinic that Tom set up and funded.

Angie and Ellen worked their way through the letters.

"I don't find anything startling here so far,' Angie said. "In one letter," she continued, "he mentioned opening his own practice after leaving a partnership. He later commented on

James's distress over a bill that would enable young women to get family planning information. Tom seemed to be in favor of it but said that he could understand the position James was taking given his Roman Catholic beliefs."

"I'm finding the same events from a public perspective in the newspaper clippings," I said. "They were obviously the things that Tom was interested in at that time but I'm not sure they help us. It does look like some articles are missing. If not, Tom was pretty erratic in what he clipped and kept." At that moment, I had to interrupt my reading to help out some customers that walked in the door.

"Wait a minute," Ellen said when I came back to the table after finishing with my customers. "This might be something: 'I can tell you, James, that I am very much relieved to have the trial behind me. It was probably the hardest thing that I've had to go through. I'm thinking that I may just change the whole focus of my career. This experience has made me rethink a lot of things.'"

"That is interesting," I said. "I wonder what trial he is talking about."

"Maybe reading further will give us a clue," Angie said.

"Possibly," I said and we continued with our reading.

"Well, he comments on the divorce in passing but doesn't go into it much," Angie said as they finished the letters. "He does assure James that the arrangements for the ranch will stay the same. Tom will maintain sole ownership."

"Hmmm," Ellen said. "Wasn't Lenore yelling something about the ranch when she left David's office? Has it been a bone of contention all these years? Could it have been motive enough for murder?"

"People have killed for less, and that aqua print would look wonderful with her red hair. Could she be the one who wore that blouse? Also, the trial is totally missing from the clippings," I continued. "That might be an important clue. Why isn't it there? We see the other parts of Tom's life that are mentioned in the letters paralleled in the clippings. So why not something as public as a trial?"

We all sat thinking in silence for a moment, and then I had an idea. "I wonder if we could fill in the blanks with online archives from newspapers."

I walked over to the computer to turn it on and get on line.

"I hadn't thought of that," Angie said. "We might find something there."

"I have it ready to go. Ellen, this is your forte. Why don't you take over?" I said as I moved away from the computer.

"OK, let's see what we get. Well, the Albuquerque *Journal* is online. I'll bring up their home page. They do have archives. We may be in luck. Nope. They don't go back as far as the dates we would need. But they aren't that far off. Let's try typing in Tom's name just for kicks and see if we get anything."

"Whoa. Listen to this," Ellen said and began to read.

Thomas Jamison Walker, M.D., cleared of wrongful death. The New Mexico Supreme Court refused to hear the case brought against Dr. Walker by the family of a patient claiming that he had killed their daughter through faulty medical practices, thus letting stand the lower court's decision of his innocence.

"What else does it say?" Angie asked.

"Nothing that we are interested in," Ellen said. "It is a recap of the Supreme Court decisions and not actually an article about Tom or the case."

"That's interesting," I said. "But I wonder if it really has anything to do with Tom's murder or with his decision to move here or the divorce. Why don't you check and see if the Santa Fe papers have anything, Ellen?"

"I'm a step ahead of you, but no luck. Their archives are a little older but still don't cover our time period."

"So we know that Tom was sued for wrongful death, but not much more," I summed up. "That was a long time ago. Could it have anything to do with his death? Or is that too far-fetched?"

"If it did, though, it puts another hole in Jonathon's case against Jack. I very much doubt that Jack was anywhere near Albuquerque during our time period," Ellen said.

"Remember, Jack was in the Air Force," I responded. "He could have been stationed in Albuquerque; and saying that, if Brenda is who I think she is, she could have been there too. I wonder if Jonathon has asked her that question yet. I need to let Jonathon know what little we found out and then I'd say that it is time for us to go next door for lunch."

"Jonathon, this is Martha," I said, when Jonathon came on the line. "I wanted to let you know what we have found out." I went on to recap for him the information that we had gleaned from the computer, the clippings, and the letters and then listened as he gave me some information.

"It was what? That's very interesting. Yes, we'll be careful. Don't worry. I'll let Ellen and Angie know both items since they're here. I assume that this isn't really for the local grapevine. Right. We will keep our mouths shut. I hope you'll keep us posted on anything you might find out that we can help with. Talk to you later."

I hung up to two faces with very questioning looks. "Let's go next door and I'll fill you in. Ellen may not be hungry but I am."

Chapter 18

"OK, Miss Secretive, spill," Ellen said as we walked into my kitchen. "Just what did Jonathon tell you?"

"Let's get lunch on the table and then I'll let you know. It will take a bit for us to digest it once you hear it."

It took us just a few minutes to get things ready and gather at the table.

"Now give," Ellen said.

"Jonathon said that they had gotten the ballistics report back on the gun," I started.

"And?" interrupted Ellen.

"And it is the murder weapon. Jonathon could find no information using the serial number, but a social security number was etched into the handle. Jonathon decided to check out that number. Now this is the weird part. It belonged to a woman named Janet Cortez and she died in Albuquerque in 1992."

"You are kidding!" Ellen said.

"Nope, I'm not. That is all the information that Jonathon has right now. They are trying to find out more about her but that's it for now. The gun belonged to a woman who is dead. And she died in Albuquerque during the time frame we think might be critical."

"Very strange. How did the gun get up here? Is there any connection to Tom at all, or is it just a gun that someone bought from a dead woman's estate? And if they did, why shoot Tom with it?" Angie was talking half to herself.

"Good questions, Angie," Ellen said. "Is there any chance that the gun might have actually belonged to Tom? Could a burglar have found it in the office and then used it to shoot Tom?"

"I don't think so," Angie answered. "Tom was a fanatic about gun safety. If someone had found it in the office, it wouldn't have been loaded. I can't imagine Tom keeping a gun in the office at all, but he is the only person that we know of who has moved here from Albuquerque."

"However, Lenore was in town, and she lives in Albuquerque," I said. "Should we look at her more closely?"

"I don't know," Angie replied. "She was really angry over the ranch, and she didn't know about the will change before Tom was killed."

"She hasn't been here for years. Then she shows up and Tom is shot. Something seems fishy to me," Ellen said. "Didn't you say Jonathon had given you two pieces of information?" she continued. "So far you've only told us one."

"He told me that Brenda was released on bail late this morning."

"She was what? He didn't give us a clue that was happening this morning. How come?" Ellen was incredulous.

"He was blindsided. The prosecutor had forgotten to tell him. Anyway, she is free for now."

"I don't like that, Martha," Angie said. "The gun was dropped near your house, so the murderer was close. Now one of the major suspects is loose. We don't know why they chose that location. Was it because of you or just a coincidence?"

"It was probably dropped there because the woods are easy to get to from the road. It might even say that the person didn't know the area very well, someone who had no idea how often people hike that trail. Someone who thought it would be hidden for a long time. And that could be any of the people we've suspected: Jack, Lenore and Brenda are all newcomers to the area. I wonder if Jonathon will find anything else about Janet Cortez," I added. "A lot of information goes away real fast if someone isn't of particular interest to the public at large."

"Hope he clues us in if he finds anything interesting," Ellen said.

"He said he would."

"Well, for now, I want to change the subject," Angie said. "I need to run the final memorial service plans by the two of you and catch you up on who is coming from Albuquerque."

"Sounds good but do we want to talk about dessert first?" I asked.

"None for me right now," Ellen said. "I'm stuffed but I would take some tea. Want me to put the water on?"

"Tea sounds good to me too, and I'll also pass on dessert," Angie said.

"OK, three for tea then," I responded. "But let's move back over to the shop so I'll be there for customers this afternoon. We have tea water ready over there and maybe, given the information that we just got on the gun, we should look at those letters again as well as go over the memorial service information."

"Sounds good to me," Ellen said as she started clearing the table. "I wonder if there's any chance that Tom had an affair."

"Tom?" Angie said. "He didn't take time to eat many days, let alone have an affair. My guess is the divorce had more to do with lack of attention than with too much attention to another woman."

"And if he had, would it catch up to him now after all these years?" I added.

"Probably you're right," Ellen said. "Just trying to look at all angles. The woman scorned and all that."

Angie and I just laughed at Ellen as we started clearing the table. In no time, we had the dishes in the dishwasher and leftovers in the refrigerator.

The rain had stopped and the sun was actually peeking through as we walked across the driveway to the shop. We might actually have a nice afternoon.

We were soon seated with our tea.

"Now tell us about the memorial service, Angie," I said.

"It will be Saturday afternoon starting at two o'clock. I've made arrangements with the garden club to meet me at the high school around noon to help decorate and to set things up. Sally is providing the food. She is shutting the café down for the service. Says that all her regulars will be there anyway and she wants to go. She has recruited a bunch of the local teens to help with the serving of the food. Music will be provided by the pipe and drum group from Leslie's church and the handbell choir from mine. David and Elizabeth will sing, and the student orchestra asked me if they could play as people are gathering and at the end of the service. You will be presiding, Martha.

I have two poems for you to read. One is Robert Frost's 'A Road Not Taken' and the other is one by Dawna Markova called 'I Will Not Die An Unlived Life.'"

"I know both of those and like them a lot," I interrupted.

"Good," Angie continued. "I'll let you decide where you want to place them in the service. Jonathon and Bob have called and let me know that they want to say something about Tom. Also, his nurse from Albuquerque has asked to speak. You can let them talk and then ask for any others who want to say something. I'm sure we will have some although I have no idea how many. I thought the handbell choir could play just before we have people talk. Elizabeth and David will sing after people talk, followed by you, Ellen. Then we will close with the pipe and drum group and their final piece will be 'Amazing Grace' on the bagpipes."

"That sounds great, Angie," Ellen said. "Will you have a CD player there or do I need to bring my own for my music?"

"I'm sure they have one but it means I have to have them get it set up. Since yours is portable, why don't you just bring it?"

"I can do that," Ellen responded. "How do you like it, Martha?"

"I think it will be beautiful and a great tribute to Tom. I think I'll start after just a few opening words with 'The Road Not Taken.' Then I'll read 'I Will Not Die An Unlived Life' just before you go on, Ellen. That will give you a definite cue. And I think I'll tell people there will be refreshments after the service just before I do that. That way, we can have a seamless transition from the poem to Ellen to the pipe and drum band without any speech interruption. Then the orchestra can begin and the people in the front row can proceed out. That will be the cue for the rest of the group to break up and join us for the refreshments."

"I like that, Martha," Angie said. "I think it will go well."

"It will be because of your planning, I'm sure. Who is coming from New Mexico?" I asked.

"Marilyn Davis, Tom's nurse, will be here, and James Hernandez and his son, Tom, who live on the ranch. Lenore is staying for it, and two of the doctors that worked closely with Tom are coming. A cousin that I knew nothing about called and she also will be here. So we'll have a nice contingent."

"Good, maybe some of those can clue us in on what happened back then and why Tom really left New Mexico. I still think that it somehow ties in with his death," I said.

"I do too," Ellen said.

"Well, do we want to look at those letters again?" I asked.

"Not me right now," Angie said. "I still need to run a couple of errands this afternoon so I had better take off."

"I probably should too," Ellen said. "I left very early this morning and I still have some computer work to do today. After all, that is what puts food on the table at my house."

"OK, we can each take our copies and go over them individually and see if anything jumps out at us."

Both women gathered up their things and put on their coats. I followed them out onto the porch of the shop. The sun was still out and it had turned into a lovely winter afternoon.

"Angie, will I talk to you by phone before the service on Saturday?" I asked.

"I'll call you early Saturday with any last-minute stuff," Angie said as she got into her car. Ellen and I waved as she drove out of the gate.

"Well, I'll see you Friday," Ellen said.

"Which reminds me, are you going to bring in the fleece

that you mentioned before we started class or do I need to dig one out from my stash upstairs?"

"I'll bring one in. It's not a wonderful fleece but it is usable and it will give you a way to describe the problems to people. It has been skirted but not heavily so the class will need to do some cleaning."

"That's OK. That is all fodder for teaching. I do have a prize-winning Churo fleece. Maybe we should compare the two. I'm not willing to let it go for student practice, but we could still look it over and see what the differences are."

"I like that idea," Ellen said. "A comparison of the two would be interesting and then we can work on mine to get it clean for spinning. Sounds like a great class. Want me to come early and bring dinner?"

"Sure, if you want to."

"It will probably be pizza."

"Pizza is good. I'm sure I'll talk to you before then," I said.

I walked her to her truck and watched as she drove away with a send off from the dogs. I returned to the shop. My spinning wheel was beckoning. I had finished the Samoyed yarn and I had some bright purple merino I wanted to work with. I settled close to the fire and began the soothing work. As my hands and feet worked together, my mind wandered back over the events of the last few days. It hadn't even been a week since Tom was murdered and we seemed to have a lot more questions than answers when it came to finding the killer.

Was my business card a clue? How did it get under Tom's body? I knew that Lenore had one in both a coat pocket and her package. Could it have fallen out when she pulled a gun from her pocket? But then, all of my customers also had access to my business cards. Was it possible that one of my friends and fellow fiber enthusiasts was a killer? I didn't want to think that, but Tom was dead, and someone had pulled that trigger.

What about Brenda? The woman I was acquainted with had a consistent victim mentality but I would have never thought her capable of violence. However when cornered even the most timid animal will fight. Had Tom cornered her? The Kokopelli fabric seemed more consistent with a woman than a man. Could it be hers? Or was it Lenore's? I still couldn't conceive it being something that Jack would wear.

Then there was Jack. Was I letting Leslie's obvious love and trust in the guy blind me to the possibilities that it might be him? His fingerprints were in the office and he did admit to an old drug problem. But still, he had an explanation for the fingerprints. Why wouldn't he tell us where he was on Thursday? It would clear him right away. It all made my head ache and I seemed to be just going in circles.

Just then, Falcor let out a warning bark. This wasn't a greeting bark but one that said we had a trespasser. I raced out to the porch to see what was going on. He took off across the pasture, barking fiercely, with Denali in hot pursuit. I could hear the growl in her voice. I thought I saw a shadow along the back fence line but couldn't be sure. However, the dogs seemed to be sure and they were telling whatever or whoever it was that they weren't welcome. Just then, I heard the yip of a coyote. Maybe that was all that it was. The dogs had hit the edge of the pasture and were checking the fence line with much posturing and noise. Had I seen a person? Or was it just the coyote? Did I need to worry? I thought back to the car last night. Was it deliberate? I didn't have any more answers to these questions than I did to the ones around Tom's death. As I stood there wondering, the dogs seemed to have satisfied themselves that all was now well and were returning across the pasture. I turned and went back into the shop. I'd close it down now and prepare for the evening by getting my barn chores done.

As I fed and watered the animals, I got an idea. John had an old buddy, Elmore Harding, who had been with him in Korea and Charleston. Would he remember Brenda? We still stayed in touch at the holidays and I had his phone number. Maybe I'd give him a call. I still didn't completely buy the Tom-was dead-scenario.

Once in the house, I pulled out my address book and looked up Elmore's phone number. He was in California.

"Hello," a woman's voice said.

"Hi, this is Martha Williamson. Is Elmore there?"

"Hi, Martha. This is Georgia." She was Elmore's wife. "We haven't heard from you in ages. Any chance we are going to get a visit?" I smiled as I remembered the willingness of Air Force families to open their doors for others from the force.

"No. I just ran into a name up here and wondered if Elmore could remember any more than I could about the person. Is he there?"

"I'm sorry but he's in D.C. right now, Martha. Could I be of any help?"

"You might be. Do you remember anything about Brenda O'Brien? She was in the unit in Charleston."

"Oh, yes," Georgia replied, "we kept in contact for some time. I felt sorry for her at first, and then began to realize that she caused most of her problems herself. She went to Albuquerque after Charleston and then on to McChord. I heard rumors that she got into some kind of trouble up there that had to do with missing items from the unit's stores. Nothing was proved but a cloud of suspicion remained. I think she got out after that tour. I haven't heard anything since then. She may even be near you. Why do you ask?"

"Well, a Brenda O'Brien was arrested here for burglary. I was wondering if there was any chance that it was the same woman. Sounds like it might be possible. It might make a difference in some other possible charges against her," I answered.

"Other charges?"

"Our physician was murdered the same night the woman burgled his office. She says that he was dead when she arrived, but that is still in question," I answered.

"Well, I'm not sure I would have expected her to kill, but burglary—that doesn't surprise me. I'm afraid that I don't know anything else, though, that might help. How have you been?" Georgia asked. "I haven't really talked to you since John's death."

I caught her up on the latest happenings in my life and found out about theirs. Thirty minutes later found me hanging up with at least a little more information. It was quite probable that the Brenda I remembered was the Brenda Jonathon had arrested. And more to the point, she was in Albuquerque at a time frame that would have let her acquire the gun. I'd call Jonathon in the morning and let him know.

Chapter 19

"Well, you sure didn't do me any favor," the tall redhead snarled as she walked in the door of the shop. It seemed Tom's ex-wife was still feeling out of sorts with the world, and today, me in particular.

"I'm not sure I understand," I replied.

"Calling the sheriff and telling him that I had one of your business cards. I was back in his office again today going over where I was the night that Tom was murdered."

"I'm sure that Jonathon was just doing his job, and if you didn't drop the card, you should have nothing to worry about," I said.

"What I don't understand is why you would even think that I might harm Tom," she said.

"I can't understand why anyone would harm Tom," I replied. "Therefore, it seems possible that the person who did is someone we wouldn't dream could have done it."

"Well, it wasn't I and I just wish the people in this town would get off my back."

With that she turned on her heel and stormed out of my shop.

I walked to the door and watched from the porch as she got into her car and spun her wheels pulling out of the driveway. As she turned onto the road, I noticed for the first time that she was in her own car, not a rental, and it had a New Mexico license plate. I would have liked to ask her a million questions, but she obviously wasn't in the mood. I just hoped that Jonathon had gotten some more information on why Tom left New Mexico. I was sure that it held the clues to why he was dead now. And though she was protesting her innocence, could Lenore have done it? She didn't know about the will change until after Tom was dead so the inheritance could have been a motive. Did she still hold a huge grudge of some sort from the marriage and divorce? Why was she in town before the murder, and was she driving the car that almost ran me down on Tuesday? Obviously if Jonathon called her in today, he still had some questions. He might have Jack locked up but it looked like he was still pursuing other possibilities.

I thought about it for a few moments and decided that I still needed some answers. I didn't care what Sean and Jonathon said; I still thought the things that happened in Albuquerque were important. I got an idea.

"Angie," I said as she answered her phone, "do you have the number for James Hernandez?"

"I think so. Why?"

"I just decided that I don't want to wait for the memorial service. I want some answers to my questions now if I can get them."

"Here it is," Angie said and read it to me.

"Thanks, Angie. If I find out anything exciting, I'll let you know."

I dialed the number Angie gave me and almost held my breath. Would this get me what I wanted to know?

"Hello," a man's voice answered but it sounded younger than I imagined James Hernandez to be.

"Hello, this is Martha Williamson in Black Hills, Washington. Is James Hernandez there?"

"I'm sorry but Dad left for Albuquerque two days ago. He had some business to take care of before he flew out for Uncle Tom's service. As a matter of fact, you just caught me. I'm leaving this afternoon to join him."

"You must be Tom," I said.

"Yes, I am. Can I help you with anything?"

"I doubt it, Tom. I wanted to ask him some questions about Tom's previous life in Albuquerque. Did you know Tom's wife, Lenore?"

"I don't remember her when she was Uncle Tom's wife but I know her or I should say that I know who she is. We don't socialize. She's not about to spend time with a bunch of Mexicans."

Hmmm, that sounded a little bitter from someone who sounded like he was in his teens. "What do you mean, Tom?"

"Well, she wanted this ranch. But Dad told me that Uncle Tom was adamant that it would stay in his possession and we could continue to live here. I think they had some big fights over it at the time of the divorce. Her father owns the adjoining ranch. She had visions of a huge mountain estate or something. But her father had allowed some development at the edge of his property and Uncle Tom wouldn't consider that. He didn't want to even take the chance that it would happen on this piece of property. She decided that it was our fault that he wouldn't divide their property so that she got it."

"But didn't she realize that it was Tom's childhood home? Why would he want to let go of it in a divorce?"

"Exactly. He loved this ranch and its wide open beauty. He would come up here to unwind sometimes and we had wonderful times riding the horses together. He was great. But every time she's caught sight of me on a horse even near her property line, she's shouted at me to get out of there. One time she yelled that she didn't want any Mexican brats on her ranch. I wasn't on her ranch. I was on ours. I don't like her and I don't trust her. I think she's a bitch. I even wonder if she killed Uncle Tom. I mentioned that to Dad. He doesn't agree with me, but still I wonder."

I wondered too. I could tell that Tom was too young to answer any of my questions about the trial. It looked like I would have to wait for the memorial service.

"She doesn't seem to have been very agreeable, Tom. It sounds like you have good reason to feel the way you do. Well, I know that you need to drive south so I'll let you go. I'll look forward to meeting you on Saturday."

"I'll tell Dad that you called. I'm sorry I wasn't more help."

"Oh, I think you were," I said. "Goodbye for now."

"Goodbye," he answered and hung up. Well, young Tom seemed to confirm that Lenore could be one angry bitch but was that enough for her to murder Tom? I wasn't sure I'd gained any information that helped. I'd have to think about it.

I looked at my watch and figured that I had enough time before the Ewephoric group arrived to run over to the house to start a load of wash and fix me something for lunch. I'd also call Angie and let her know how little information I'd obtained.

I put a note on the shop door telling any customer who might stop to ring the bell.

The day was overcast, but the property was beginning to show small signs that spring was not too far away. The weeping willow near the front porch had its lovely gray catkins and the witch hazel was still in bloom. As I looked across the front yard, I noticed Sable was in a hunting position and her tail was twitching big time. I couldn't see what she was after but she was very much the fierce lioness on the prowl at the moment. Just as I stepped onto the ground she pounced and I saw one of the chickadees take flight. I was glad that she had missed it. I know it is her nature to hunt, but I hate it when she catches one of my wild birds. On hearing my steps, she turned and started toward the back door at a pace to get there just ahead of me.

"Hi, pretty girl. Are you ready to go inside for your afternoon snooze?"

"Yowwwl."

"I thought so."

I opened the door and she streaked toward the window seat in the living room. She would probably sleep the afternoon away hoping for sunshine through the window.

I had finished my chores and just started out the back door when I heard the first car come into the parking lot. I waved at Elizabeth as she got out of her car.

"Leslie called me," Elizabeth said. "She and Jeevana are going up to Seattle today. I think Jeevana decided that Leslie needed a break from the stress here."

"Thanks. We'll miss them but I agree. Leslie does need the break."

As I opened the door, additional cars filled the parking lot and I noticed that Michael was in one of them.

"Hi," Michael said as he bounded up the steps. "If you women can put up with me, I thought I'd join you and get some practice on my spinning. My schedule gives me Thursday afternoons off this quarter."

"Great to see you, Michael," Elizabeth said. "I thought I'd do my spinning instead of knitting too. Maybe Martha can give us some private pointers. That way, I won't look quite so much like a dunce tomorrow night."

Kerry, Linda and Mary had joined us while we were standing at the door talking.

We were soon seated in our favorite spots and working on our projects.

"Michael and Elizabeth, you are both doing very well on your spinning," I said. "You are moving quickly to a more uniform thread. Anything you want particular help with?"

"You'll like my request," Michael said. "I want to buy a real spindle and some fiber that I'd use in an actual project."

"I just want you to watch me and see how I'm doing at this point," Elizabeth added.

"OK, Michael, I'll handle your request first so we can get you spinning with your own spindle. Then, I'll watch you, Elizabeth."

Michael had soon picked out a spindle that he liked the feel of and some lovely Cormo batts.

"I think I'm going to enjoy spinning with these. Thanks for the help, Martha."

"My pleasure. Why don't you start using it and we will see if it really does what you want. If not, you can exchange it."

I settled down next to Elizabeth with my knitting so that I could watch her spinning.

"Hey, did you all hear that they let the burglar out on bail?" Mary asked.

"I'm not surprised," Michael responded without looking up from his spinning. "They don't usually keep people in jail waiting trial if they can come up with bail."

"But I thought she was a suspect in the murder," Kerry said.

"She is," I said, "but not the major one, and they let murder suspects out on bail too."

"True," Mary said. "It just feels kind of creepy knowing that she is free to roam the territory. If she is the murderer, then what's to keep her from doing another one?"

"I'd be more apt to expect her to do another burglary," I responded. "After all, if she did kill Tom, it was because he surprised her during a burglary. Her pattern was burglary, not murder."

"Hmmm," Mary said, "I'm still not happy having her loose."

I had been watching Elizabeth as she spun during this conversation. "You are doing very well, Elizabeth. Did you have specific questions or did you just need to know that you were on the right path?"

"My biggest problem is connecting two pieces of wool together," Elizabeth answered.

"You're about to the end of that piece so let me watch when you get there."

Elizabeth was having problems with her connection not holding long enough to get adequate twist in the thread.

"Elizabeth, I think it will help you if you turn your spindle by hand slowly while you are doing your connection. That way, you have more control, and you don't have the weight of the spindle until you have the splice made. Why don't you try that and see how it works?"

"Where are Leslie and Jeevana?" Kerry asked.

"They went to Seattle," Elizabeth answered, looking up

from her spindle. "Jeevana wanted to get Leslie out of town for the day. She is really stressing over this thing with Jack. They can't get the bail hearing until Monday and he still isn't saying where he was on Thursday evening. Just that he had some personal business to take care of."

"You know, I saw someone that was a dead ringer for Jack when I was in Portland a couple of weeks ago," Linda chimed in. "And he was walking with a very attractive young woman and a little boy who looked a lot like the man. I almost hailed him and then thought better of it. But I still wonder if it was Jack."

"Ouch," Mary said. "You think he could have a family in Portland? Has our Leslie fallen hard for a married man?"

"It would make sense of the fact that he won't talk about where he was and why he goes to Portland every free moment he has," Linda answered.

"I don't know, gang," I said. "He didn't strike me as the type of man who would lead Leslie along just for a lark." But at the same time, I wondered. Could he not be the nice upstanding young man I thought he was?

"I agree," Elizabeth chimed in. "I bet it was someone else."

"Well, it sure looked like him—even walked like Jack does," Linda said.

"Whether it was or not," I said. "Let's not say a word to Leslie or Jeevana about it. She doesn't need any more to stress over right now."

I received a bunch of nods in agreement.

"Tom's ex-wife, Lenore, was here this morning," I said.

"What did she want and what is she like?" Linda asked.

"She wanted to chew me out for giving Jonathon some information," I answered. "As to what she is like, I really don't know. She is a very attractive woman, tall with red hair and the ability to dress in a manner that makes you take notice even when she is in jeans, which she was this morning."

"She has a nasty temper," Elizabeth chimed in. "She really gave David the riot act when he refused to discuss the will with her on Saturday. He told her she could find out the contents when the will was filed with the court. Didn't make her a happy camper at all."

"She does seem to have an angry streak," I added. "She basically came by to give me a piece of her mind also."

"Did you get any answers on why Tom moved up here or what caused the divorce or any of that stuff?" Kerry asked.

"No, she didn't give me a chance. Chewed me out for letting Jonathon know that she had one of my business cards and stormed out."

"Wonder if she could have taken that anger out on Tom?" Michael said.

"I was wondering the same thing this morning," I said. "Maybe one of us can talk to her some more at the service. I'd still like to know more about what happened in Albuquerque."

Conversation then turned to other happenings around the town and comments on the projects that people were working on. We were interrupted when Nali came through her door and gave a good shake.

"Looks like it's raining again," Linda said.

"Well, at least it's not snow," Kerry added. "I hate driving in the snow, and I understand you do too, Martha."

"Yep, your husband was my rescuing angel on Tuesday night."

"What happened?" Mary asked.

"You must be the only one in town who hasn't heard," I said and laughed. "I was driving to Ellen's to help look for Shasta, who had disappeared, when the little fluff ball ran across the road in front of me. I hit the brakes without thinking and ended up with my truck stuck in the ditch. Mark Begay came along and let me use his cell phone to call Triple A, who called Bob. So Bob and Mark got my truck out of the ditch and Shasta ended up back home safe with Ellen. It was an adventuresome night that I have no desire to repeat."

Everyone laughed. Most of them could see themselves in the same circumstances because many of us here do not have snow driving skills.

"Speaking of driving," Elizabeth said, "I need to get my things packed up and start running my errands. David and I have to be at the church tonight to practice our piece for the memorial service."

"I'm so glad you agreed to sing," I said.

"We couldn't turn down Angie's request," Elizabeth said. "Tom was a good friend. My only worry is that I'll break up in the middle of it."

"I'm sure you'll do fine."

Elizabeth's move to leave started everyone else packing up their things.

"Martha, I'm ready to buy that yarn this week," Linda said. "I also think I need to get a set of double points to go with it."

"It's over there on the right side of the yarn collection. I'll pull the double points for you. Do you want four or five needles and what size?"

"Size one and five Brittany needles, please," Linda said.

Linda and I finished her purchase and walked to the porch in time for me to wave at the others as they left.

"I'll see you at the service on Saturday," I said.

"I'll be there. I think the whole town is going to turn out. I expect to see that room as full as it is on graduation."

"I wouldn't be surprised."

Linda made a dash through the rain to her car and I returned to the shop.

I had a number of tasks to work on before I closed the shop and settled in for the evening.

Chapter 20

T he Spider's Web," I answered the phone. I had been working in the shop for most of the morning.

"Hi, Martha, this is Jonathon."

"Hi, Jonathon, what's up?"

"I thought you'd like to know we have received the lab report on that piece of fabric and the stain on it is Tom's blood. So the person who owns that item of clothing has some significant explaining to do."

"It is probably the person who owned the piece of clothing, Jonathon. Anyone with a lick of sense will have destroyed the item by now."

"I'm sure you are right, but I can hope, can't I? By the way, we did get a search warrant to search Jack's aunt's house for it."

"But you really don't expect to find anything, do you?"

"I have no idea," Jonathon responded. "I have seen criminals do some pretty silly things. I would be shirking my duty if I didn't go looking for it."

"I can understand that. But I'd be less than honest if I told you that I hoped you found something. I really still think we will find out that someone else murdered Tom."

"And that someone else may be another friend," Jonathon responded. "Martha, I know you don't want to suspect your friends or customers but it will probably be one of them. You are too trusting and not nearly cynical enough. I worry that you may walk into a situation that gets you in trouble. People know you are interested in this murder. If Jack isn't the murderer, one of those people may decide you are getting too close. Be careful."

As I thought about what Jonathon had just said and wondered if I should tell him about the shadow on the edge of the pasture, he continued.

"We have also found that Jack was stationed in Albuquerque from 1993 to 1994 so he could have acquired that gun in some way. He says he's never seen it but it does give him possible access."

"I was there for a month around my high school tenth reunion in 1995 and that would also give me access to it if you think about it."

"I didn't know that you had Albuquerque ties. Hmmm, maybe I should move you to my list of subjects," Jonathon said and laughed.

"Better hope I didn't do it. You've given me all your clues for solving it," I answered. "Also, as I told you, Brenda was stationed in Albuquerque so she had access too."

"Well, she's quit answering questions since she got an attorney, so I don't know yet for sure that they are the same woman.

I've requested her military records but such requests take a little time. So that continues to leave Jack as my prime suspect. He was seen near the office the night of the murder. His fingerprints were found in the office and we did find the type of drugs that were missing from Tom's office. I've known more than one person who stayed clean for a long time and then started drugging again."

"I understand that, Jonathon, but he has given you a very rational explanation for why those things are true and there is nothing about him that gives the impression that he is back on drugs. Have you seen any evidence of him coming off them while he has been using your hospitality?"

"There is nothing except his word for his explanations, Martha. And he isn't willing to come straight on what he was really doing Thursday night. But, I do have to admit that I haven't seen any evidence of serious withdrawal."

"Well, I'm not convinced, Jonathon. I still think that, of your two major suspects, Brenda is your best candidate to have owned that piece of fabric. I guess I'm just going to have to find that murderer for you so that you can let Jack go free." I was half joking and half serious when I said this.

"Don't you do anything stupid. I meant what I said about you being too trusting. Better to leave the police work to those who are paid to do it."

"I won't, Jonathon. Believe me—I have no desire to put myself into danger. I'm just hoping I'll think of something that will help."

"Well, Tammie is signaling me that I have another call coming in so I need to take it. I'll see you tomorrow, Martha."

"Thanks for calling, Jonathon. I'll keep my thinking cap on. Bye."

I hung up the phone and turned back to the spinning I was doing when the phone rang. I was working on some silk I wanted to use for a shawl. It was a beautiful shade of green with highlights of yellow, blue and teal in it. I started my wheel and was soon lost in the soothing sounds of the wheel and the feel of the fiber running through my fingers. Spinning is one of the most relaxing things I do. My mind wandered to Janet Cortez. Who was this woman? Was she young, old, a mother, a professional or what? How did she die and most of all how did her gun end up in western Washington hundreds of miles from the city of her death? And was Jonathon correct? Was I in danger? Lots of questions and no answers. Many times the tranquility of spinning could help me sort things out, but today I was getting nowhere.

The crunch of tires on the drive and a joyful bark from Denali told me that someone she liked had just arrived. I looked out the window to see Sean's county vehicle. I got up to go outside as I saw him heading for the fence to give his girl an ear scratch.

"Hey what brings you this way?"

"I had to make another trip to Montesano for the boss and thought you might like to join me for lunch."

"I'd love to have lunch with you but why don't we eat here? My gallivanting because of all the stuff around Tom's death has taken a major toll in my usual shop time. If I didn't have the class tonight and the purchases from yesterday, I would have very little income this week."

"No problem. You know I love eating here. I just wanted to give you the option of eating on me."

"I'll take you up on that after the memorial service on Saturday. I figure the town will get back to some semblance of normal after that. Speaking of—are you coming for the service?"

"No. I didn't know Tom very well, and one of our deputies who's scheduled for duty did. He wants to come so I said I'd trade duty with him to free him up."

"That's nice of you since it means you lose your weekend. Well, let's go into the house and see what we can find for food. If nothing else, there is always toasted cheese."

"Actually, that sounds pretty good to me. Why don't we do that? I don't have a lot of time but did want to see you. I don't think I've talked to you since Jonathon chewed me out over the scrap of fabric."

"Nope, you haven't. Did he just chew you out or did he talk to your boss too?"

"Just chewed on me. Actually called me at home so he would be sure not to get me in trouble at the office. Nice guy, that Jonathon."

"He is. And you know you did deserve it, although I'm kind of glad you told me. I think that piece of material is the major clue. Now if Ellen and I can just remember seeing it somewhere."

"I think he is glad too but he can't say that. I was speaking out of school."

We had made our way into the kitchen while talking. We were soon seated at the table with our sandwiches, some apple slices, pretzels and coffee.

"Looks good, Sis. I always said this place was the best feed in town."

"Thanks. Now, what has been happening in your life?"

"Not a whole lot. Brenda is out on bail and we are waiting for a trial date. She hasn't admitted to doing any of them except the one where she was caught and Tom's office. We've had some domestic violence cases. Boy, do I hate those; they are always nasty. A couple of other incidents. Pretty much the usual for a week in a county this size. So how is the case coming on Tom's murder?" Sean continued. "I haven't really heard anything since the piece of fabric."

I told him about my escapade with Shasta, the information from the lab reports on the gun and the fabric, and the interesting information from Tom's letters to James Hernandez.

I finished with, "My week has centered on Tom's death. I keep asking mental questions about it. I just can't quite let it go. I've also done what I could to support Angie. She has done a great job of organizing the memorial service. It will be a wonderful way to say goodbye to a good friend."

"Maybe you need to let the police ask those questions," Sean said. "But the information on the ownership of the gun is interesting. I bet it is a major piece to the puzzle if we just knew how to fit it in."

"I think so too," I said. "I'm hoping that one of the folks from New Mexico may be able to fill in some gaps for us. I talked to Tom Hernandez yesterday but he's too young to remember that time period. His father wasn't home, but I hope to talk to him at the service."

"I'll be interested to know what you find out, but right now, I need to get back to work. I've already stretched my lunch hour some."

"I'm glad you stopped by. I always enjoy your company."

I walked out to the porch with Sean and sent him on his way with a hug. Sable came running from the barn as he walked to his car and Sean stooped down to give her some ear scratches before he climbed in to drive away.

"Yowwwl," said Sable. She entwined my legs as I continued to stand on the porch enjoying the sun that was peeking through the clouds.

"You want a treat, pretty girl?"

"Yowwl."

"OK." I returned to the kitchen and gave Sable a kitty treat which she promptly took to the middle of an Oriental rug to consume.

Back at the shop, I had tasks to do before Ellen arrived. I wanted to spin some more of the silk and I needed to get things set up for the spinning class tonight. Since I can get lost in my spinning, I decided to put a CD on. When the music ended, I would move to setting up for class. I was soon lost in the music and the tranquility of the spinning, and before I knew it the CD was finished and I had almost filled the bobbin on my wheel. It was going to be a lovely yarn and would make a wonderful weft for the shawl I wanted to make.

Now I needed to get things ready for class. I was going to talk about choosing raw fleece and about cleaning it and preparing it for spinning. I love working with raw fleece but some spinners never want to touch the stuff. It can be a dirty smelly process. I wondered how the members of tonight's class would fall out on the raw fleece spectrum. I got my supplies set out in the classroom and climbed upstairs to find the fleece I would compare to Ellen's. It was a beautiful dark brown fleece—purchased from a friend who is Navajo—that had taken prizes at the Taos Wool Festival. I carried the tub containing it downstairs and was just putting it under the table when I heard the crunch of tires. Ellen was here.

"Do you need any help?" I called as I walked out onto the shop porch. "You look like you have quite a load there."

"If you can come get my spinning stuff, I'll carry in this fleece."

I walked out and took Ellen's spinning bag and purse from her. Her fleece was in a plastic bag and from the smell of it, I was pretty sure that we would have quite a bit of skirting to do this evening. It should be a good contrast to my lovely fleece. We carried both into the shop.

"I have a pizza in the truck for us too," Ellen said. "Figured you probably had salad makings."

"I do. We should have time for a glass of wine before dinner and you can show me how you are doing on your spinning."

"A glass of wine sounds wonderful. This has been one of those days at the computer. I think I took out three lines of code for every two I put in. I'm ready for something totally different."

I turned around to walk out of the shop when a white streak came running in through the dog door.

"Woof," said Denali as her tail wagged as it only wags for Ellen.

"Snuck in on you, did I, big girl?" Ellen laughed. "And where were you when I drove in?"

Denali just grinned and sat for Ellen to give her a hug and an ear scratch. Falcor hadn't come in. He was probably further out in the pasture or just figured that he was too busy.

"Enough for now, Nali," Ellen said as she gave her a thump on the side. "I want to go over to the house and relax with your mom."

As we turned to go out of the shop, Nali turned and went out her door. She would see us on the outside.

Ellen gathered up her spinning and purse and I stopped by her truck and picked up the pizza.

Back in my kitchen, I put the pizza in the oven on warm and turned to find Ellen's head already in my fridge looking for wine.

"Looks like you have sparkling or chardonnay. Which do you want?" she asked.

"Sparkling, I think. That's been open for a bit and the bottle tops only hold in the bubbles so long."

"Sparkling it is then."

I reached up and got the glasses and took them into the sitting area while Ellen followed with the bottle. I curled up on the couch in the corner, which is my favorite spot and Ellen landed on a pillow on the floor, which is usually her favorite area. Sable immediately took advantage of Ellen's position and curled up next to her for some loves.

Ellen quickly caught me up on her day of programming and Shasta's antics.

"Change of subject," I said. "Jonathon called me today and the stain on the scrap of material was Tom's blood."

"That means we do need to remember if we have seen that fabric before," Ellen said. "I don't remember it at all, but then I can be so dense sometimes about what people are wearing."

"If it isn't a local person, we may have never seen it before," I added. "But I still believe that a woman wore that fabric; so to my mind, it moves Brenda and Lenore to the top of the list."

"Is Jonathon looking at them seriously?" Ellen asked.

"I don't know, but I do know that we need to move onto food if we are going to be ready on time. And I need to feed the critters. Do you want to raid my fridge for salad makings while I go out to the barn?"

"Sure, give me the hard work," Ellen teased.

I threw a pillow at her and got up to go outside. It didn't take me long to do my chores at the barn. By the time I got back, Ellen had fed Sable and had everything ready for us to eat. The pizza did smell good. I hadn't had one in a long time and the local pizza shop excelled in making their product.

Chapter 21

We'd finished dinner, cleaned up, and were walking back over to the shop when Jane drove in.

"Hi, Jane. It's good to see you tonight."

"Hi, Martha, would you be willing to meet with me Sunday afternoon to talk about your spinning unit for my class? It is difficult for me to get away during the week and I'd really like to have that planned out or at least have a general outline of what we are going to do."

"No problem, Jane. Why don't we meet here at the shop about two o'clock? Most of my equipment and books are over here so we can look at things and decide what we want to cover. I also like to have things planned ahead."

"Good, I'll plan on being here then. That is a good time for me as I have a lunch date after church."

The other students had been arriving while Jane and I were talking.

"Eeew, what is that smell?" Linda asked.

"I can tell you don't deal with livestock, Linda," Ellen said. "That is eau de sheep. Martha seems to think that we all want to learn the ins and outs of raw fleece."

"I may be willing to pass on that experience," Linda said.

"Many people do, Linda. However, since we do have some local producers of wonderful fleece, I decided to at least introduce you to the possibilities. Let's gather into the classroom area," I said to the group that was rapidly becoming noisy with all the individual conversations.

As people were moving in that direction, I saw Leslie come in and go over and say something softly to Ellen. She didn't look too chipper tonight and I wondered what was up. Had something happened with Jack? However, right now I had a class to teach and Leslie moved over to join the group.

"As Ellen said and the aroma indicates, we are going to work with raw fleece tonight. Before I start on the pains and joys of raw fleece, do any of you have questions on what we did last week?"

I got the look that said there were questions but let's get on with the subject at hand. I've found that students usually prefer to catch me to ask questions when we are actually working with the fiber.

"Ellen was good enough to bring us a fleece from one of her sheep. This one is pretty much as it would come off the sheep. We also have a prize-winning fleece to look at. Those of you who want to can gather around the table to get hands-on."

Michael and Judy decided to use thin gloves to protect their hands and I noticed that Linda, Jane and Theresa were hanging well back where they could see me and watch, but they had no intention of getting their hands into the fleece.

"Let's do some of the gross skirting right now. We want to remove all of this and just throw it away. It can be used for compost, by the way, but you are not going to do anything with it as far as your spinning is concerned."

As I was talking, I was removing some fairly large sections of fleece that had obvious feces in it or huge clumps of vegetable matter.

"Once caution on working with raw fleece," I added as I continued with the skirting. "You should have an up to date tetanus shot just to be totally safe."

"How can I know that I'll get a good fleece?" Allison asked.

"If possible, try to actually see the fleece before you buy it. I like to buy mine at the local wool festivals. All of the fleece has been judged before they are entered into the sale. So you not only see it, but you have the judge's opinion to guide you. Your other option is to buy from someone you know is reputable. You can find reputable sources by talking to your friends or joining some of the email lists spinners and weavers belong to."

"Before I have you start working with Ellen's fleece, I want to show you another fleece from the same breed." I opened my fleece and put it next to Ellen's on the table. "Notice the differences. This one has been heavily skirted, which we would expect from a fleece that was entered at a festival. Second, notice that there is very little vegetable matter in the fleece. You really have to look for it. And third, the tips are not weathered as badly. Tippy wool can be difficult to dye and the tips can break off during preparation."

"Now, notice one of the characteristics of the Navajo Churro, which is that it has a double coat. If you look closely at a lock, you can see that there are longer, coarser fibers that are the outer protective coat and then shorter, finer fibers that are the inner coat. Whether you separate the two fibers and spin them alone or card them together depends on what you want to do with the finished yarn. This is the traditional sheep of the Navajo people, and the one many of the Navajo use to make the yarn for their lovely rugs.

"Now before we move on, come up and actually handle the locks from the two fleece. For the most part both of these are strong healthy fleece. Take a lock and gently snap it like this by holding it in your two hands and giving it a quick snap. It should not break. If it does, you have a weak fleece."

Eager hands moved into the fleece and comments of all kinds started to fly.

"No way am I going to touch that stuff," Jane said.

"Aw, come on, Jane," Leslie countered. "It really isn't that bad. It feels a little tacky but not bad and you can even feel the softness with it not being washed."

"It doesn't even smell so bad when you get one of the cleaner locks," Allison said as she put one up to her nose.

"I'll still take your word for it," Jane said sticking by her opinion. "I'll take my fiber already prepared and ready to spin."

"There are many advantages to that, Jane," I responded. "Cleaning a fleece is a lot of work. There is no sense in doing it if you don't enjoy it. You can get prepared fiber in just about any type you want."

"OK, class, let me put my fleece away and then I'll use Ellen's to show you how to clean raw wool." I put my fleece back in its tub and proceeded to take the group through the steps of soaking, rinsing and drying raw wool. "This is just a brief introduction so you can start playing with the wool if you want to. Let's take a break now, and then after the break those of you who want to continue working with the raw fleece may and those of you who want to work on your current spinning may. I'll be here to answer questions and work with you on an individual basis for the second half of the class. There is coffee and tea water over in the sitting area. Also some cold bottled water in the little fridge."

The group began to break up, chattering as they moved to get their drinks. Ellen walked over to me.

"Leslie wants to talk to us after class. She seemed quite upset but said it could wait until everyone is gone."

"OK, guess we wait until then to find out what is happening. I noticed she wasn't her usual cheerful self."

"Is everyone going to the memorial service tomorrow?" Theresa asked.

Almost everyone answered in the affirmative.

"Angie has done a great job of planning it," I commented. "I hope that many of you have wonderful Doctor Tom stories to add to it."

"Bob has a good one about one time when they went fishing," Kerry said.

"I'll probably say something about how wonderful he was when my husband was sick," Linda added. "That is, if I can get through it without breaking up completely."

"I still don't get it," Jane said. "From what you all say, he was a saint. Why would anyone kill him?"

"Good question, Jane," Ellen responded. "If we knew that, we might know who the killer was."

"Well, I'm just sure it's not Jack," Leslie said with a vehemence that caused no one to respond quickly.

"I just hope that Jonathon figures out who it is soon," I replied and then noticed the look of pain that Leslie shot at me. Just what did she want to tell us this evening?

Conversation continued to ebb and flow for the next few minutes until I felt the need to get people back to their tasks.

"All right, let's get back to work. Those of you who want to divide up Ellen's fleece among yourselves, there are plastic bags on the shelf above the table. Ellen says she doesn't want any of it back so it is all yours. Your assignment will be to wash at least part of it so that we can use it to practice carding next week. Once you are done, you can join the rest of us over here with our spinning. Ellen, would you help with the organization over there?"

"Those of you who don't want anything to do with raw fleece, get out your spinning and let me see how you are doing. This is your chance to corner me with your questions."

The spindles came out and I was soon busy answering questions and helping people with the fine points of their spinning. The rest of the class time disappeared quickly.

"All right, gang, it is time for us to break up. We will meet again next week and talk about carding wool as well as continuing to work on the spinning. If you have any questions, please don't hesitate to call me or come by. Officially the shop is open Tuesday through Saturday, although this week our schedule has been a little weird, and I'll be closed tomorrow for the memorial service."

As I helped people with purchases they had made, the others began to pack up their things and say their goodbyes. I walked out the door with Theresa to say good night and watched as she drove off followed by the last car in the parking lot except for Leslie's and Ellen's.

I turned back into the shop and noticed that Leslie had started to cry.

"What happened?" I asked. "You obviously were having problems this evening."

"Jack's attorney called me just before I left to come over here. Jonathon found some burnt material in the burn barrel on the back of Jo's lot that he feels clinches his case against Jack. He is going to ask that the judge deny bail on Monday."

"He found what!" Ellen exclaimed.

"Jonathon found some material in the burn barrel behind Jo's house. Evidently it wasn't completely burned and he was able to tell what kind it was. Anyway, he says that it is evidence that Jack did kill Tom. I don't know what Jack is hiding but I know he didn't kill Tom; I just know it," Leslie wailed. Ellen put her arms around Leslie and held her while the younger woman broke down completely.

"I think someone is trying to frame Jack," I said. "Everyone in this town knows that Jonathon has him in jail. I think our killer took advantage of that. It wasn't found inside Jo's house. It was found in a burn barrel outside that anyone could have access to when Jo was teaching. My guess is that his attorney will say the same thing at the bail hearing."

"Do you think the judge will believe that?" Leslie asked as she got control of her crying. "I keep thinking that everyone would like to blame it on Jack and have the murder solved."

"I don't know, but I think it is a fairly good argument. I won't say don't worry because you are going to worry. However, I suggest that you try to get some sleep tonight and we will see what tomorrow brings. Some of the Albuquerque people are going to be here for the memorial service. Both Ellen and I think one of them may hold a key to our mystery with the knowledge they have. We haven't given up, Leslie. Neither of us thinks Jack did it. We just have to find the right piece to the puzzle and it will all fit together."

"I hope you are right. It all seems so hopeless some days."

"It does," Ellen responded. "But I'm sure it will get figured out. Something will break for us."

"It helps that you two believe in him along with me. Well, I need to get home. We will be opening the store in the morning as usual but we are going to close it at one o'clock so all of us can go to the service. We figure no one will be shopping anyway."

"We'll see you tomorrow," I said as I gave Leslie a hug. "Get some sleep tonight."

I walked her to the door and watched as she got into her truck. I turned back into the shop as Ellen was packing up her spinning.

"Wait a minute while I shut things down and lock up and I'll walk out with you. It has been a long day."

Ellen and I were soon walking out to her truck.

"Thank you again for bringing in the fleece," I said. "It was a great teaching tool."

"No problem. I wouldn't have used it and I learned a lot about how I want to take care of the fleece on my sheep by listening to you."

"See you tomorrow," I said as I gave her a hug.

"Will do," she said as she climbed into her truck.

Ellen beeped her horn and waved as she drove out of my gate. I followed and closed the gate then turned and headed back to let the dogs loose for the night.

Chapter 22

Dogs were barking as I tried to climb the cliff to see the danger, but I wasn't going fast enough. I was out of breath and starting to stumble when I surfaced from a deep sleep and realized that the alarm barks were real. As I leapt out of bed and raced to the window, I heard the sound of a car engine start. I pulled back the curtains just in time to see the taillights of a car rounding the curve just beyond my house. Both Denali and Falcor were still barking at the front gate. Good dogs! But who was it? I looked at the clock radio. It was one A.M. Why was someone at my front gate at this hour?

I was wide awake now and the pit of my stomach felt like someone had kicked it. I entered the kitchen just as the dogs flew in to let me know about the intruder.

"Good work, guys."

They both came over make sure that I was unhurt, and Falcor went back toward the door looking at me.

"They're gone, big guy. You chased them off. It's OK now. How about a cookie?"

I got a look that said I might not understand but both dogs decided to accept the cookie anyway. I fixed a cup of peppermint tea and curled up on the window seat to think. Just what was going on? Was this connected to Tom's murder? Or was some idiot just lost? I shivered in the night chill and pulled an afghan up over me. I knew one thing, I was very glad for my big, white protectors. I didn't lock that outside gate. It was just latched. Without their vigilance, the person might have gotten inside. But that brought me back to the point. Why did they want in? I finished my cup of tea and returned to bed. I thought I would have trouble falling to sleep but the next thing I knew Nali was waking me for morning chores.

After taking care of the animals, I walked out to the outer gate. I could see footprints. Whoever it was, they weren't very large. You wouldn't find that size foot on a six-foot man. I couldn't remember Brenda very well, but I bet she could have left them. I had no idea as to the size of Lenore's feet. I guessed that these prints might fit either one of them. That brought me back to the question: Was this related to Tom's death? Again, I had no answer. But someone was here; and at one A.M.., I didn't think their appearance was totally benign.

I wasn't going to open the shop because of the memorial service but I had some paperwork to do so I headed over there later in the morning. As I walked in the door, I noticed that the message light was blinking on the answering machine. I hit the play button.

"Those big white dogs won't always protect you. Back off."

I looked at the machine and played it again. Same words. It was date stamped at about three this morning, after the episode at the gate. I played it again. I couldn't recognize the voice. It was muffled as if someone might be talking through something like a scarf. I couldn't even tell for sure whether it was male or female.

My stomach clenched again. Someone thought I was getting too close. Too close to whom? What was I missing? What had dropped in my lap that I wasn't recognizing as a major clue? Had my recent phone calls caused the warning? But how would they know that I'd made the calls? Then again, this town is a gossip's dream and I hadn't kept the calls a secret. The files and the gun both had Albuquerque connections. Did the murder have the same connection? I thought so, but I sure wasn't connecting the dots. None of it made any sense to me. I knew one thing, though: It was time to tell Jonathon about my visitors and the phone call. I'd do it at the service this afternoon.

I drove into the high school parking lot about one-fifteen. From the cars in the parking lot, it looked like a number of people had arrived early to help with whatever tasks needed to be done. I found a place to park and walked toward the all purpose-room. There was a gentle breeze and the temperature was in the 50s. The crocus and pansies were in bloom in the beds close to the building. There wasn't a cloud in the sky, and in the distance, I could hear the cry of a red-tailed hawk. I almost wished we'd planned to hold the service outdoors but then it could have just as easily have been pouring rain and 35 degrees.

"Hi, Martha," Marian said as I entered the building. "Angie is looking for you."

"Any idea where I might find her?"

"I think she is in the kitchen with Sally."

"Thanks, I'll look there."

I started to walk across the all-purpose room as Angie walked out of the kitchen.

"There you are," Angie said. "I need your opinion. Who should sit in the front reserved row?"

"You, of course, and probably Ellen as it would make it easier for her to move into her dance. I think the other people should be the New Mexico contingent since they actually have the longest history with Tom."

"Sounds good to me. I'll make sure that our people at the guest book and the door know to steer them in that direction. Didn't the garden club do a wonderful job with the decorations?"

"They sure did. Especially since this isn't the greatest time of the year to gather flowers from our yards. And the memory altar is beautiful. Did you do that, Angie?"

"Elizabeth helped. We both went through Tom's house and picked out the things to put on it, and James Hernandez brought the knife that Tom had given him. It is one that belonged to both Tom and Tom's father. I think Marilyn Davis has something to add also when she gets here."

"I'm glad so many people that were important to Tom were able to add to it."

"Martha, can you help me with this?" Ellen called as she came in the building. Her hands were full as she was juggling to carry both her CD player and her costume all at once.

"I suppose it never dawned on you to make two trips," I said with a laugh as I relieved her of the CD player.

"Never, that would be too easy. Would you put that where one of the band members can turn it on? The song is track five."

"Sure thing," I said as she turned to go to the restroom to change.

"Hi, Bill," I said as I approached the band director. "Would one of your students be willing to turn the CD on for Ellen for her dance? She says it is track five on the CD."

"Of course, Martha. How will we know when Ellen is to come on?"

"She'll follow immediately after I read 'I Will Not Die An Unlived Life.' Did you get copies of the program?"

"No. Guess I should send a student after them."

"I'll go get them for you. They will need to start playing soon. I see people starting to congregate in the parking lot outside."

"Thanks, Martha."

I retrieved some programs for Bill and his band students and then went to the restroom to make sure I was presentable. Ellen was just finishing changing her clothes. She was also in conversation with a woman I didn't know. She was shorter than I and slightly plump. Her silk dress and the beautiful cut of her gray hair were elegant and her smile brightened her eyes and her face.

"Martha, this is Marilyn Davis," Ellen said. "She was Tom's nurse in Albuquerque."

"Hi, Marilyn," I said. "I'm glad to meet you and looking forward to your comments."

"Tom was a special man. I wanted to share his part in my life."

"Good. You are listed on the program between Jonathon and Bob. When the three of you are done, I'll ask if anyone else wants to share memories. Well, we will be starting soon. I hope to visit more with you after the service, Marilyn."

"I'll look for you, Martha. I'd like to talk to you also."

I sat in the chair Angie had provided for me on the stage

and looked out over the gathering crowd. It appeared the whole town and then some had turned out. It was obvious that Tom was much loved. I noticed that Jane was clear in the back. I was a little surprised to see her since she had made such a point earlier of not really knowing Tom. Oh well, maybe she just felt it was her civic duty as a local teacher. The New Mexico people were all in the front row on the left as well as Angie and Ellen. Jonathon was in the second row on the aisle but I noticed that his staff was spread throughout the room. I wondered if they were watching for anything in particular. I would have to talk to Jonathon after the service. I smiled at Angie and Ellen and got to my feet as the last strains of the music filled the room.

"Good afternoon, my friends. I think Tom might be surprised at the large turnout today. He was always surprised when someone pointed out to him that he just might be a little special in this world. I'm glad you have joined us to celebrate his life. This is going to be a time for us to share our joy in knowing Tom and I hope all of you who so desire will share your stories as we move through the afternoon. And now I'd like to read a favorite poem. It is 'The Road Not Taken' by Robert Frost. 'Two roads diverged in a yellow wood…'"

As I finished the poem, the handbell choir moved seamlessly into their first piece. It looked like all of Angie's careful preparation was paying off. The handbell choir was beautiful. They played three pieces ending with 'Over The Rainbow' which Angie had said was a favorite of Tom's.

I nodded to Jonathon and he got up to speak. "All of you have wonderful memories of Tom, I know. As a police officer, I have had to call him out to help with the most horrific of tasks and at the most inopportune times. Never did I have him grumble about the timing, and never did he refuse to come. No matter the problem, he was the soul of gentleness as he dealt with people who were injured and often afraid. He was always there when I needed him and I feel like I have lost a good friend and a partner."

As Jonathon sat down, Marilyn rose and moved to the front of the room. "I know few of you," she began. "But we have one connection and that connection was Tom Walker. I worked in his office for fifteen years. He was the finest employer, doctor and friend that one could possibly have. But I want to tell you of his ongoing work in New Mexico. I am the manger of a women's health clinic." Marilyn stopped for a second and seemed to be focused on something in the back of the room. Then she went on. "This clinic was founded by Tom so that no woman would need to have inferior gynecological medical care just because she was unable to pay for it or because she was afraid to go to her family doctor or normal health care provider. We provide whatever care that woman needs. We do not ask a lot of questions and we offer total privacy. I have seen the clinic make remarkable changes in the lives of many women and in their health. None of this would be possible if it had not been for Tom, and even in his death, this work will go on because he has provided amply for the clinic in his will. He was a remarkable man."

As Marilyn moved to her seat, I saw her look to the rear of the room one more time, then shake her head and turn to be seated.

Bob followed Marilyn with a wonderful, funny story about Tom on a fishing trip and then one after another people came up to share their stories and their memories. It became more and more obvious that he was going to leave a huge hole in this community. When people were finished, Elizabeth and David came forward. Their voices blended beautifully as they sang a favorite of Tom's, "The Impossible Dream."

As their voices died down, I moved forward once more. "I am going to read another favorite poem of Tom's, but before I do, I want to invite all of you to join your friends and neighbors after the service to share in the wonderful refreshments that Sally has provided and to continue to celebrate Tom's life. This final poem is by Dawna Markova. 'I will not die an unlived life...'"

When I had finished the poem, the strains of R. Carlos Nakai's flute music began and Ellen was on her feet and moving into her dance. Her choreography was wonderful and her movement reminded me of a bird as it floats on the thermals in the desert sky. She was beauty and grace itself. And in total contrast, as the music of the flute came to an end, the swirl of a bagpipe began. There is nothing that can get the blood going so much as pipes and drums, and these members of the community were good. They played two numbers and then ended with "Amazing Grace." There was silence for a moment after the bagpipes were done. Again with a total shift of mood, the school band broke the silence with Beethoven's "Ode to Joy." Taking her queue from the music, Angie rose to her feet and led the people in the front row out of the group and to the area where the refreshments were to be served. Once they had moved out, the rest of the people began to move and to break up into small groups of chattering neighbors.

"Wonderful service, Martha," Ted Larson, Leslie's father, said.

"It was, Ted," I said, "but it is Angie who deserves the credit. She organized it and put all the pieces together. I just did the part she assigned to me. How is Leslie doing? I didn't see her in the group."

"She's here. She headed for the restroom as soon as it was over. She was mumbling something about lines. She is doing

OK. Of course, this problem with Jack is putting a strain on her; but so far she is holding up. I just wish I had as much faith in him as she does."

"I think she is correct as far as the murder is concerned. I don't think Jack did it either. As far as him not taking her into his confidence over where he was that night, we shall just have to see how it all shakes out in the end. I'm hoping it is a mountain made out of a mole hill." In spite of my words, I still wondered about this.

"I hope you both are right, Martha. Well, I see a couple of people I need to talk to. See you soon, I hope."

"You will. I'll need feed shortly."

I turned and spotted Jonathon across the room and walked over to him.

"I have to talk to you. I had a scare last night," I said as I approached.

"You what? Why didn't you call me?"

"Because it was over by the time I realized it was happening." I told him about the dogs waking me up. "But more important, I got a phone call in the wee hours of the morning. Someone left a threatening message on my shop answering machine."

"And you didn't call me this morning? Martha, I don't want you hurt." Jonathon was looking grim and I could tell he wasn't happy with me.

"I probably should have," I admitted. "But I knew I'd see you this afternoon. I brought the tape with me. The shop machine is old and still uses them." I pulled it out of my pocket, handed it to him, and continued. "I didn't recognize the voice. I think it was disguised. Sort of sounds muffled. I couldn't even tell if it was male or female."

"Thanks, but I still wish you'd have called me this morning. I'll have my people get on this, though, and see if we can get the voice to come in clearer. In the meantime, please stay out of this investigation. You have obviously already caused alarm for someone."

"I will. I promise," I said as Jonathon headed over to hand the tape to Walter. But I knew that I would continue to ask questions. I couldn't let it drop as long as I thought Tom's murderer was walking free. I looked around and spotted James Hernandez. I also noticed that Lenore Walker seemed to have disappeared from the crowd. I wondered if she had left right after the service. I walked over to talk to James.

"Hi, James, I'm Martha Williamson."

"Good to meet you, Martha. Tom told me that you called on Thursday. Sorry I wasn't there."

"No problem. I just had some questions about Tom's divorce and the trial. We found some mention of both in some of his papers but little in the way of details. I was hoping you might be able to fill in some gaps."

As we talked we walked over to some chairs and sat down.

"I won't be any help on the trial," James said. "Tom came to the ranch to get away from his problems during that time and he refused to talk about it. I don't take the Albuquerque paper so I didn't see anything that was in it. I decided I was a better friend just by providing him a place to hike, ride his horses and generally relax so I never pressed for details. However, I'm sure that Marilyn will know them. She was with Tom through the whole messy time. Lenore would too if you can get her to talk to you."

"I gather that your opinion of her isn't a whole lot better than your son's," I commented.

"No, it's not. I felt she made Tom's life miserable during a time when he deserved all the support he could get. She decided the trial was done just to make her life difficult. You'd have thought that Tom asked to go on trial. Then when they finally got divorced, she tried to obtain the ranch in the settlement. That ranch was Tom's childhood home. It had been passed down to him by his parents and was in no way part of their mutual property. Tom did keep it, but the fight added extra stress."

"Yet, Tom did leave it to her in his will to begin with," I said.

"He did. I was never sure why, but I think it was a case of he hadn't thought through what he really wanted to do with it. Later he set up the trust, which was reflected in the last will. I can tell you that I breathed a sigh of relief when the trust was finalized. Needless to say, I didn't like the idea of Lenore taking over the ranch. My family would have been out on the street very fast if that had happened. She has never liked us."

"Do you have any idea why she was still under the impression that the ranch was hers when Tom died?"

"I have no idea except that the trust wasn't finalized for very long before his last will was written and he was killed. They had resolved their differences for the most part and were friendly but I don't think they communicated very often. My guess is that he was avoiding the confrontation. Men are prone to do that, you know."

"Not just men," I said. "I don't like confrontation either and can procrastinate quite a bit when I know it's necessary. Maybe he was waiting until he had Angie up to speed on the will, and he never got a chance to do that."

"That's possible. I'm sure she wasn't a happy camper when she learned the truth."

"From what I heard," I said, "that was putting it mildly."

At that moment, Marilyn walked toward us.

"Hi, Marilyn," James said. "Have you met, Martha?"

"Yes, I did just before the service," Marilyn answered.

"Thank you for your part, Marilyn," I said. "It gave us another side of Tom that many of us did not know."

"I only wish that I could have conveyed in words how really important he was. But they always fail me at such times."

"That's true of all of us. Have you had some of Sally's wonderful food?"

"I'm going to skip it because the New Mexico group is having an early dinner together. Carter and Eugene are flying back tonight and we all wanted to have a chance to talk before they left. That's why I wandered over here. James, are you and Tom ready to go?"

"We are. Is the ice lady joining us?"

Marilyn grinned at his description of Lenore. "No, she isn't. She said she had another engagement."

"Good. We'll have a better time without her."

"Since you are eating early, I hope you are trying Anthony's in Olympia," I joined in. "They have a great early bird menu."

"That is where we are going. I do want to talk to you, though, Martha. Could we get together tomorrow?"

"How about brunch? I could pick you up about ten-thirty and we could go to Bud Bay Café in Olympia."

"That sounds good. I'm staying at Lavender Nights."

"That's Linda Matheson's place. I know it. Linda and I are good friends. OK, I'll see you in the morning then."

Marilyn, James and Tom walked toward the door of the building and I went over to the food table.

"More food, Sally?" I said as she came out from the kitchen with another full tray of pastries. "You have done a marvelous job of feeding everyone. I do want to give you a donation to help with the cost."

"Not on your life, Martha Williamson. This is my gift to Tom. He was not only one of my regulars at the café, he was a good friend and the best doctor I ever had. It is the least I can do."

"Then thank you, and I'll honor your gift by enjoying the food," I said as I began to make my choices. I decided on some of the salmon spread on French bread, a small spinach tart, some fresh fruit and one of the small cream cheese pastries; but I didn't make a dent in the possibilities that Sally offered.

"Did you leave any for me?" Ellen asked as she came up behind me.

"I think so but with your appetite, the people coming after you may have a problem." I laughed.

"Give me a minute to fill my plate and we can take it and sit down someplace. I figure that we will be here awhile to help Angie clean up after everyone leaves."

"I agree. People don't seem to be in a hurry to leave. They are enjoying the chance to talk together and Sally is feeding everyone well."

"This should keep me going for awhile," Ellen said as she started toward some chairs at the side of the room.

"I should hope so. Did you leave any for those who came after you?"

"Nope, I cleaned the place," Ellen responded with a twinkle in her eyes. "Come on, smarty, let's get seated so I can eat some of this instead of just talking about it."

While Ellen and I were eating, I filled her in on my late-night visitor. Like me, she was all questions and no answers. Friends drifted over, talked and then moved on to speak to other people. Slowly the room was starting to empty out and

Angie was walking toward us, although it was taking her some time because she kept stopping to talk to people.

"I think we may need to start cleaning up to get the last of them out of the place," she commented as she came and sat next to Ellen. "People are enjoying remembering Tom. I've heard some pretty good stories as I've moved around the room."

"You really did organize a beautiful service for Tom, Angie," I said. "Thank you for letting me be part of it."

"I couldn't have done it without the help of the whole community. I think it does show how important he was to all of us. I doubt we will find another like him. However, I am going to try to find us another doctor. I'll advertise the practice for sale as soon as David and I work out the details. This town needs a doctor. I just hope we can find someone who comes at least a little close to filling Tom's shoes."

"We do need one," Ellen said. "But those shoes are very big to fill. It will be hard."

"I know it," Angie said. Then on looking around the room, she added, "I see Sally is starting to clear off the food tables and Bill has the students putting away their band equipment so maybe we can start to clear up the mess."

It actually took us very little time and we had the room back to what it was before we started.

"Thanks," Marian said as she joined us. "You would be surprised at how often groups use this room and then leave the mess for my staff to clean up."

"We wouldn't think of leaving it a mess," Angie said. "Tom would roll over in his grave if we treated you that way. Besides, it just isn't right."

"Well, I still appreciate it. It means I don't have to come back here tomorrow and can actually have a day off."

"Speaking of, Angie, are you actually going to get some rest tomorrow?" I asked.

"I am. I have every intention of sleeping in tomorrow, and then I'm just going to putter around my house," Angie said. "I'll also have to start making some serious decisions about Tom's house and things next week but for tomorrow I'm going to just let everything slide."

"Good. I'm glad. You need a break."

"How would you like to help me carry some of this out to my truck?" Ellen asked as she came up with her costume, CD player and it looked like some of the leftover food from Sally.

"Sure. I need to get home too and take care of the livestock before it gets too dark."

"Not before you get some of this food to take home," Sally said as she came up and handed me a large box.

"Thanks, Sally. From the size of this box, I may not have to cook for a week. You really are special," I said as I took the box and gave her a hug at the same time.

"OK, Ellen. Put your box on top of mine and we will get ourselves homeward bound. Thanks again, Sally. And thanks to you too, Angie. I'll talk to you next week."

"I'm going to have brunch with Marilyn tomorrow," I said to Ellen as we reached her truck. "Do you want to join us?"

"No, I don't think so," Ellen answered. "I have let my work slide this week and I really need to get some programming done. I'm hoping to sleep in and then do some work."

"I can understand that. Jane is coming by tomorrow afternoon to talk about my program at the school next month. I'm hoping that may also move me back into the groove of the shop and my job. This week has taken its toll on our normal routines."

I gave Ellen a hug and walked over to my car carrying the

box that Sally had given me. It had been a wonderful service but I couldn't help but wonder when we would find out who really killed Tom. As far as I could see, we were no closer to figuring it out than we had been the day Tom died. I still did not think that Jack was the guilty party. But if not Jack, who?

Chapter 23

I t was not quite dawn when a cold, wet nose nudged me. "Hey you, can't a person even sleep in on Sunday?" Another nudge and a snuffle said that the answer to that question was no. "I'm coming, I'm coming," I said as I climbed out of my warm bed into a very chilly bedroom.

I pulled on a pair of sweats and some wool socks and followed an anxious Denali out of the house and into the cold winter morning. I stopped to check for any strangers only to have Nali give me another nudge.

"OK show me what it is, big girl." Nali took off at that point and went into the barn. As I followed, the cries of a newborn lamb told me one of the ewes was lambing. The first lamb was fine but Lani was obviously exhausted and struggling to birth another one.

I quickly scrubbed my hands and arms, slipped on surgical gloves, and after applying lubricating jelly to my right hand,

I slid it into her vagina. I could feel two little hooves and the head so the lamb was in the correct position but for some reason it wasn't coming easily. I decided to give her a little help with this one and gently pulled on one leg. I moved to the second leg and repeated the movement. Then with both of the its legs extended, I again coaxed the lamb. With my gentle, steady pressure the lamb slipped into the world. I wiped the membrane from her face and she gasped, started breathing strongly and yelling her presence in the world.

She was quite large for a twin and the extra size may have been what was causing the problem. Lani, tired though she was, clambered to her feet and started cleaning her baby. I dipped the umbilical cord in iodine and clipped it short. By then the lamb was moving to its feet and starting to nurse. The first lamb was also joining her sister. Lani would be fine, thanks to Nali.

"Good girl, Nali," I said. "You were a big help. Now I suppose you are ready for breakfast."

She answered me with one wag of a tail and a trot toward her food bowl. Falcor had come in while we were tending to Lani and he was standing near the food bowl patiently waiting for his breakfast. After feeding the dogs, I put out the food for the other animals and checked on the other ewe. She was fine and giving no indication that this was going to be the day for her to lamb. I went to the back of the barn once more and checked on Lani and her lambs. They seemed to be doing fine. I made sure that Lani had some good alfalfa and fresh water within her area. She would stay in there with the lambs for the next few days. Feeling the need for a shower but very exhilarated by the new lambs, I walked back to the house. The sun was just beginning to show above the hills and the sky was a wonderful mix of pink, apricot and lavender.

I stopped in the kitchen just long enough to start the coffee and then headed for the shower. The hot water pouring over my shoulders began to release tension I hadn't realized was there. For awhile, I just stood under it and relished the comfort that it brought. Turning off the shower, I reached for my warm towel. Shortly after we moved in, John had given me a gift of a towel warming drawer. I thanked him every time I stepped from my shower and wrapped myself in the warm towel.

My coffee was ready when I returned to the kitchen. I filled my cup and moved to the window seat to watch the day brighten. Sable came to join me after finishing her breakfast. She loved the window seat and was soon curled up and snoozing by my feet. It looked like we would have a second day in a row of sun and warmth. I reached over and picked up a seed catalog. A favorite pastime at this time of year was deciding what I wanted to plant in the kitchen garden. I would buy most of my seeds and bedding plants from Ted, but it was fun to look at the catalog. Once in awhile I would order something that was a little more exotic than what Ted carried.

As I was thinking about a second cup of coffee, both Denali and Falcor wandered into the house. "Everything all right out there, big guys?" I was answered with a grin and a flop as they both settled down close to me for a bit of companionship. I got up and poured my coffee and turned on *Weekend Edition*. Might as well find out if the outside world was still functioning. With its company, I settled down once more on the window seat. Sable stretched and accepted my scratching of her stomach with all the elegance a Siamese can summon and then purring loudly curled up close to me. I sipped my coffee and let the wonder of the new birth, my terrific animals and my life in general seep into my bones. Life felt good and there was no forewarning of the day's events.

I finished my second cup of coffee and decided to go for a walk with the dogs before I had to get dressed for my brunch date with Marilyn. I hadn't planned on being up and functioning this early but farm life had changed those plans. Rather than leash the dogs, I would just walk on my property and see what changes spring was starting to bring.

"Come on, monsters. Show me your territory this morning," I said as I picked up my jacket and slipped my feet into my barn boots. Happy to have me for company, the dogs raced a number of yards ahead and then raced back again to make sure I was still following. Outside of my main pasture area, there was a small stream that meandered through the back of my property. It was a favorite place for both the dogs and me, and they were delighted when I opened the gate and we started in that direction. Someone before me had planted crocus by the hundreds and they had naturalized. In protected areas they were starting to bloom. They would be a wonderful show in a few more weeks. Here and there wild violets were also just starting to bloom. The Steller's jays were calling to each other and in the distance I could hear the mating call of a song sparrow. He must have just returned as they don't winter over with us like the jays do. As we turned to walk down the stream, I saw a rabbit show its head and then, on catching sight of the dogs, make a dash for cover.

The dogs were in heaven as they went from smell to smell, checking out the changes in this part of their territory since the last time I had let them come out here. The fencing in this area was not as secure and they only came this way when I could come with them. As we moved toward the outer fence, Falcor's head came up and he made a beeline for the fence. Once there his nose went down and he started smelling all along the fence.

"What'd you find, big guy?" I walked over to where he and Denali, who had joined him, continued to scour the fence line with their noses. As I bent down to look closer, I caught my breath. It wasn't a coyote the other afternoon after all. All along that section of the fence, I could see footprints. Someone had been here. But why? Just to make me uneasy, or were they searching for a way onto my property? A shiver went up my spine in spite of the warm morning sunshine. They were gone now but I had never felt as exposed as I did just then.

I called the dogs and we continued our walk. No sense in messing up their morning just because mine had been disrupted. I sat on a large rock by the edge of the stream and watched as it tumbled its way over and around the rocks and branches that had fallen into it. Right now it was quite deep and rapid. In the height of the summer, it would slow to just a trickle but the recent rains had caused it to swell to its winter glory.

As I gazed at the water, my mind went back over the events of the past week. I thought of my business card under Tom's body. If it was dropped by the killer, that pointed a finger right at Lenore. She had a couple of them I knew. Then what about the car that almost hit me? Were those license plates from New Mexico? She appeared to have motive. She could have obtained the gun in Albuquerque, and she would have had no problem getting close to Tom. Could a woman who had actually loved Tom and lived with him for many years come to hate him enough to kill him? I had trouble with the concept, but then, who else fit the clues that we had? I would have to talk to Marilyn this morning and get more information. But I was getting a feeling that maybe I was close to figuring it out.

A cloud slid over the sun and the change in temperature brought me out of my thoughts. "Come on Nali, Falcor. It is time for us to go back." They turned from their wandering and came back to me. I patted each one and we joined together to walk back to the pasture.

Once inside the main pasture area, the dogs took off in different directions to check on the sheep and llamas that had come outside to graze. I decided to go into the barn to check on Lani one more time before I closed dogs and livestock into their fenced area for the day. The lambs were nursing hungrily and Lani just gave me a quick look before she nuzzled one of them. They were obviously doing just fine.

"They are pretty girls, Lani. Thanks for giving them to me."

I moved my van from the garage into the outer parking area and shut the gate that would keep the Pyrs back with their charges while I was gone. It was time for me to get ready to meet Marilyn. I was looking forward to our talk.

Chapter 24

Marilyn was waiting for me on Linda's porch when I arrived to pick her up.

"Good morning," I said as she climbed into the van. "I hope you had a good evening and a good night's sleep."

"I did and you were right. Anthony's was a wonderful place to eat. We even saw an eagle through the window just about dusk. He was sitting on a piling and then rose with such grace and flew down the bay. They are so wonderful."

"I'm glad you saw them. They live in that area and can often be seen from the walk along the bay. I decided that we would stay here in Black Hills for brunch," I continued as I pulled into the parking lot of the Lodge at Black Hills. "I realized that the Budd Bay Café was very close to where you ate last night and thought maybe you'd enjoy Holly's cooking and the charm of her bed and breakfast. Her menu is small but the food she does prepare is exquisite and everything is homemade on the premises, including her croissants, which I highly recommend."

"Sounds just right," Marilyn said as we walked in the door. "Look at those beautiful quilts, and that rocker just beckons you to come in and get comfortable, doesn't it? What a wonderful place you have," she added as Holly walked toward us.

"Thank you. You are Marilyn, right? I enjoyed your comments on Dr. Tom yesterday."

"Yes, I am," Marilyn responded. "I can see why Tom loved it here. The people are so friendly and it is such a beautiful place."

"Hi, Martha," Holly said as she turned to me. "I have your reserved table over here where you can see both the garden and the fireplace. The garden is starting to come to life and I have the fountain going today for the first day of the season. It just seemed right to turn it on."

"Thanks, Holly. It really has turned into a beautiful day."

"Here you are," Holly said as we reached our table. "Do both of you want coffee?"

"I do," I answered and Marilyn nodded her agreement.

"I'll leave a carafe then, and here are the menus. The special this morning is homemade bagels with lightly smoked local salmon and cream cheese. And Martha, I have some fresh papaya from Hawai`i if you are interested. I'll leave you for a minute to look at the menu."

I poured both Marilyn and me some coffee from the carafe. "I think I'll have the special with the papaya."

"I had salmon last night," Marilyn responded, "but her fresh baked croissant with homemade preserves and brie cheese sounds interesting. I'll pass on the papaya. They are not a favorite fruit for me but the fresh California strawberries sound good."

"I'm a strawberry snob," I said. "I'll wait for the local ones to come on, but I love papaya. John and I lived in Hawai`i for four years and I fell in love with the local fruit. Rambutan and lychee are also favorites but I seldom ever find them fresh here."

"Sorry, Martha, but I never see those available," Holly said as she walked up to take our order. Marilyn and I told her what we wanted and then continued our conversation as she left.

"You speak of your husband fondly, Martha, so I'm assuming that you aren't divorced. Are you a widow?"

"Yes, John was killed in an auto accident. I had a terrible time at first but life is now fulfilling again. Different but good."

"I'm sorry. It is hard when we lose a life partner early. I've never married but sometimes it feels like I'm married to that clinic. It was actually good to get away for a few days, even if the reason for coming was not a happy one. This really is beautiful country. I can't get over how green it is."

"It is different from Albuquerque. My father was stationed there and I loved the stark beauty of the desert. There is a grandeur there that hasn't been matched in any other place that I've lived."

"Here you are," Holly said as she placed our food before us. "Let me know if I can get you anything else."

"It looks wonderful," Marilyn said. "I can't think of another thing I would need at the moment."

"Me either," I commented.

"Hmmm," I said. "There is no comparison between this bagel and one that I buy from Safeway."

"I have to agree on the croissant also," Marilyn said. "And her preserves are wonderful—not too sweet and lots of fruit flavor. I wouldn't have thought of using brie this way but it really works. I'm glad I ordered it."

We continued with general conversation about Holly's garden and places to see in the area since Marilyn was going to be here a week. Then I got down to the question that I really wanted to ask.

"Marilyn, what happened that caused Tom to be sued and was that why he moved up here?"

"To answer your second question first and with a simple answer, yes, that is why he moved to Washington. The suit was a terrible tragedy that should have never happened but people in grief sometimes do stupid things. Tom was on call one Saturday evening. A young woman came into the emergency room hemorrhaging and scared to death. She told him that she had tried to induce an abortion herself a week before. She was in the military and did not want her career ruined. Also, the father of the child was married. She was Catholic, and for some reason in her mixed-up mind, a safe abortion by a doctor seemed to have more sin connected with it than a self-induced abortion. Anyway by the time she came to the hospital, she had a massive uterine infection and her bleeding had turned into a hemorrhage. Tom was able to control the hemorrhage but the infection did not respond to antibiotics and she died."

Marilyn paused to take a sip of coffee and continued. "Although he had done everything correctly, the family blamed him for her death. They were in total shock over the fact that their daughter was pregnant and they would not believe that she could possibly induce an abortion. They actually accused Tom of inducing it himself without her permission. It was a very nasty trial. Their attorney did everything possible to smear Tom's name and to discredit him as a physician and a man. In the end, he was found to be completely without fault. However,

Tom always blamed himself. He would go over and over what he might have done to change the outcome."

She shifted and gazed out the window for a moment. Was she was reliving those sad days?

"The whole thing took a terrible toll on his practice and his life. The stress of the trial was also the final blow to his marriage. He and Lenore were high school sweethearts. The marriage was having some of the problems that happen in relationships as partners grow and change, but I think they might have worked through it if the suit had not happened. However, she was furious about the bad publicity the trial caused. She felt that it damaged her medical practice and her father's reputation. He was a state senator. It was an election year and he was in a fight for his seat, which he subsequently lost. I doubt that it had anything to do with the media circus around the trial, but you couldn't have convinced Lenore of that."

"Was the fight over the ranch as nasty as the Hernandezes have let me to believe?" I asked.

"Yes, it was. I don't know what possessed Lenore but she was fixated on owning the ranch. It really wasn't part of their community property and had been in Tom's family for generations. But she had this image of a huge spread up there in the northern mountains and she fought him long and hard for it. When the dust settled, Tom still owned the ranch. Over the years they settled most of their differences but that ranch was always a sore point. I could never understand why he left it to her in his first will after the divorce, but he did. I was not surprised when I learned that he had made other arrangements recently."

As I listened, I once again wondered if Lenore could be angry enough to murder Tom. But I was also struck by the tragedy of the whole situation.

"How terrible," I said, "that something so tragic should harm not only the life of the young woman but of everyone involved. It is beyond me how anyone could accuse Tom of such a thing, but as you say, grief does cause one to do terrible things sometimes. Did this have anything to do with the clinic that Tom founded?"

"Yes. He hoped that having such a clinic available might help another young woman going through the same thing. We spend a lot of our time counseling women. We help them see all of their options. We provide whatever medical help they may need, but we also have a large circle of social and spiritual resources that we can refer them to for help in those areas. We also provide medical care for any other problem that women might have where they don't have another physician to help them. It is fulfilling work and I'm glad it can continue."

"I'm glad it can continue too. Do you remember the name of the young woman?" I asked.

"I've been trying to remember it since we started this conversation but it has completely left my mind," Marilyn answered. "I should know it. It should be seared into my brain but it isn't. You know, though, something odd happened yesterday afternoon. When I was talking at the memorial service, I thought for just a moment that I saw her in the group. Then when I looked again, she was gone. I must have just imagined it since I was talking about the clinic. It was very odd."

"That is odd," I said. "What you've told me fills in a piece in the puzzle of Tom's life but I'm not sure it helps with the puzzle of his death. I'll have to think on it some more. Let's walk in Holly's garden for a bit before I take you back to Linda's. I have an appointment at two o'clock but we still have some time."

"I'd like that but, you don't have to take me back. It couldn't be more than a mile from here and I'd enjoy the walk," Marilyn said. "It is such a lovely day."

"It's slightly over a mile but not too far to walk. I'll give you directions when I leave. I agree it is a great day for a walk. The dogs and I took one early this morning."

I paid Holly for our food and we walked through the French doors into the garden. The pussy willow tree still had a few catkins on it and just a smidgeon of early green was starting to show. The crocuses were everywhere, and in a protected area there were a few daffodils in bloom. She also had pansies and decorative kale.

"What kind of dogs do you have?" Marilyn asked.

"They are Great Pyrenees. They guard my livestock and give me wonderful companionship. Then to add to their value, they produce fiber for me to spin. I can't imagine life without them. Denali really helped me get through the death of John and this morning she woke me up and led me out to the barn where a ewe was in trouble. She probably saved the life of the lamb and possibly the ewe too."

"They sound like they really are terrific dogs."

"Why don't you come by the shop before you leave and you can meet them? You aren't leaving until Thursday and I'm open Tuesday through Saturday. Or if tomorrow works better for your schedule just give me a call. I'll probably be out in the morning but should be back by the afternoon. I'd love to show you my place of creativity."

"I may just do that," Marilyn answered. "I'd like to see your shop. I do knit and crochet so it would be fun to see what you have available."

"I carry most of the usual yarns, needles, and hooks, but

I also have a selection of handspun yarns that you might find interesting, including some with Great Pyrenees hair in it."

"Dog hair in yarn. Isn't that rather unusual?" Marilyn asked.

"Not as unusual as you might think when you are talking handspun. A lot of people spin the hair from their own dogs. It even has a name, chiengora."

"I'll come by. If it is to be tomorrow, I'll call you."

As we continued to talk, we wandered further out into the garden; you could see where the rhododendrons and the camellias would be covered with blooms later in the spring. I would have to remember to come back in late April or early May. Circling back toward the lodge, we came upon a hidden Japanese-style garden. It was a small area that called for one to sit and just enjoy the day.

"I think I'll just sit here for awhile," Marilyn said. "It is so peaceful. I think that I'd like to just spend some time doing nothing."

"I'll leave you here then and look forward to seeing you later in the week," I said as I gave her a hug. I turned and walked down the path toward my van. As I climbed into the van, some of the things Marilyn said to me began to replay in my mind. Could I be totally wrong in thinking that it was Lenore? As a matter of fact, had we all been blind to the real killer? Jonathon was focusing on the robbery with the idea that Tom had surprised the burglar. I had been focusing on people who knew Tom in Albuquerque. What if it were someone who only knew Tom by reputation—a reputation tainted by grief and despair?

As I started the van and drove out of the parking lot, my thoughts went to events and conversations of the past week: a sister who died from an infection; a marriage and divorce which could easily change a name; someone who didn't trust male doctors and who avoided handsome sheriff's officers; and someone who was new in town. I didn't like where my thoughts were leading me but I was almost certain that I knew who Tom's killer was. Now, how was I going to get the proof that I needed? Right now others would think I was nuts.

I almost missed the turn into my driveway because I was so busy sorting and resorting the new ideas. Was I totally crazy? Could it be true? I would be looking at things differently as we met this afternoon. Was I crazy to see her at all? Maybe, but I still needed proof.

Chapter 25

The dogs were nowhere in sight when I drove up but as I walked to the barn, I could see them ambling back in that direction from the far side of the pasture. Obviously I was not important enough at this time to cause them to hurry. I went inside to check on Lani. She and the lambs were doing great.

As I entered the shop, I noticed that the dogs had decided to move back into the pasture. Maybe they'd come visit later. I considered what I would need for this afternoon and pulled *The Ashland Book of Spinning* along with two of Bette Hochberg's books and Connie Delaney's book on spindle spinning. These would give us a starting point for discussing the classes on spinning. I wondered if this planning was a total waste of time. Was I correct? I thought so, but for now, I'd move forward as if nothing had changed. I wasn't sure whether Jane wanted me to do quite a bit of demonstrating and talking or if she wanted me to teach the children to spin. I could go either way. It was really her call. Once I had the books on the coffee table in the sitting area, I put on some tea water. As I finished, I heard Jane's car come into the driveway.

"What a beautiful day," Jane said as she entered the shop. "I didn't even feel like I needed a coat today."

"It is beautiful. I'm really enjoying it while I can. I know we will still have more cold weather, but I love these warm February days when they come.

"Come on over here and pull a chair up to the coffee table," I added. "I thought we'd look at a couple of books and then talk about what you wanted me to cover. Do you want some tea?"

"Yes, please. Peppermint if you have it," Jane said as she pulled up an ottoman next to the table.

I fixed our tea and moved back over to the table. "Now what do you want me to do?" I said as I settled down on the couch.

"Well, I hoped you would be willing to come for more than one day. I'd like to have the children have a chance to take a fleece from sheep to yarn."

"You want smelly raw fleece in your classroom?" I laughed.

"Well, I don't like it particularly but I think it is an important part of their learning process so I think we should do it. I'll keep my prejudices to myself."

"Do you want me to take up the whole day when I'm there or just part of it?"

"Maybe just the afternoon," Jane answered. "It will give them a way to dissipate some of the nervous energy that comes after sitting in the classroom all morning."

"I think we should take four afternoons then," I continued. "Maybe two one week and two the next. Mondays are good for me because the shop is closed. Then how about Wednesday? I'll just have to close the shop but I think I can manage that as long as I let people know ahead of time."

"That would work. I'd like to do it the last two weeks of March if that is all right."

"I can do that. It will give me enough time to prepare. I'll refine this but how does this outline sound? The first afternoon, I'll give a brief history of spinning and we can talk about the wool and where it comes from. Then we can wash some of the wool. We will put each child's wet wool in a labeled plastic bag and I can take it home to dry. The second day, we will card the wool and get it ready for spinning. Then the last two days, we can spin our yarn and make a friendship bracelet or a bookmark or something like that out of it. We could have the children make their own spindles but I think that it would be simpler if I just brought in enough toy wheel spindles for each of them."

"I think I'd like them to make their own spindles," Jane said, "but I could lead that part of it. I'm sure you can show me what to do. That way, you don't have to take the time from your shop for another class session. Maybe we could put a week between your class sessions and I can use that week for them to make their spindles."

"I can handle that schedule shift and the spindles are easy to make. I can show you how after spinning class this week."

"That would be good. It will give me a chance to make sure I can do it well before I show the children. I'm so glad that you are willing to do this, Martha. I have found the members of this community to be so committed to helping in the schools. It is quite a change from the big city school that I left."

"Teachers like you are hard to find, Jane. I think you will find that the parents will do everything they can to keep you."

As I said that, Jane turned slightly to reach for the Connie

Delaney book and I caught a glimpse of a patch on the shoulder of her vest. My heart sank as I realized that my suspicions were true and I now had my proof.

"What a beautiful patchwork vest, Jane. Did you make it?"

"Yes, it was my first try at crazy quilting. All the pieces come from clothing that I've made myself."

"Would you mind if I looked at it more closely? I love quilting."

Jane took it off and just as she handed it to me, the phone rang. I walked over to answer it with the vest in my hands.

"Spider's Web."

"Martha, this is Marilyn. I just remembered the name of the young woman. It was Janet Cortez. Does that help at all?"

"Yes it does, Marilyn. Thanks for calling me. I have Jane here right now but I'll call you back later. Are you going to be in this evening?"

"Yes, I will. I'll talk to you then."

While I was talking to Marilyn, Jane had walked over to the area with the books. She now turned with Rachel Brown's *Spinning, Weaving and Dyeing* book in her hands. I walked back over to the sitting area while I considered my next move. I looked down at the vest I held in my hands and looked up at Jane. "Janet Cortez was your older sister, wasn't she?"

"What do you mean?" Jane dropped the book and strode back toward me.

"Was that why you killed Dr. Tom, Jane?"

Would she admit it? I realized my hands were sweating. Was I crazy? My stomach was in a knot, but I continued. "Were you extracting revenge for the death of your sister and did it seem fitting to use her gun to do it? Your vest has a patch in it of the fabric that was found with Dr. Tom's blood on it. You burned the blouse but you forgot about the patch on the vest."

Jane's face contorted. Her mouth became grim and at the same time tears welled up in her eyes.

"He killed my beautiful sister. That man murdered her as sure as I'm standing here and then he just walked away. 'I'm sorry,' he said. 'We did all we could but we couldn't save her.' That was supposed to somehow make it better. That was supposed to take away his culpability. And then he had the gall to say that she had induced an abortion. My sister wouldn't do that. My sister knew that it would be a grave sin. Whatever happened, he caused it. He gave her the infection with his sloppy medical practices and he let her die."

The words tumbled out and almost ran into each other. She was shaking and her voice had risen to a shout. I wondered if the dogs had heard her. Would they notice something was amiss in the shop? Did I want them to? I had no idea what I was going to do next.

"Were you there, Jane? Did you go to the trial?"

"No! They wouldn't let me come! My parents said I had to stay at boarding school. They brought her body home for the funeral and I attended that; then as soon as it was over, they shipped me back to school. 'Janet wouldn't want you to mess up your school year,' they said. How did they know what Janet would want? I wanted to look him in the eye. I wanted to accuse him of the murder of my sister. And I did. Just before I shot him, I let him know who I was and why I was doing it. I let him know that in the long run he couldn't escape justice."

"How did you get him to meet you at the office?" I asked. I was actually stalling as I tried to think of how I was going to handle things. I knew that Tom would come if anyone called and said they needed him.

"That was easy." Jane actually laughed. "I just called and said I was running a high fever and couldn't stop the vomiting and diarrhea. All of you had told me how he was such a saint and how he would come out anytime he was called. You were right. He said he'd meet me at the office and he did. When I walked in and it was obvious that I wasn't sick, he asked me what was wrong and I told him. Then I pulled out Janet's gun and I shot him." She actually looked triumphant when she finished that sentence. Did she have any idea how unhinged she sounded at the moment?

"Why did you take the Albuquerque files from the office?"

"I was destroying the office to make it look like a robbery when I found them. I thought they might have something about Janet in them so I grabbed them. I was right."

"So when you were done with them, you threw them out beside the road. Why?"

"I just wanted them out of my car. I realized they were still there the day it snowed. So I just got rid of them. There wasn't any way that you'd connect them with me or so I thought."

"And you dumped the gun on the trail up the mountain never figuring that anyone would find it in that deep hole by the tree. You must have thought that the heavy snow was a miracle since it helped mask your trail and the gun. But you didn't really understand the power of a dog's nose to find things long hidden. So Falcor found the gun and then Blackie found the scrap of material. But why did you put the burned blouse in Jo's burn barrel? At least I assume you burned it first since burning it in her barrel might be pretty obvious."

"I thought the police might go looking there again and it seemed like a good way to keep their suspicion on Jack. It almost worked too. But you are right. I had forgotten about the patch on the vest. Funny how you look at things without really seeing them after awhile. I figured that I could just wait until the school year was over and then leave at the end of my contract. The weather would be a good excuse. As you said, a lot of people can't stand the gray up here. It wouldn't be particularly noteworthy that I only stayed a year. And even if they found Jack innocent, which I figured they would do, I would still have time the way court cases go to be out of here before they started looking again. But I hadn't figured on one of the people I liked the best also being one of the nosiest. And now I have to decide what I'm going to do."

"I think that what we are going to do is call Jonathon," I said as I reached for the phone.

"No, I don't think so," Jane said coldly as she pulled a gun out of her purse. "Janet wasn't the only one with a gun. My father taught all of his children how to use a gun at an early age. That is why he didn't think it was odd when I asked him for Janet's gun. We all own them and we are all excellent shots so I would recommend that you move your hand away from that phone, Martha."

I did as I was told. Where were the dogs? How could I attract their attention without letting Jane know what I was doing? "And just what do you plan on doing now?" I asked.

"I don't know, but it is obvious that I'll have to leave here faster than I had expected. And I must do something to keep you quiet while I go. I really don't want to hurt you, Martha. I am not a murderer. I am a teacher. Tom Walker deserved what he got. All I did was provide the justice that the courts failed to give. But you are my friend and so I need to think about what to do. However, calling the police is not an option."

"Are you sure, Jane?" I asked as I again stalled for time while I considered my options.

"Of course I'm sure. I have no desire to spend time in jail, and the justice system that failed me once is probably not going to see how right my actions were. They will fail me again. No, I think I should go to Canada, and I think you are going with me as a hostage. If we make it there safely, I'll tie you up somewhere and leave you. It should delay you long enough for me to get well out of the area. And if I get stopped, well, you will be my bargaining chip, Martha."

"I don't think that is a very good plan, Jane."

"Maybe not but it is the only one I have now. I want you to get whatever cash you have here and coats for both of us. We are going to take a trip. Now I suggest you start to move slowly so I can watch you but start getting the things we need."

I started to move toward the door, wondering if I could make a break for it.

"Stop!" Jane yelled. "Don't even think about it!"

I heard a dog bark and Jane turned for just a moment. I took advantage of it, and in one swoop, I picked it up a chair and swung it at Jane. I missed but the chair hit a display of needles and the whole thing landed with a crash. I made a leap toward Jane as she leveled the gun back to cover me. We faced off with me panting and Jane's face showing panic. My attack was probably a mistake.

"That was a very stupid thing to do." Jane's voice rose to a shriek. "I'll kill you if you force me to."

"Jane," I started, but at that moment I heard a cacophony of barking and then a deep growl as a blur of white came through the dog door. Jane whirled to face them as Falcor leapt. I screamed as Jane's gun went off and I heard her howl of anger and Denali's yelp of pain. Jane was sprawled on her back on the floor with Falcor standing over her. A low growl was coming from his throat and his head was poised over her throat but was not touching her.

I saw Jane's gun just a few inches from her grasp where it had fallen when she went down. Although my instinct was to go to Nali, I knew I had to get the gun first.

"Keep her there, Falcor," I said. As I reached for the gun, I could see Jane's face. It had crumpled and she was crying, although I couldn't tell whether it was fear, anger or frustration and I didn't care. Right now, I was a whole lot more worried about my dog.

I knelt beside Nali and could see the red blooming on her side. She was breathing heavily but she was still alive. Her eyes were filled with pain but she tried to get up when I approached.

"It will be all right, big girl, lie down."

She lay back down. When she rose up, I hadn't noticed any evidence of blood on the far side so the bullet was still in her.

"Let me get something to try to stop the bleeding,"

I was talking to her to keep my own feelings in check. I went to one of the cupboards and took out a couple of small clean towels I kept there. I snagged the phone with one hand on my way back to Nali. I gently pressed the towel to her side and then dialed Jonathon's number.

"Tammie," I said, not even giving her time to finish her greeting. "Get Jonathon to my shop now. I have Tom's killer, or rather, I should say that Falcor has Tom's killer. I can't answer questions, I have to call Mark. Nali's been shot. Just get someone here and hurry."

I hung up without giving Tammie a chance to say anything. She would get one of the men here right away. I pressed the speed dial for Mark's office knowing that I would get the answering service. But I didn't.

"Hello." It was Mark. I didn't think any voice ever sounded so beautiful.

"Mark, this is Martha Williamson. Denali has been shot in the side by Tom Walker's killer and I think it's pretty bad."

"By Tom's killer?"

"Yes, Falcor is standing over her right now and I can't leave but Nali needs medical attention now."

One wonderful thing about Mark is he has his priorities straight. I knew he was probably dying of curiosity but he didn't ask any questions.

"I'll be there as quickly as I can. Tell that girl to hold on. She is too important for her to do something foolish like die on us."

"I'll tell her, Mark. We are in the shop. Please hurry," I said as I started to cry.

"I'm coming now, Martha. You hang in there."

I hung up the phone and turned to where Falcor was still standing over Jane. "Keep her there, big guy, and don't let her move. I need to stay here with Nali."

Falcor looked at me and then gave another growl for Jane's sake to make sure she knew that her best option was to stay motionless.

"Martha," Jane started.

"No," I said. "I don't want to hear it, Jane. You killed my friend and now you've shot my dog. Nothing you can say will help."

I heard the sirens of the police cars and two of them barreled into my drive. Moments later, Jonathon came rushing in the door with his gun drawn.

"Put that thing away, Jonathon," I said. We've had too many guns in here already today. Falcor has your prisoner well in hand, or maybe I should say paw."

Jonathon looked over to where Falcor was standing on Jane then, he looked back at me.

"Jane?" he asked. "Tom's killer is Jane?"

"Yes," I said, "and I think she would be very happy if you took control of her so I could release Falcor from his post."

Jonathon walked over to where Jane was sprawled on the floor and I spoke to Falcor. "OK, big guy, you can let her up now. Jonathon will take over,"

Falcor looked at me to make sure I meant it.

"Enough, Falcor, come over here."

He slowly backed off but stood next to Jane, growling until Jonathon had her handcuffed and on her feet. Then he walked over to where I was sitting on the floor with Nali.

"That dog tried to kill me," Jane shouted.

"Stuff it, lady," I replied. "If he had wanted to kill you, you would be dead. All he did was hold you for Jonathon."

"Now, if you will tell me—" Jonathon started but at that moment Mark came into the shop and all my attention focused on him and Nali.

"I'll talk to you later, Jonathon. I need to help Mark. Just get that woman out of my shop. Oh, and by the way, you will want these for evidence. They're hers," I said as I handed him the vest and gun.

Jonathon started to say something else to me and then just shook his head. "Come on, Jane," he said. "You are going for a ride with me. I'll talk to you later, Martha. Take good care of Nali."

Mark was already examining Nali.

"She has lost some blood, Martha, but I can't tell a whole lot without an x-ray to see where the bullet is. I need to move her to the clinic. Do you have something that we can use to move her and keep her stable?"

At that moment another vehicle running a siren careened into my drive and almost immediately feet were on the porch.

"Are you OK, Sis?" Sean yelled as he rushed into the shop.

"Slow down, Little Brother, I'm fine."

"But the radio said something about a shooting in your shop."

"There was and Nali is badly hurt," I said. "But I'm fine. Now, since you are here, I need you to help Mark get Nali to his van. Is there any chance your vehicle has the kind of backboards that they use for auto accidents in it?"

Sean thought a minute. "I think it does. Let me go look."

He turned and went back out to his vehicle. He was back shortly with just what we needed. I put an old blanket over it and we gently moved Nali onto it. She whimpered with pain when we moved her but made no effort to move on her own. Sean and Mark carried her to Mark's van and lay her on the floor in the back. We secured her with straps he had in there.

"Stay still, big girl," I said. "We are going to get you taken care of real soon."

I turned to Sean. "I know you're on duty but could you stay here for awhile? I think Jonathon will be back but I want to go with Mark and Nali."

"I'll lock your place up, get Falcor back with the animals, and call Jonathon to let him know where you are, but I really do need to get back on the road as soon as possible."

"That will be enough help. Thanks."

"I'll follow you, Mark, so that I have my van to come home in. Just let me get my purse and coat."

"OK, Martha," Mark said as he climbed into the front seat of his van. I saw him look over his shoulder and speak to Nali before he made a call on his cell phone.

Mark was hooking his seat belt and starting his van as I came out of the house and got into mine. The short trip to his clinic seemed to take forever. I was so worried about Nali and every possible scenario played in my mind as I wondered what I could have done to prevent the tragedy.

I was relieved to see that another car was in the parking lot. Maggie, Mark's vet tech, was already there to meet us. That must have been the call that Mark made. By the time both Mark and I had parked, Maggie was outside with a rolling gurney. She and Mark gently transferred Nali to it.

"Martha, you can't do any more here. Why don't you go home? I'll call you when we are done with the surgery."

"No, Mark. I'll stay here. I can pace here as readily as I can at home."

"OK."

Mark and Maggie rolled Nali into the office and into the back while I stood in the waiting room looking out the window, praying that my girl would recover and thinking about the surprises that the day had brought. I hadn't been standing there too long before Jonathon drove up and came in.

"How is Nali?"

"She's in surgery right now. I don't know," I said as I fought back the tears that were so close to the surface.

"Mark is a remarkable veterinary surgeon. If anyone can save her, he can."

"I know, Jonathon, but I still blame myself. I was pretty sure Jane was the killer. I shouldn't have met with her today. But I needed proof."

"You misjudged Jane, Martha. You still thought that her better side would prevail. If the dogs hadn't shown up, the outcome could have been a lot worse. By the way, Jane is still spitting about Falcor attacking her. Says she'll sue over the vicious dog. I told her to try it."

"Falcor never touched her except to send her sprawling on her back. She would be hard pressed to show any real injuries."

"I know. He did a magnificent job. I think he earned a steak for dinner tonight. Now tell me exactly what happened."

I took Jonathon through the events of the afternoon, and the fact that her vest was the proof that cinched it.

"You know, Jonathon, you said earlier that we might not be happy about finding Tom's killer and I feel like that. Jane was a gifted teacher. She was a very likable human being, but she had this one terrible blind spot over the death of her sister and that twisted her completely when it came to Tom."

"Yes, I agree. She tried to convince me that her actions were justified. She has been planning this for years. The opening for a teacher at Black Hills Elementary was a sign as far as she was concerned that she was supposed to carry out her mission."

"Oh, I bet that is who it was," I said half to myself.

"What?" Jonathon asked.

"Marilyn saw someone at the memorial service who reminded her of Janet Cortez but when she looked that way again the person was gone. She thought it was weird but didn't think too much about it. It was Jane. I had seen her earlier at the back of the room but she wasn't in the group that stayed for food and conversation after the service. I bet she caught a glimpse of the puzzlement on Marilyn's face and decided that she needed to leave."

Just then Mark walked back into the waiting room.

"I have removed the bullet. It had just nicked a lung but it missed her heart. Now it's up to Nali to recover. She has lost quite a bit of blood but I think she'll make it. She's got a lot of strength. You can see her for a minute or so, but my prescription for you is to go home and take care of yourself and the other critters at your place."

"I agree with that," Jonathon said. "I have called Ellen and she'll be waiting for you at home. My guess is she'll already have the livestock fed and bedded. You need to have some pampering yourself."

I looked at my wonderful friends and just nodded. I was once again close to tears. I turned and walked back to where Nali was with Maggie. Right now all I wanted was see my girl with my own eyes and know that she was all right.

Chapter 26

I was rearranging the area of the shop that had all the roving in it. It was a rainy afternoon two weeks after Jane had been captured. Falcor was asleep in the classroom and Nali was resting by the stove. She was recovering from her gunshot wound but I was still keeping her fairly close to me. Right now Falcor had the livestock duty.

I was musing over the events of the last few weeks. It turned out that Lenore was in Washington to speak at a medical conference in Seattle. She may not be the nicest person in the world, but she hadn't killed Tom. Brenda had told the truth. Tom was dead when she entered his office. She would be tried for the burglaries but that was all. Just then Nali raised her head and I heard the crunch of tires on the drive. I looked out and saw that it was Leslie's pickup. It would be good to see her. I had talked to her on the phone when she called to thank me for getting Jack released, but I hadn't seen her since the memorial service. I walked toward the door as they came in. Along with Leslie was Jack and between them was the cutest, small, redheaded boy that I'd seen in a long time.

"Hello. You two look very happy. Who is this?" I asked as I knelt in front of the boy.

"I'm Tyler and I'm three years old," he said.

"This is Jack's son," Leslie added. "He is the reason Jack wouldn't tell me where he was. He was with Tyler, who was living with Jack's mom and his sister. The silly man hadn't said anything about having a child when he first came to work for us for fear that it would keep him from getting the job. Then when we started to care for each other, he thought it might change my feelings for him. Can you tell me, Martha, why this adorable little boy would change my feelings for Jack?"

"No, I can't. Tyler, do you like big dogs?" I could see that he was looking at Nali. He nodded. "Do you want to pet the dog?" He nodded again. "Then come with me. You must be very gentle because the dog has been sick."

I took his hand and we walked over to Nali. She raised her head but made no move to leave her spot by the fire. Tyler squatted down as only little children seem able to do and gently patted her upper shoulder. He was very careful to not touch the area that had been shaved for her surgery.

"Why is the doggie sick?" He asked.

"A bad lady shot her," Jack responded. "It was the bad lady that got Daddy in trouble for awhile. Nali and Falcor saved Martha and got Daddy out of trouble."

Hearing his name, Falcor got up and ambled over to where all of us were. Tyler's eyes got round as he saw how big the dog was.

"Oooh," he said. "Are you a wolf?"

"No," I said. "He is just a dog but he is a very brave dog."

"Which brings us back to why we are here," Leslie chimed in. "Tyler, do you want to give one of these to each of the dogs?" She asked as she pulled two large rawhide bones from her tote bag. "And we also brought this," she added as she pulled a piece of paper from the bag as well.

She handed it to me and I laughed before I read it aloud to the dogs.

"We hereby certify that as Falcor and Denali are dogs of a heroic stature and as they risked their lives to save their owner and bring about justice, they shall be supplied with free dog food for the rest of their lives. Plus anytime they put their heads into Black Hills Feed, they shall be awarded the treat of their choice from whatever is in stock at the time."

It was signed by Leslie, Ted and Jack.

"Thanks, guys," I said with the often present tears coming to the surface again. I still shuddered at how close I had come to losing my beautiful girl. "I really appreciate this and the dogs will too."

"It is the least we could do," Leslie said. "We have no way of knowing what the outcome might have been if you and the dogs hadn't caught Jane. Hopefully Jack would have been found innocent but one never knows. Other innocent people have ended up spending years in jail. And," she added, "this is an informal invitation so you can mark your calendar. We want you and the dogs to attend our wedding."

"Your wedding!" I laughed. "How wonderful. When and where?"

"It will be the first of May and it will be at a friend's house on Summit Lake. Hopefully we can have it outside but if we can't, they have a huge family room and deck that will hold the people that we plan on inviting. You and the dogs are the first beyond family and the hosts to learn of it. You are to be honored guests."

"We will be delighted to come. Won't we, big guys?" The dogs answered with a single tail wag. "Now, can you come next door for something to eat?" I asked.

"No, we really need to get back and relieve Dad at the store. He promised Mom that he'd take her to dinner and a movie in Olympia tonight," Leslie said.

"Thank you again so much, Martha," Jack said. "If you ever need any help around here, you let me know. I owe you more than I can ever repay."

"Thank you, Jack. I'll call on you if I need to. I'm just glad that it came out so well for all three of you. And I'm very glad to meet you, Tyler. Next time you come, you can see the baby lambs."

"Can I, Daddy? Can we come tomorrow?"

Jack laughed. "Well, I don't know about tomorrow but we will come back soon. Now give the doggies a goodbye pat and then we must be going."

Tyler gave Nali a pat and Falcor a hug. I walked them to the door and gave all three of them hugs. "Come back soon, and thanks again."

"We will," Leslie said and then they turned and walked out to their truck.

Falcor and I watched as they drove out. I was so glad to have friends like them and so happy for Leslie. She deserved the lovely life that appeared to be stretching ahead of her. I closed the door and looked back over my shop. My life wasn't so bad either. Ellen was coming over for dinner and some spinning tonight. It would be a quiet evening with my best friend, my dogs and my favorite pastime. Life couldn't get better than that.